Freedom
Stone

Jeffrey Kluger

PHILOMEL BOOKS

An Imprint of Penguin Group (USA) Inc.

PHILOMEL BOOKS
A division of Penguin Young Readers Group.
Published by The Penguin Group.
Penguin Group (USA) Inc., 375 Hudson Street, New York, NY 10014, U.S.A.
Penguin Group (Canada), 90 Eglinton Avenue East, Suite 700, Toronto, Ontario
M4P 2Y3, Canada (a division of Pearson Penguin Canada Inc.).
Penguin Books Ltd, 80 Strand, London WC2R 0RL, England.
Penguin Ireland, 25 St. Stephen's Green, Dublin 2, Ireland
(a division of Penguin Books Ltd).
Penguin Group (Australia), 250 Camberwell Road, Camberwell, Victoria 3124,
Australia (a division of Pearson Australia Group Pty Ltd).
Penguin Books India Pvt Ltd, 11 Community Centre, Panchsheel Park,
New Delhi—110 017, India.
Penguin Group (NZ), 67 Apollo Drive, Rosedale, North Shore 0632,
New Zealand (a division of Pearson New Zealand Ltd).
Penguin Books (South Africa) (Pty) Ltd, 24 Sturdee Avenue, Rosebank,
Johannesburg 2196, South Africa.
Penguin Books Ltd, Registered Offices: 80 Strand, London WC2R 0RL, England.

Published simultaneously in Canada.   Printed in the United States of America.
Design by Semadar Megged.   Text set in 12-point Horley Old Style.

Library of Congress Cataloging-in-Publication Data
Kluger, Jeffrey.
Freedom stone / Jeffrey Kluger.—1st ed.   p. cm.   Summary: With the help of a
magical stone from Africa, a thirteen-year-old slave travels to the battle of Vicksburg
to clear her father's name and free her family from bondage.
[1. Slavery—Fiction. 2. African Americans—Fiction. 3. United States—History—
Civil War, 1861–1865—Fiction. 4. Magic—Fiction.] I. Title.   PZ7.K6875Fr 2011
[Fic]—dc22   2010006028
ISBN 978-0-399-25214-3
1 3 5 7 9 10 8 6 4 2

With love to
Elisa and Paloma,
my brave and clever girls

Chapter 1

THERE WERE TWO kinds of slaves on the plantation Lillie and her family called home: those who could sleep on the night before the slave seller came and those who couldn't. Lillie's little brother was too young to understand exactly what the job of the slave seller was, so this morning, just before sunrise on the day the terrible man was going to arrive, the boy lay deeply sleeping beside her in the narrow bed the two of them shared. Mama knew the slave seller well, having seen too many of his visits over the years and watched too many people she knew and even loved get sold off like prize heads of livestock. For much of the night, Mama had thus tossed and thrashed in her bed on the other side of the family's little cabin, giving in to sleep only in the last hour or so. Lillie had slept even less than Mama, drifting in and out of a fitful doze for much of the night and awakening fully a short time ago, just as the sky was beginning to show a faint shimmer of dawn outside her window.

As most of the slaves on the plantation knew, the slave seller was not actually a slave seller at all. What he was—or at least what the white family called him—was a slave appraiser, a man whose sole job was to visit plantations throughout the county, examine the slaves working there and report back to the auctioneers about which ones looked likely to bring the highest price. Slaves who were selected this way were usually gone within a month and almost never seen again. Rumors had been swirling for weeks that the appraiser would be making his rounds soon, and that was no surprise.

The last harvest had been a poor one at Greenfog— which was what the plantation where Lillie lived was called—and the war between the North and South, now in its third year, was making money even harder to come by throughout Beaufort County and the rest of South Carolina too. Masters who could not raise enough cash selling their crops would often turn to selling some slaves. Yesterday, just after the quitting horn sounded, the overseer called the Greenfog slaves together in a field near the stables and announced that their Master had decided that some of them would have to go, and they'd all be priced for sale in the morning.

This, of course, was the worst news a group of slaves could hear, but the Master had tricks to try to make them forget that—or at least to think about it less. Last night, as on all nights before the appraiser came, an extra ration of pork—pink and fresh-killed, not salted and dried—was distributed to all the cabins. Fresh pork was said to brighten moods and soften skin, giving slaves the healthy, well-fed look the auctioneers liked to see. The pork had been delicious—it was always delicious before slave appraiser days—and Lillie's little brother had stuffed himself with it. Despite her worries, Lillie could not resist it either. Mama would not eat a bite.

Even better than the ham the slaves ate was the rest they'd get. Today, the morning horn would sound a bit later than usual and there would be no fieldwork to do. Well-rested slaves were also thought to be more appealing to the appraiser. For Lillie, however—and for all the other slaves who lay awake on the night before the slave seller came—extra time to sleep just meant extra time to brood, and as morning now broke, Lillie found herself staring ahead into the shadows of the cabin, her mind filled with thoughts of the sorrow that at least one family would feel before the sun went down on Greenfog again.

Lillie stole a glance at her sleeping brother, who was called Plato, and envied him the things he did not know. She was thirteen now, old enough to understand when trouble was coming. But she had been barely the boy's age—which was six—the first time the appraiser called. Back then, if Mama and Papa told her not to worry about what was going on, she wouldn't worry. If they told her that none of them would ever be sold away or flogged, she believed that too. When a child was marked for sale and its mother dropped to her knees and wailed with a terrible, animal sound, Mama would pick Lillie up and carry her off and sing in her ear so close and strong that the sound of the weeping woman's screams would seem to fall away.

But Lillie was too old to pick up now, too old to sing to and too old to believe good things were going to happen just because Mama said they were. All the other children who'd lost a family member to the slave traders had had mamas who told them the same things, and that hadn't helped them a lick.

As Lillie lay in bed, lost in these dark thoughts, a terrible, choking feeling came over her, and her skin went prickly hot with fear. In time, the sun would be up and she would face the day as well as she could—which she reckoned would probably be good enough. But here in the still-dark cabin, the low ceiling and the deep silence and even the thin, scratchy blanket under which she lay seemed all at once as if they would suffocate her. She flung off the blanket, causing her brother to stir slightly, and drew three or four deep, trembly breaths. She needed to get up, she needed to be outside, at least until day broke and her mama awoke. And she needed to go see her friend Bett.

Ever since Lillie had been old enough to explore the plantation on her own, spending time with Bett had lifted her mood. Bett was an old slave who lived on a tiny patch of unfarmed land just beyond the tobacco field. She had spent nearly all her adult life working the ovens in the Master's kitchen, baking cakes and muffins and loaves of bread and all manner of sweets and treats. When Bett was too old for Big House work, the Master had allowed the other slaves to build her a cabin of her own where she could live out her remaining years. She would still be required to work, of course, but now it would be for the other slaves alone, baking their weekly portion of bread, which the mamas were usually too busy in the fields to make on their own.

Bett had been old for as long as Lillie could remember, but no one seemed to know her exact age, including Bett herself—who also didn't seem to care. "There ain't but two states of things," she liked to say. "There's alive, and there's dead. I expect I'll be one until I'm the other."

When Lillie was feeling sad or cross, she'd often as not find her way to Bett's cabin, where she would help with the cleaning or water fetching or sometimes even the baking itself, and would always get something fine and fresh-baked for her troubles.

All the same, Lillie had not visited Bett much in the last year. She had an older girl's thoughts and an older girl's troubles now, and was not so easily soothed by a child's work and a child's reward. This morning, however, the comforts of Bett felt like just what she needed. Lillie glanced toward the window at the faintly brightening sky. Bett, she knew, would surely be awake now; she made it her business to be up before the sun. If Lillie hurried to her cabin now, she could help herself to one of the old woman's smiles—and perhaps a bite of her fresh-baked bread—and be back before her brother and Mama even knew she was gone.

Quietly, Lillie climbed out of bed. She was wearing nothing but her nightshirt, but it was long enough—nearly to her knees—to protect her against the morning chill and against being punished for going about undressed should anyone spot her. She tiptoed toward the door, taking care not to make the floorboards creak. She cast a nervous glance back toward Plato and Mama and then, before her courage could fail her, slipped out the front door.

The pebbly soil outside the cabin felt damp and gritty against Lillie's feet, and she shuddered a bit at the touch of it. She looked ahead toward the tobacco field and set off in its direction in a light trot. It was early September, and the days were still hot in the Carolinas, but the mornings were cool and pleasant, and Lillie enjoyed the feel of the air against her face and her bare arms and legs. Running through the tobacco plants, she squinted toward the end of the field where Bett's cabin lay. As she drew closer, she picked up the scent of baking on the air and smiled. It smelled like cornbread, and it smelled fine—but it also surprised her. Bett always baked her morning bread the night before, and on most days, she did not light her oven much before noon. Still, the smell alone helped lift Lillie's mood. It was almost as if Bett knew she'd be coming and knew what she'd need. Bett did seem to know such things without being told, a fact that delighted Lillie most of the time—and spooked her a little at other times.

At last, Lillie broke out of the field and into the clearing where the little cabin stood. She could see the curl of white cook smoke rising from the small chimney, and she came to a stop, scanning the quiet scene. As she did, her eyes widened in surprise. Bett raised a thick garden of flowers and vegetables behind her cabin, and that garden often drew a thick cloud of bees. But there was something queer about Bett's bees—or at least sometimes there was. Unlike most bees, which could fly a lot faster than a person could duck and run, Bett's bees were often strangely slow. Their wings moved with the sleepy sweep of swan wings; they floated from flower to hive so lazily that Lillie could sometimes beat them there at a walk. And if one of them came at her cross enough to sting, she could step out of the way and brush it out of the air with barely a thought. Few other people ever saw the bees, just a slave child now and then who might be playing nearby and whose story of having seen such a thing was never believed by any adult. Lillie and her brother did see the bees. They took to calling them the slowbees and loved to watch them when they appeared.

"Quick!" Lillie would call. "The slowbees is about!" And Plato would come running.

Now, in the just-breaking sun, Lillie could see that the slowbees were everywhere, massing around the garden thick and dark as a rain cloud, as if they too had been drawn by the baking. This many bees could sting a horse to death no matter how slowly they were moving. Lillie didn't want to consider what they could do to a child like her. She took a step back and started to turn away. But at that moment, the door to the cabin creaked open and Bett appeared. She looked as she always did—small, stout, strong. But she looked older and wearier too, as if baking so early in the day were too much for her.

"I reckoned I'd see you this morning, child," she said with a small smile. "But it's best you not be here now."

Lillie was surprised. Bett had never turned her away before. "I felt like visitin'," she said uncertainly.

"I know," Bett said. "I expected you would. But there's matters I have to mind this morning." Lillie glanced toward the bees, but Bett didn't follow her gaze. "Come later," Bett said. "Later there'll be cornbread for you."

Bett closed the door, and Lillie stood where she was for a moment. Then she turned and walked off—thoughts of the slave appraiser once again filling her head, and the low buzzing of the bees filling her ears.

Chapter Two

BETT DID NOT FEEL good about sending Lillie away. The old woman had not been called to the stable yesterday to hear the overseer's announcement—she was never required to do such things anymore—but she'd heard the rumors about the appraiser's visit and reckoned when the assembly horn blew that that was what it was about. This morning was surely the kind of morning Lillie would want to come visit. She was a fool child sometimes—all children were—but she was a good child too. Still, Bett had other matters to tend to and she needed to turn her full thoughts to them.

The tray of cornbread that had been baking in the oven was finished, and Bett took it out and set it aside. It looked fine, and it smelled proper, but it was not up to the job she needed it to do. She'd have to start over with something different. With a sigh, she selected another of her bread pans, carefully scraped off the crust from the last baking and then washed it to a shine. She gathered up nearly all the flour, yeast, salt and eggs she had left and mixed them into a dense, gummy dough—denser and gummier than she'd usually abide. She looked at what she'd made and frowned. This was not the kind of bread she'd eat herself, nor the kind she'd offer to the other slaves. It was, however, suited to her purposes, and when those purposes had been served, she would feed it to the geese around her cabin, who would gobble it up and like it just fine.

Bett glanced out her window and saw that the sun had risen to two fingers above the horizon. Lillie was gone, but when Bett cocked her ear to the tobacco field, she could already make out the sound of two or three slave children laughing and calling out. The youngest boys often came to the fields early to play chasing and hiding games while their mamas made breakfast. Today they'd be especially likely to do so, since the morning horn would be sounding late, but boys—by their nature—would still be awake with the sun. Bett walked to her door, stepped outside and called into the field.

"Boy!" she shouted as loudly as she could. She didn't much care which boy heard her; they all looked to be the proper age. "Boy!" she repeated. The closest child turned and pointed to himself questioningly. Bett nodded a large yes, one the child could see at a distance, and waved him over.

The boy trotted out of the field with an ease Bett remembered from her own girlhood and presented himself to her.

"Yes'm?" he said.

"I'm bakin', child. I need you to taste somethin' for me."

The boy brightened; if Bett was making sweets it would be a rare treat to taste them before they went into the oven. Bett stepped back into her cabin, and the boy followed. She withdrew a wooden spoon from her apron pocket, dipped it in the fresh dough and presented it to the boy. He looked uncertainly at the gray, sticky blob that stuck to the wood. This wasn't at all what he'd expected.

"Taste it," Bett said.

The boy hesitated. "Is this conjurin'?" he asked with a frightened look.

Bett smiled at the question. Most plantations did have conjurers—older slaves whose grandpapas and great-grandpapas had remembered Africa well and learned some of the old land's good-luck spells and healing charms. No one knew for sure if Bett practiced any such magic. She did have a keen way of finding things when they were lost, a keen way of spotting liars and a keen way of knowing when folks were coming down sick—even when they didn't know it themselves. She reckoned most of this just came from paying attention, but other folks always imagined there was more to it.

"No, child," she said with a laugh. "This ain't conjurin'."

"Cause I ain't done nothin', so you got no reason to do me harm."

Bett smiled again. "I know. I just need you to taste somethin' my old tongue can't anymore."

She held out the spoon again and the boy wrinkled up his nose again, but he tasted a bit of it. It was terrible—Bett knew it would be. "Once more," she said, sorry that she had to ask.

The boy looked set to cry, but again did as Bett instructed.

"Thank you, child. You done good work," she said, taking his chin, turning up his face and seeing that his eyes had indeed begun to well. She gave the boy a dipper of water and daubed at his eyes with her apron. "You come back here with your mama day after tomorrow," she said. "I'll have a proper loaf of bread for her, and see if I don't have a sweet cake for you too."

The boy smiled at that, turned and bounded out of the cabin. Bett sighed and closed the door. She returned to her work, pressing and mixing the dough with the spoon. Yes, she thought, this sorry loaf would probably serve. It was well suited to what was sure to be an equally sorry day.

Chapter Three

LILLIE RETURNED HOME at a brisk run, glancing all the while at the slowly rising sun and trying to guess whether Mama would be awake by now. When she drew near the large patch of pebbly dirt that surrounded the line of little slave cabins, she slowed. Here she would step lightly, the better to mask the sound of her feet crunching the soil. She tiptoed to the door of her cabin, opened it slowly—thankful that it didn't squeak—and peeked in toward her bed. Plato was still deeply asleep and had not, near as Lillie could tell, even shifted his position since she left. She sighed in relief and opened the door further—then slumped. Mama was sitting at the little eating table, sipping a mug of sassafras tea and looking at her sharply.

"Mama—" Lillie began, but Mama silenced her with an even harder glare. Lillie's brother stirred slightly, and Mama glanced toward him, then summoned Lillie to the eating table with a tick of her head. Lillie stepped quietly across the cabin, trying not to meet Mama's gaze. She did glance up to see that there was a second mug on the table, and this gave her hope. It had always been Mama's habit to make herself tea in the morning, but just in the last year, she had begun making some for Lillie as well. They had never spoken about this new practice; one day Mama was putting out a single mug, and the next day there were two. Lillie still smiled when she picked up her tea each morning. The fact that it was there waiting for her today might mean that Mama wasn't as cross with her as she feared.

"Child," Mama now hissed, in a voice that said yes, she was surely mad, "where have you been?"

Lillie sat at the table and wrapped her hands around her mug, feeling its warmth. She hesitated. "To see Bett," she answered. She knew better than to fib now.

Mama rolled her eyes. She'd surely reckoned as much, which explained why she didn't look angrier. She liked Bett, and she had been sorry in the last year when Lillie seemed to have lost interest in the company of the old woman, but today was not the day to go out on adventures without asking first.

"You know what happens to slaves when the appraiser man comes?" Mama asked in a hard whisper.

"They gets sold off," Lillie answered.

"You know what happens to the ones what misbehaves?"

"They gets sold first." It was a lesson Lillie had been taught when she was small and had been made to repeat many times since.

Mama nodded. "Bett ain't no help on a day like today, child," she said. "Mindin' yourself—and mindin' me—is all you gots to do."

Lillie said nothing and nodded, then picked up her mug and sipped the tea. It was hot and it was good, sweetened with a drop or two of the little bit of honey Mama kept and used only on days when she reckoned they all needed a treat. Lillie glanced up and smiled at Mama. From across the cabin came a small snort, and Lillie's brother rolled over, breathed deeply and stretched. Lillie stifled a giggle.

"Plato's wakin'," she said, and Mama looked toward the boy warmly.

Mama had not been happy about giving her son an odd name like Plato, but Lillie's papa had insisted upon it for reasons he held dear but didn't much discuss. Mama herself had an unusual name. She was known as Phibbi, which was an African name for a girl child born on a Friday. The overseer and the Master forbade anyone to use the name and addressed Mama instead as Franny, so the other slaves did as well—at least when they were in the company of white folks. In private, they used Mama's true name, and Mama was grateful to them for that. Lillie too had a proper African name—Quashee, which meant a girl child born on a Sunday. Papa had given her the name, told her about it as soon as she was old enough to understand it and explained that she should never use it outside of their cabin until the day she was free, when she could carry it with the pride she should.

As slave cabins went, Lillie's family's was a good one—particularly to Lillie and Plato themselves, who had been born here and knew no other home. It had a strong plank floor; a good chimney that Papa had built of oyster shells, sand and lime; and enough dishes, mugs and spoons to fill the cupboards Papa had also built. There was a small table where the family took their meals and there were two chests of drawers for the clothes Mama made. A curtain down the center of the cabin separated the children's bed from Mama and Papa's, but now that Papa was gone, Mama mostly kept it open. The only times she'd pull it shut were on those nights, which still happened now and then, when she would slip into bed and cry till near sunup—something Lillie and Plato learned not to ask her about, since she always answered the same way.

"Mind the things what're yours to mind," she'd say, and Lillie would know to do as she was told.

It had been four months now since Papa had died—on the twenty-second of May, the dispatch had said, in the siege of Vicksburg, in Mississippi. Only last week, Mama had removed the black mourning rag she'd nailed to the cabin door—and only then because the overseer had ordered her to.

"It spooks the other slaves, Franny," he snapped. "Take it off or I'll take the rag and the door along with it."

Lillie herself still cried most every day for Papa. The pain at first had been like a solid thing—a hot stone inside her belly. Now it was more of a terrible, heavy everywhere-ache. She could stand it until something would remind her of Papa—a slave's laugh that sounded like his, a whiff of pipe tobacco that smelled like his. Once she'd even cried at the rough touch of a hog's bristly back, because it reminded her of the rough feel of Papa's unshaven face when he gave her a kiss. And when anyone on the plantation spoke of freedom, she thought of Papa most powerfully of all.

Freedom for all the slaves—but mostly for his own family—was something Papa had talked about all the time. And for a while, it seemed that it was coming. It was late in 1863 now, and at the beginning of the year, word went 'round that even as the war between the armies of the North and the South raged on, Mr. Lincoln had signed a paper—a proclamation, Lillie's mama said it was called—ordering freedom for all the slaves in all the Rebel states. The news crept slowly from plantation to plantation and everywhere was met with scowls from the white folks and secret smiles from the black folks. But smart people of both colors knew the paper didn't change much.

"This mean we can pack up our things and walk North tonight?" Lillie's papa asked her when she and Plato had jumped and whooped enough over the news.

"No," she answered.

"Does it mean I can earn my own livin' and work my own land?"

"No," she repeated.

"Just so," he said. "The South is a weasel, and we is the chickens. Weasel don't let go of a bird when you read him a rule tellin' him to. He lets go when you shoot him."

Papa soon decided that he wanted to help out with that shooting himself. Just last spring, word was sent out that the Army of the South, desperate for more men, had begun accepting slaves as soldiers, assigning them to battle-field jobs like cooking, nursing, horse-shoeing or digging. All able-bodied male slaves over sixteen would be accepted with the promise that if they survived, they would be freed. When not enough family men volunteered in the coastal counties of South Carolina, the promise of freedom was extended to their wives and children too—even if the men themselves were killed in the fighting. And when a plantation owner complained that he'd paid good coin for his workers and didn't want them shot up in the war or freed by the Army, the Army just threatened to confiscate his other male slaves too, which quieted the objections fast.

Going to war in exchange for his family's freedom was an idea that appealed to a sensible man like Papa, and one evening after work was finished and dinner was done, he announced that that was what he planned to do. The family argued, the children cried and Mama even threatened to stand and block the door. But they knew that Papa had made up his mind, and the next morning he was gone. Before he left, he hugged Lillie tight.

"I'll come home again, Quashee," he said.

But Lillie's papa never did come home. Just three months after he left, he died, one of the many, many casualties at Vicksburg. The family grieved terribly, but took some comfort from the thought that the freedom Papa had wanted for them would now be theirs. Just two days later, however, they learned that even that wasn't to be. A telegraph message was delivered to the Big House telling the Master that upon Papa's death, he had been found in possession of a small purse of coins—gold coins, and Yankee ones at that—that he was assumed to have stolen. Since he couldn't pay for his crime, the family would have to, and the promise of freedom that had been made to them would be denied. Later, the Army delivered the bag of coins to the Master—a common practice when a slave had stolen something and the rightful owner could not be found. The Master was pleased with this arrangement and, like all Southerners who came across Northern money, vowed not to spend any of it till he had gone through all his Confederate money first and had no other choice. If the South won, he could melt the coins down for their gold; if the North won, Southern currency would be useless and he'd need to hold tight to any Yankee wealth he had. Either way, the arrangement suited him fine, and he liked to boast that he had turned a far tidier profit than he could have from simply selling Papa at auction.

Lillie knew—*knew*—her father could not have done any thieving, but only weeks later, a slave who'd served along-side him and lost a leg in the fighting was freed and sent home to South Carolina. He brought word to the plantation that, yes, the coins had been found in Papa's pocket, and, yes, they were Yankee gold. Lillie cursed the coins and cursed the war and cursed the South and cursed slavery itself, but she had no thought at all of cursing her papa. He was an honest man who'd lived an honest life and, she was certain, had died an honest death.

None of that, of course, could possibly help her or her family on slave appraiser day, and as the sun rose higher, the appraiser's visit drew closer by the minute. Lillie finished her tea and sat in silence as Mama quietly prepared the family's breakfast—mush, a bit more honey and some stunted but sweet melon she'd been able to raise in her garden. Finally, the morning horn sounded—a hoarse blast from an old bugle. All the slaves would be expected to be awake before the last echo of it had died away.

The noise from the horn made Plato jump, then he murmured and climbed out of bed. As he had every night for the past four months, he had worn one of Papa's old shirts to bed. It hung down closer to his ankles than his knees and even now, seeing it on him made Lillie's eyes well up. He walked sleepily over to the table and sat down without a word, then picked up his spoon and began eating his mush. Mama and Lillie exchanged a smile. It always took Lillie a while in the morning to wake up and find her appetite. Mama was the same way, but Plato would go straight from bed to breakfast, sometimes without even fully opening his eyes.

"Boy," Mama said, "one day you're gonna put your spoon in a bowl o' mud if you don't look at what you're eatin' first."

"S'mush, Mama," Plato said with his mouth full. "S'good."

Lillie tried to eat too, but she had no stomach for food—and would not have much time to linger over it anyway. Once the horn sounded, it meant the appraiser was already on the grounds and was visiting with the Master and the Missus in the Big House, where he'd be given a small breakfast before setting about the day's business. Mama hurried the children through their meal—Lillie managing a few spoons of mush and a few bites of melon—and then began to take out the clothes they'd all be wearing.

When the appraiser was here, the slaves did not wear what they wore every day, but instead were instructed to dress in the best clothes they had—or at least the cleanest ones—and to wash and comb with particular care. The girls would be expected to decorate their hair with bits of ribbon if their mamas had any. The boys would be expected to close their top shirt button—if their shirts had a top button. This, like the extra food and the extra sleep, was believed to make the slaves more appealing.

Unlike many slave girls, Lillie did own a proper dress, one that had belonged to Mama until the night before a recent plantation dance, when she had brought it out and asked Lillie if she'd like it for her own. Lillie at first thought she was being teased. Her shape had been changing this season, that was sure, rounding out in a way that made her clothes a snugger fit than they once were. Still, if she favored anyone's looks, it was less those of her mother—who remained shapely and lovely even deep in her thirties—than those of her father, a tall, rangy man who'd seemed to have been made up mostly of straight lines and sharp angles. Lillie had always felt cheated by that, reckoning that a girl ought to resemble her mama and a boy ought to resemble his papa. But now that her own papa was gone, she told herself it was good there was someone whose appearance would always call him to mind. Mama's dress did fit Lillie, but not without some cutting and stitching to make it more suited to her.

What Plato would be wearing today was not clear. The boy did not yet have a fancy suit of clothes, but in recent months Mama had been quietly making him one at night, as a treat for his sixth birthday. When Papa died, she stopped for a while and the birthday passed without a gift. But she'd picked the work up again lately—the better to busy herself on those nights when she couldn't sleep.

Now, as Lillie slid into her dress, Mama went over to her drawer and took out what she'd made: a pair of brown pants, a scratchy white shirt and a little green jacket that looked like it belonged more to a squire than a slave boy. "Seems like you're growed enough for a good suit o' clothes," she said, turning around and showing them to Plato. "I reckon these'll serve."

Plato beamed—a bigger smile than Lillie or Mama had seen from him at any time since Papa died—and began dancing excitedly from foot to foot. "Mama, Mama, Mama!" he said. "Can I put it on? Can I put it on? Can I put it on?"

"Yes, you can," Mama said with a laugh, holding the clothes higher to prevent him from grabbing them straight from her hand. Then she settled him down and helped him into the little outfit, showing him how to fasten all the buttons. When she was done, Plato stood, looking himself up and down.

"I look just like the Little Master!" he exclaimed, having often seen the Master's eight-year-old son walking about the plantation in his many fine suits of clothes.

"No!" Mama snapped, with a suddenness that startled both Lillie and Plato. "The Little Master looks like the Little Master. You look like Plato. Do you understand that?"

"Yes, Mama," Plato answered meekly.

"Good," Mama said. She smoothed the jacket on his shoulders and tugged the sleeves until they hung properly. "Fine a child as this," she muttered to herself, "the Little Master would be lucky to look like you."

At last Mama took her own best dress down from a hook and began putting it on. Just as she was finishing, there was a loud rapping at the cabin door; before she could answer, the door flung open and the overseer stepped in.

The overseer at Greenfog was a man called Mr. Willis, and he was more or less like all the other overseers on all the other plantations. He was perhaps forty years old—young enough that he was still capable of moving fast and handling a whip, but old enough to have been doing plantation work for many years and to know how to keep such a big place running. He was a small, wiry man, with a large bald patch on the top of his head that would turn a deep, fiery red at the first flash of springtime. Lillie sometimes fancied that she could read his temper at any moment by looking at just how dark a shade of red his head had become.

"Franny," Mr. Willis now said brusquely, "finish yourselves up and get outside. Lineup's already started."

Mama accepted that the white folks would never address her as Phibbi, but she always hesitated a bit before responding to the name Franny, as if she could never quite accustom herself to the form of address. "Yes, sir," she said after a moment. "We'll be along presently."

"See that you are," Willis answered. He looked Plato, Lillie and Mama up and down. "I expect the traders will be interested in the lot of you," he said with a sharp little laugh. Then he turned his eyes particularly to Mama, allowing them to linger there in a way Lillie didn't like. "I'll be 'specially sorry to see you go, Franny." He barked his little laugh again and left the cabin as abruptly as he'd entered it.

Mama watched the man go without a word, then looked at the children and nodded toward the door. Plato didn't move, and Lillie too felt rooted where she was. Mama put her arms around their shoulders and smiled.

"Ain't no different than when Papa was here," she said. "Hold him in mind, and you'll be fine." She nudged both children gently, and they all stepped outside.

Just as the overseer had said, the lineup was already forming. Every slave on the plantation would be present except Bett, who was too old to sell and had been for a while. All the others were now clustering in ragged groups in front of their cabins, and Mr. Willis, along with two slave drivers, strode back and forth in front of them, flicking their whips and summoning them forward into a neat row. The bigger of the two whip men was known as Bull, because that seemed to capture both his build and his wits. The other one—who was called by his proper name, which was Louis—was a tick smaller and a bit brighter. Neither man was shy about using his whip, but Bull seemed truly to love it. He was known as a marksman with almost any lash and was said to be able to whip a blueberry off a fencepost without touching the wood or leaving a stain of blue juice behind. The slaves crossed the whip men at their peril, and this morning none of them chose to. They assembled side to side as they were instructed, mothers and fathers holding their children's hands.

From behind the cabins, they could soon hear a clopping of hooves, and the Master and the slave appraiser, mounted atop their horses, trotted into view. The appraiser was dressed in old and worn traveling clothes, with a slouchy leather hat on his head and boots so scuffed that it wasn't easy to say what their original color had been. The same clothes would not have looked out of place on a slave. The Master was dressed in a fine morning suit—much finer than he would wear on any ordinary day. Such fancy clothes meant a prosperous man, one who didn't need to sell off any of his slaves unless he could get a top price for them. Of course, the appraiser would not have been there at all if the Master were really as wealthy as he was trying to appear—something everyone assembled today knew.

"Impressive crop o' workers," the appraiser said as the men's horses slowed and they dismounted. He scanned up and down the line, casting a practiced eye over them and making a brief notation in his ledger. "You look after 'em well."

"Fair portions of food and lots of hard work," the Master said. "That keeps them strong."

The two men began to pace the line while Bull, Louis and Willis stood nearby. Lillie squeezed Mama's hand, and Mama squeezed back. Then Lillie craned her neck forward, looking left and right, in the hope of getting a glimpse of Cal. Cal was a boy about her age whom she'd never much noticed in the past, but was becoming fonder of lately. Like Lillie, he was growing this year, and she reckoned he was turning out handsomer—if skinnier—than she'd thought he would. Cal had a quiet, sometimes worried way about him, which she found dear, as well as a quick temper and a taste for trouble, which she found less so. Plato had seemed to have taken a shine to Cal too of late—ever since Papa had died. Sometimes, he'd trail after the bigger boy when they were walking to work in the tobacco fields, and Cal would pick him up and swing him about till he giggled—which figured high in Lillie's estimation too. As always in the last few years, when there was a slave lineup, Cal would be standing not with his own family, but with another one that had taken him in.

Cal's mama had died giving birth to him—her first child and, as it turned out, her only one. Cal's papa never quite got past the death of his wife, reckoning that if the Master had allowed a doctor to tend her properly, she might have survived. Ever since then, he'd had a hot turn of temper, and four years ago, during a lineup just like this one, the Master had sold him South to Louisiana, far enough away that he was never likely to see his son again.

Cal moved into the cabin next to his family's, where a couple named George and Nelly lived. They had never had children of their own, and now that they were getting old—past forty, most people reckoned—were not likely to. Cal accepted the bed they gave him, ate the food they made him and minded them as well as he could. Now and again, he even looked as if he cared for them. One sleepy afternoon, Lillie spotted him napping on the porch of his cabin with his head in Nelly's lap and her hand smoothing his hair, like a real mama and her real boy.

As the slave appraiser paced the line, Lillie spotted Cal far at the left end, and she didn't like what she saw. He was looking down—not straight ahead as the slaves were supposed to so that the appraiser could examine their eyes and teeth—and he was looking cross. This was just how his papa used to behave himself, and though George and Nelly warned the boy to mind himself better, he never seemed to listen. Even at a distance, Lillie could see Cal's jaw working and his hands clenching. George and Nelly were standing on either side of him and both nudged him to soften his expression and unknot his hands. The appraiser saw all this too.

"Who's that boy?" he asked, pointing Cal's way.

The Master, who didn't hold on well to names, glanced questioningly toward the overseer.

"That one's called Cal," Willis said.

Even on hearing his name, Cal did not change his pose.

"Boy . . . ," rumbled Bull. He gave off with a small snap of his whip and Cal raised his head and looked forward. The appraiser and the Master approached him.

"Looks like a strong one," the appraiser said, "and he ain't near full growth yet." The man took Cal's chin in his hand and turned his face right and left. Cal's expression was stony. Lillie watched and held her breath.

"Good eyes, good skin," the appraiser said. "How's his spirit?"

The Master again turned to Willis.

"High sometimes," the overseer said. "He needs some breaking still, but that's always the way when they's this age."

The appraiser turned Cal's face forward and regarded

him closely once more. Then he let go of his chin, made a notation in his ledger and turned away. Lillie released her breath.

The appraiser now walked slowly back up the line. There were three other boys Cal's age on the plantation, and they all drew his interest. Men much beyond their middle thirties were less valuable; they'd been worked out or would be soon enough, but the Master might add one to a sale of two or three other slaves if that would round out the price he was getting. Girls a little older than Lillie were of special interest since they were almost as strong as boys their age and had all their baby-making years ahead of them. Buy a slave girl who later had three children and you got four workers for a single price. There were four girls on the plantation about this age, and the appraiser stopped in front of them all.

Finally, he approached Lillie and her family and, as Lillie had hoped, did not show much interest. Mama was too old for his needs, Lillie was still a little too young, and a boy as small as Plato was all but useless. The appraiser passed them by without slowing, then stopped. He turned back and looked squarely at Plato. Lillie snapped her head from the appraiser to Plato and back again, and then moved as if she were about to jump at him. Mama squeezed her hand and kept her still.

"How old's the boy?" the appraiser asked.

The Master shrugged. "Seven?" he guessed.

"Six," said Willis. He ticked his head at Bull, who moved a step closer.

"What's your name?" the appraiser asked Plato.

The boy didn't answer.

"It's Plato," said Willis.

The appraiser laughed at that.

"His papa give it to him," Willis said. "You can change it if you like."

"Plato'll do for now," the appraiser said and turned back to the boy. "You look like a strong, boy. Are you?"

Plato looked to Mama, who glanced fleetingly toward the appraiser with ice in her eyes. Then she turned to the boy and nodded for him to answer.

"Yes, sir," he said.

"Then how 'bout you jump for me?"

"Sir?" Plato asked.

"Jump," the appraiser repeated.

Mama grabbed Plato and pulled him back to her.

"Franny . . . ," Bull said, staring at her hard and flicking his whip.

Mama looked at the whip, raised her chin and held the boy tighter. Bull then smiled thinly, turned his eyes to Plato instead and flicked the whip again. Lillie drew a small gasp. She'd seen Bull give a child Plato's age three hard strokes for stealing, and she didn't doubt he'd do it again. Neither did Mama. She released him slowly.

"Jump, baby," Mama said softly.

"Why?" Plato asked.

Mama smiled but her eyes looked wet. "The man's got a son just your age at home. He's bettin' my boy can't jump higher than his."

Plato smiled, crouched down and jumped back up as high as he could.

"Again," the appraiser said, and Plato obeyed. Then the man waved the boy absently back into line and made a notation in his book. Mama pulled Plato to her hard, and he looked up at her, smiling.

"Did I jump higher, Mama?" he asked.

"I believe you did, child," she said, fighting to give him a smile.

The appraiser turned to the Master and spoke quietly. "Boys his age can go for more'n you think," he said. "Useless for farm work, but merchant ships like 'em as cabin hands. Train 'em early and you got a proper sailor when they're growed. I sold a child his size for two hundred dollars down in Cuba last year." The Master smiled.

Even with the appraiser's soft tone, Lillie could make out a few of his words, especially "merchant ships," "cabin boy" and, most awful of all, "Cuba." She couldn't place

Cuba on a map—having never seen a map—but knew it was a distant place where the slave trade was hard and cruel. Mama heard the words too, and the pair of them exchanged a terrible glance.

The appraiser now turned away, scanned the remaining slaves and at last appeared to be done with his morning's work. He might have gone on his way too if Cal, who had been standing still with his eyes to the ground and his fists still balled up at his sides, hadn't reckoned he'd had enough. The slaves weren't permitted to leave the lineup until the overseer dismissed them—all the more so on a day like today when the Master had a visitor who needed to be impressed. Cal, however, did not much care about making an impression, and he suddenly turned hard on his heel—so hard that he made a loud crunching sound in the dry dirt underfoot. The overseer, the slave drivers and everyone else turned to look. Cal proceeded to stalk away without a glance back. Lillie's mouth dropped open and she had to hold down the urge to call him back. The overseer needed show no such restraint.

"Boy!" he shouted. "You turn back!"

Cal ignored him.

"Boy, you heard Mr. Willis," Bull bellowed.

Cal walked on.

"Cal, come back here, 'fore they whip you!" Nelly cried.

But Cal still walked on.

Bull glanced at the overseer, who nodded in approval, and the big, muscled driver bounded toward Cal's retreating back, spinning his whip in a fierce, loud whirl. Nelly and George made a move toward Cal.

"You two stay where you are!" Willis commanded.

Lillie looked on in horror as Bull snapped his arm back and the whip emitted a sound like a board snapping. He then flashed the lash forward again with a speed and ferocity that would surely flay the very flesh off Cal's back.

But the whip never touched the boy. As Lillie and the others watched, Bull's arm suddenly seemed to seize up— or, Lillie realized, to slow, as if it were all at once not moving through air, but through molasses. The whip itself, which had been snapped so fast it was nearly invisible, seemed to slow down too, and for an instant moved with the gentle, flowing motion of a length of cloth being twirled underwater. The scene was at once graceful and mystifying and utterly terrifying. No sooner had things seemed to slow down this way, however, than they sped back up again. The slave driver's arm snapped forward, pulling him violently off balance—so violently that with an audible pop, the bone of his shoulder jumped free from its socket. Bull dropped the whip and fell to the ground, howling in pain and clutching his shoulder as his arm hung limply by his side. Cal walked on, untouched.

For the second night in a row, Lillie took to her bed but got almost no sleep, spending the night living and reliving the events of the day. Bull's arm had been set right as quickly as it had been hurt. Louis and the overseer needed merely to pull it hard and twist it proper for the bone to pop back into place—just as they sometimes did when a slave dislocated his shoulder in the field. The arm would be fine again in time, but it would be weeks before Bull would be fit to whip anyone. No one could quite explain what had made his whip slow the way it had, but most people reckoned it had simply been caught by the wind or a muscle had seized up in his arm. Bull himself was in too much pain to think about the matter much.

Cal was flogged as Lillie knew he would be, but it was Louis, with his much lighter lash, who administered the punishment. What's more, with the appraiser still on the grounds, the Master wanted to appear stern but humane, so Louis was told to apply just three strokes. The pain was still terrible—judging at least from the way Cal cried out— but any damage to the skin of his back was small and would heal quickly.

Far, far worse was the matter of Plato. No one knew precisely what happened to slaves who vanished into the Cuban shipping trade, mostly because they were almost never seen again. They led a hard life that—with the threat of shipwreck, drowning and disease—often ended early. Plato himself had not understood the day's goings-on and had chattered for much of the afternoon about the fine jumping he'd done. He now slept peacefully beside his sister. Mama refused to discuss the matter, but she did close the curtain in the cabin tonight after getting in bed.

As Lillie lay awake, her thoughts finally turned to her papa. If he'd come back from the war, they would all be free today. And if he'd not been found in possession of the coins at his death, the same freedom would at least have come to his family. Instead, the family—like the coins themselves—remained the property of the Master. But that was a terrible injustice. Of all Papa's qualities, he was first of all an honest man, one who'd come by the coins in an honest way. If someone could prove that, Lillie, Mama and Plato could leave this place together—and Papa's name would be cleared.

Lillie herself was not the person to try such a thing. She was just a child—and a slave child at that—one who could never set foot off the plantation without the Master's permission, and could barely set foot outside the cabin without her mama's. But who else was there? Plato was too small, and Mama was Mama. Like all slave mamas, she had more than she could manage surviving day to day and seeing that her children did the same. So it fell to Lillie. If she herself did not set things right, they would always be wrong.

At that moment, in the silence of the cabin, she resolved that setting things right was just what she would do. She would prove Papa's innocence, she would free her family—and if she did it soon, she would keep her brother out of the appraiser's hands. Lillie had no idea how she was going to do all that, but she had no doubt that she was going to try.

Chapter Four

IKE ALL SLAVE CHILDREN, Lillie began working around the time she turned seven, fetching water or carrying tools in the field or, much better, chasing off birds that would swoop in to gobble up seeds as they were being planted. Small children loved being assigned to bird-chasing work, a job that kept them running and giggling and would usually turn into a game after the birds were gone—something that was fine with the overseer. Enough slave children engaging in a loud enough chase was more than was needed to remind the birds not to return for the rest of the day.

Lillie's mother did the more serious labor of a field slave, sometimes working alongside Plato, who was only beginning his seasons as a bird-chaser. Lillie had grown beyond bird work, and just last year she had been given a job in the nursery cabin, where the slave babies were looked after. Young mothers working in the fields would leave their babies there in the morning, come back to feed them two or three times during the day and fetch them again when the quitting horn sounded.

The job of caring for the slave babies used to be done by an old slave woman named Hannah, who had a natural gift for the work—able to silence an unruly child with a single hard stare or soothe a weepy one with a single soft touch. But Hannah died before the last planting season began, and there was no other slave woman of suitable age to handle the job. So Lillie was given the nursery cabin work, along with a young slave named Minervy. Minervy was about Lillie's age and was a hard-working girl, but also a very timid one—so nervous that other children would sometimes tease her by popping out from behind hay bales or wagons just to see who could make her leap the highest.

"There's sparrows what can spook that girl," Lillie's mama would say, and Lillie was inclined to agree. But inside the nursery cabin, Minervy seemed to have the same natural way with the babies Hannah had, which was why she had been picked for the job. Lillie—who quickly found that she liked chasing birds a lot better than chasing babies—was chosen mostly to help Minervy.

On the morning after the slave appraiser's visit, Lillie woke up with her decision to free her family still fresh in her mind. She had feared that in the full light of day it would seem like a fool idea—the kind of thing that's good for thinking about in the safety of a dark cabin deep at night, perhaps, but is best left there. Lillie, however, had a plan, one that she'd chewed over for much of the night until sleep had finally claimed her, and she reckoned it was a good one. Today she would set it in motion. The first step in doing that would be to figure out a way to sneak out of the nursery cabin during working hours—something she knew would not be easy.

Bull and Louis spent most of their time in the fields helping Mr. Willis keep the slaves from slowing down in the blaze of the afternoon sun. But now and then, they'd wander the grounds of the plantation, just to make sure that the slaves who worked in the chicken coops or hog pens didn't think that their pleasanter surroundings and softer jobs meant they didn't have to work hard too.Worse than getting caught by Bull or Louis would be getting caught by Mama, who was sometimes sent back from the fields to fetch a tool or a bundling bag or a bucket of drinking water. If she spotted Lillie getting into mischief, she'd likely thrash her harder than the slave drivers would.

The biggest reason it was hard for Lillie to slip out of the nursery cabin, however, was Minervy. As sure a hand as the girl had with the babies, she never seemed to trust that she could manage them alone. When Lillie left the cabin for so much as a privy visit, Minervy would fret and wring her hands, worrying that things would surely come undone in her absence.

"I can't quiet even one baby at a time," Lillie would remind Minervy. "You can hush a whole cabin of 'em." Minervy, however, would not be appeased.

Today, Lillie had no choice but to leave the girl on her own—at least if she wanted to follow her plan. The battle that had claimed her papa had been fought in distant Mississippi, and most anyone who had any information about how he came by the coins that stained his name would either have died along with him or scattered with the army to fight in other states. The idea that the likes of Lillie could solve a puzzle like that seemed a fool thought indeed. And yet there was a place she could begin looking: the town of Bluffton.

The wounded slave who'd served in Papa's platoon and claimed to have seen the coins was a man named Henry who'd worked at a farm not far from Greenfog. He had no money to go north when he was freed, and he wouldn't risk the travel even if he did—open roads in the midst of a war being no place for a one-legged former slave. When he'd come to Greenfog to bring the news about Papa, he'd said he was planning to settle instead in nearby Bluffton, where he was known and where he might even pick up paying work. If Lillie could somehow make her way there, she might be able to find him and learn something he wasn't telling.

Traveling to Bluffton, of course, would be well-nigh as hard as traveling to Mississippi, at least for Lillie by herself.

But Bett went there all the time. As the oldest of the slaves and the one least likely to run off, Bett was well-trusted at Greenfog and was often given traveling passes that would allow her to run errands. The most important of those errands were her once- or twice-monthly trips to Bluffton, where she would pick up the flour, cornmeal and other supplies she needed for her baking. Usually, she'd take a slave child with her for help, and once, when Lillie was nine years old, she'd been that child. Now she'd have to persuade Bett to take her again.

When the last of the mothers had dropped the last of the babies off at the nursery cabin this morning, Lillie craned her head outside to make sure they were gone, closed the door and, for extra measure, closed the shutter next to it too. Then she turned to Minervy, who was balancing a baby on her hip and glancing warily across the room at another one who had begun to fuss. Lillie spoke in a whisper.

"Minervy," she said, "I need your help."

Minervy regarded her suspiciously. "What kind o' help?"

"I need you to take care of the babies; I got to go do something."

"Do what?"

"I can't say."

"Then it has to be something you shouldn't."

Lillie shrugged. "Might be. All the same, I has to go."

"What'll you do if the slave driver sees you?" Minervy asked.

"I'll get thrashed, I expect."

"What'll you do if your mama sees you?"

"I'll get thrashed worse."

"And if someone comes by and asks me what become of you?"

"Tell 'em I took sick and will be back directly."

Minervy's eyes went wide. "Lillie, I can't tell a fib like that," she said, "at least not so's I'd be believed."

"You got to, Minervy," Lillie said.

"But I can't! It ain't fair!" Minervy pleaded, her voice rising high enough so that the fussing baby began to cry. "We'll get caught, and we'll both get whipped!"

Lillie took Minervy's shoulders, looked into her eyes and saw the whole of the other girl's fear there. She was about to tell her that she needed her help and that was that, but she stopped herself. Minervy was the uncommon kind of slave girl who watched herself so carefully she might well grow straight into her adult years without ever getting a taste of the lash, something she had told Lillie more than once she was determined to do. By asking her to lie now, Lillie could put her in the way of the whip she so wanted to avoid. Minervy was right: That wasn't fair. If Lillie was going to make trouble this morning, she would have to make it on her own—and take the consequences on her own.

"All right," she said, releasing Minervy's shoulders. "If anyone asks, tell 'em the truth. You don't know where I gone." She turned on her heel and slipped out the door before Minervy could say anything else.

Lillie stood in the soft grass in front of the nursery cabin and looked around herself warily. The route she would take to Bett's house would have to be a roundabout one—avoiding a direct run through the tobacco fields that would leave her open to getting spotted by Mama, or past the barns that might attract the notice of the slave drivers. Instead, she'd have to go a stealthier way, skirting the fields in so circular a path that she would brush up against the very boundaries of the plantation itself—an invisible line she dared not cross lest she be marked not merely a girl out on mischief but a runaway.

She set out at a light run and, despite her racing thoughts, found herself enjoying the feel of the grass beneath her feet and the fragrance of lavender on the air. Before she had gone more than a hundred yards, however, she once again noticed another smell—the smell of baking. It was crowded down by the flower smell rising from the fields, but it was there all the same, and as always, it was coming from the direction of Bett's house. Lillie picked up her pace and ran low and fast, keeping her head down to avoid being seen and following her nose as much as her eyes. At last, she doubled around the west corner of the tobacco field and Bett's cabin came into view. She stumbled to a stop in the scrub and low grass on Bett's tiny lot of land and bent forward with her hands on her knees to catch her breath and slow her pounding heart. Then she straightened up and looked about.

The slowbees were back—not many, just a few, so few that if you didn't know to look for them, you might not see them at all. And the slowbees weren't all that caught her eye. A dozen yards away, the little stream where Bett fetched her water gave off a deeper burble than it usually did, and even from here, Lillie could see that it too was behaving oddly, moving at a creep that gave it a look less of running water than of thick, cold syrup. Turning her gaze up, she saw that even the plume of oven smoke rising from Bett's chimney appeared to have slowed itself, feathering out across the sky like ink spreading in water. The water and the smoke, like the bees, could have easily escaped someone else's notice. Once again, Lillie heard the creak of the cabin door, and once again, Bett stood inside. But this time she opened the door wide and gave Lillie a fuller, more peaceful smile.

"Now you can come in, child," the old woman said. "I was wonderin' what was keepin' you."

Chapter Five

LILLIE STOOD WHERE she was for a long moment, staring at the usually friendly sight of Bett and yet feeling reluctant to move. She had known the old woman for as long as she could remember and had always found her a gentle presence. Now, however, Lillie was strangely afraid. Bett seemed to notice that. She opened the door wider and ticked her head invitingly.

"Come in," she repeated. "There's bread if you want some."

Lillie unrooted her feet, stepped across the grass and climbed the single step into the cabin. It was warm and close inside with the heat coming out of the oven, but Bett closed the door anyway, as if she already knew the reason for Lillie's visit and reckoned privacy was called for. The little house looked the way it always looked, furnished with an eating table and two chairs, a dresser with a small looking glass above it, and a bed covered with a soft, woolen throw Bett had owned for years and years and years. Lillie had always liked the colors of the worn old blanket—greens and yellows and oranges and scarlets on a background of deep black.

"Africa colors," Bett would say. "Been sleepin' under 'em my whole life."

The only part of the cabin that didn't look as tidy as the rest was the area near the hearth where Bett did her baking. There was a small wall of shelves filled with a jumble of baking trays, mixing bowls, spoons, whisks and knives. Next to it was a separate shelf stacked with an odd collection of bowls and pieces of china that were far too fine for a slave's cabin and in fact had come from the Big House. All of them were chipped or cracked or otherwise not suitable for the Master's home and had been given to Bett as a gift from the Missus.

"I expect these would look just fine in your kitchen," the Missus had said with a broad smile when she passed the battered old things to Bett.

"Yes, ma'am," was all Bett had said.

Beneath Bett's shelves was a long, well-used worktable where she mixed her batters and kneaded her doughs. Resting on the table was a fresh tray of dark bread. Lillie could see a few curls of steam rising from it and, though Mama had given her a good breakfast of hoecakes and milk, she could feel her belly rumbling. Bett saw her staring at the bread.

"You look hungry, girl," she said.

Lillie nodded mutely.

"Sit then," Bett said, gesturing to one of the two chairs.

Lillie did as she was told, and Bett sliced off a thick piece of the fresh bread. She blew the crumbs off a plate sitting on the mixing table, placed the bread on it and carried it to the eating table. Lillie inhaled the heavy, yeasty smell and took a bite. The bread, as always, was just what bread ought to be. The crust was thick and flavorful, and fought with her a little when she bit it. The inside was cloud light. It was as if two foods had come together in a single one, and Lillie ate hungrily. Bett sat down and watched her and, after a long moment, spoke.

"I reckoned today was the day you'd come," she said.

"I woulda come earlier if I coulda got away," Lillie said through a mouthful of bread.

"I know," Bett said. "You want to talk about the boy—Plato."

Lillie stopped chewing and looked up, the appetite suddenly gone from her. She nodded. "How do you know?" she asked.

"People talk, I listen," Bett said. "You want to know if I can help you."

Lillie nodded again. "Can you?" she asked.

"What is it you reckon I can do?"

"I need to get to Bluffton," Lillie said, putting down her

bread. She leaned in and spoke low and fast as if someone might be listening. "I need to go soon. We was supposed to be freed, but since they say my papa done some stealin', they ain't never gonna let us go. I got to show he didn't do it or they'll take Plato away and we won't never see him again." Lillie never found it easy to talk about Papa without the talk turning to tears—especially when she had to repeat the lie about the stealing. But she swallowed hard and her eyes stayed dry.

"What's in Bluffton?" Bett asked. She pushed Lillie's bread plate a little closer to her, but Lillie had lost interest in eating and Bett did not press her further.

"A man," Lillie said. "A slave soldier what might know somethin'."

"You think I can help you get there?"

"You can," Lillie said.

"You think you can just walk about a place like that, askin' questions like you was growed and free?"

"I got to try. I can't let 'em take Plato!"

Bett sat back. "You're askin' a lot, girl," she said. "And you're askin' for trouble too. No harm would come to me— even that Bull wouldn't lay a whip to my back, and the Master couldn't get more'n a coin if he tried to sell me off for misbehavin'. But you'd fetch a price and a flogging both if you got caught. And besides . . ." Bett trailed off as if considering whether or not she ought to continue. Then she went on, but more gently. "And besides, how do you know they wasn't tellin' the truth 'bout your papa? It ain't every slave man what comes by a bag o' Yankee gold, 'less he took it."

Lillie's eyes went fiery, and her tone went cold. "My papa weren't no thief," she said, rising to her feet, "and I won't listen to no one call him one. He lived an honest man, and he died one too! And if you don't believe me, we ain't got nothin' to talk about!" She pushed her chair back noisily, nearly knocking it over, and began to stalk toward the door.

"Girl!" Bett called after her sharply. Lillie slowed, then turned back. "Sit back down!"

Lillie hesitated and Bett's stern tone and face softened to weary amusement. "Sit," she said, with a tired wave of her hand. Lillie returned to the table and Bett looked at her thoughtfully.

"No, child," the old woman said at length. "I don't reckon your papa was a thief. A thievin' man's always lookin' about, as if he's waitin' to be caught at somethin'. An honest man got a steady way about him—and your papa was steady like a tree. You got his way about you, and you got his looks too—which I reckon pleases you less than if you had your mama's looks. But you're Ibo and your papa was Ibo, and your mama ain't."

This was not the first time Bett had mentioned that Lillie was Ibo, and Lillie could never tell if she meant it as a good thing or not. "A lot of Ibo in you, child," Bett liked to say if she caught Lillie wrestling with another child or otherwise making trouble. "Maybe too much."

Papa had had a lot more to say than Bett on the matter of the Ibo, and he had talked of it often. The Ibo were the African tribe that Bett's people and his people—and so Lillie's own people—had come from. It was something she ought to be proud of, he said. The Ibo were known as fine music-makers and storytellers and were said to be especially good with numbers, coming up with their own form of ciphering that was even better than the one the white men used. Best of all, at least to Lillie, the Ibo people didn't see much difference between an Ibo boy and an Ibo girl, an Ibo man and an Ibo woman, reckoning any Ibo could hunt or plant or fight or tend as well as any other one. Full-grown Ibo women even went into battle alongside the men, facing the same enemies and carrying the same weapons. Bett used to say that she could spot an Ibo in any group of Southern slaves, and it was that readiness to tangle when they had to that set them apart. Sitting across the table from Lillie, she now looked in the girl's face, seeming to study it closely.

"I expect you aim to do this thing," she said.

Lillie nodded.

"And I expect you won't let me be if I don't give you some help," Bett added.

Lillie shook her head no.

Bett sighed and then stood, pressing her palms down

on the table to help herself rise, grunting with the effort. "I'm too old to be of much use to you myself," she said, "but maybe I got somethin' that can serve."

She made her way over to her baking shelves and took down a small, reddish jar, holding it carefully in both hands. The jar looked like ordinary Carolina clay, but it was shaped like it had been made with another land in mind. Bett carried it back to the table, set it down and took the lid off. She withdrew a small cloth bag and opened the drawstring that kept it shut. Then she tipped the bag into her hand, and a shiny chip of black stone fell into her palm.

"That," she said, "is a piece of Africa."

Bett slowly tilted the chip this way and that. It had a surface that looked as if it had been polished, and it reflected light like a bright coin. "Your papa never knew what part of the Ibos' land his people come from," Bett said, "but I knew where mine was from. A place not far from the ocean, where the ground was cut through by rivers and streams. The water always ran fast and bright there, and my papa said his papa told him it tasted fine too—what a cloud would taste like if you could squeeze it down tight and put it in a bowl. Still, there was one place the water didn't run so quick, and that was on my granddaddy's land. When it flowed through there, it flowed like syrup. But if you scooped the water out and poured it on the ground, it spilled as quick as any water ought to. Ever see any other water behavin' like that?"

Lillie nodded.

"I reckoned you had. My granddaddy never could understand why his stream behaved that way. Then he dug beneath the mud where the fish and turtles fed and found black rock everywhere just like this chip—long, hard bones of it runnin' through the ground. The Africans called the rock firestone, 'cause it come from the hot rocks the mountains spit out. Granddaddy reckoned it was the firestone what held the magic that slowed his river, figuring stone that flowed fast and then turned hard could share its changin' nature with the water. He broke some bits offa the rock and carried them with him for luck. When the slavers caught him, he hid two of the chips under his tongue and promised himself he'd never spit them out—not when he got chained, not when he got whipped, not when they closed him in the belly of a ship and carried him across the ocean. He held on to 'em till he was sold to a plantation where he could hide 'em well and pass 'em on to his children and to their children who came after."

"And this here piece is all that's left?" Lillie asked softly.

Bett smiled again. "No, child," she said. "I got the other one too."

Bett stood again and gestured to Lillie to follow her. She walked the three steps to her still-hot oven and crouched down in front of it. Lillie did the same, flinching at the heat coming out of the bricks. Bett pointed into the oven and Lillie followed where her finger indicated. At first she noticed nothing, but then she saw what Bett wanted her to see: a single brick in the oven wall, just the same as all the other bricks except that in the middle of it was a shiny piece of black stone, about as big as a small coin. The stone was plain to see once you knew where to look, but no one other than Bett would ever have cause to use her oven, much less crouch down low and peer inside.

"I reckoned I needed a place to keep at least one of 'em safe," Bett said. "So I baked me a brick and mortared it in where no one would ever look. What I didn't figure on was that when I lit the fire, the magic o' that stone would get carried on the smoke. It flows out of the chimney and just like it slowed my granddaddy's river—"

"It slows the bees!" Lillie finished. "And the stream and the smoke!"

Bett nodded.

"What about the whip—the one what missed Cal?" Lillie asked.

"That too," Bett said.

"But how did you make it work just right—so the whip didn't hit nothin' but the air?"

"That sort o' thing comes with practice. Part of it comes from just when you light the fire and just when you put it out. Part of it's how you bake. If I bake my bread the regular way, I can slow things down a little; if I bake it too long, I can slow 'em down a lot. I can even bake it too short and speed things up. There's other things them stones can do too, but they don't bear foolin' with."

"What other things?" Lillie asked.

"Never mind. Didn't I just say they don't bear foolin' with?"

"But why not?"

"There's magic you touch and there's magic you don't," Bett said firmly, "and I'll tell you which is which."

"But s'posin'—" Lillie began.

"I said never mind!" Bett answered, and this time she spoke with a bite in her voice Lillie had never heard before.

Lillie fell silent and looked awkwardly down at her hands.

Bett softened her tone and smiled. "It was wrong o' me to make mention of such a thing. We got enough magic in this oven and this stone already without pushin' it places it ain't meant to go. Besides, I don't plan to use it at all 'less we got no other choice."

Lillie nodded. "How will we know that?" she asked.

Bett's demeanor now changed entirely and she allowed herself a laugh. "Full of questions," she said. "Too many for today. You go back to that nursery now 'fore anyone notices you missing. Ain't no one gonna bother your brother for a little while yet."

"When can I come again?" Lillie asked.

"Two days," Bett said. " 'Round about then, I reckon I'll be needin' to make a trip to Bluffton, and I could always use the help of a young pair of hands."

Lillie brightened, Bett's angry moment now entirely forgotten. "Two days!" she said excitedly. Then she jumped up from her seat as Bett struggled up from hers, and the old woman and young girl hugged good-bye at the door. Bett watched as Lillie ran off and vanished back the way she came. Then she closed the door, gathered up her stone and swaddled it carefully in its drawstring bag.

Chapter Six

MISS SARABETH was taking her morning stroll when she spied Lillie dashing out of the cabin where Bett the baker lived. That was a surprise, since near as Sarabeth could recall, the place Lillie belonged at this time of day was in the nursery cabin tending to the slave babies. The fact was, however, it had been so long since the two girls played together that neither one was entirely sure any longer how the other spent her day.

There was a time when Sarabeth—who was the Master's daughter—and Lillie, who was the Master's property, played together all the time. They played on Saturdays, when Lillie and Plato were done with their cabin chores and Mama let them go outside; they played on Sundays, when Miss Sarabeth had her afternoons free and the Missus gave her permission to go down to the slave cabins. They would sometimes even play after work was done on weekdays, when both of them had an hour or so before Lillie was called back to the cabin for a dinner of possum or fatback and Miss Sarabeth was called back to the big house for whatever grand meal she would be served that night—a meal that Lillie would ask her about the next day and that Miss Sarabeth would describe in detail, from the creamy soups to the venison or fowl to the tiny sweet cakes she and her brother would eat and the strong brown spirits the men would drink.

Nobody thought it especially strange that Lillie and Miss Sarabeth liked to play together. Plantation children of both colors often fancied one another's company—there being few other boys or girls anywhere nearby—and it was only the sternest masters who thought it unfitting for the colors to mix when they were so young. But when the children reached Miss Sarabeth's and Lillie's age, it was time for the white boys and girls to start behaving like the Southern ladies and gentlemen they were becoming and the black boys and girls to start acting like the slaves they already were and would always be.

Before long, Miss Sarabeth started coming to visit Lillie less and less. While she still sometimes stopped by on the weekends, it was usually in the company of the Missus, who liked to put on fine clothes and tour the slave quarters, smiling in a way Lillie never cared for.

"They look after themselves just fine, don't they?" the

Missus would ask Sarabeth as if Lillie and the other slaves weren't there. "Your father was right to let them build good cabins that they'd be inclined to keep well."

It had been about a month since Miss Sarabeth had made such a visit, and it had thus been that long since she'd last set eyes on Lillie. Part of her smiled this morning as she was taking her walk along the path by the tobacco field and saw her old friend leaving Bett's cabin—but another part frowned. Even before Miss Sarabeth drew near the cabin, she caught the scent of baking on the air. When she was small and she and Lillie would smell that smell, they would steal away from wherever they were supposed to be and run to see Bett, who would break off a piece of whatever bread or cake she was making and let them have some— always taking care to brush the crumbs off their clothes before they left, so that the fact that they'd been there at all would be a secret only the three of them shared. But after a time, Miss Sarabeth had begun to tire of the old baker woman. Bett always tried to give the girls equal helpings of bread, knowing that small children quarrel about such things. But the portions could never be exactly the same, and on those occasions that Lillie got the bigger one, Miss Sarabeth made her trade.

Lillie didn't appear to mind at first—that was how things were supposed to be—but Bett sometimes did. A disapproving look would flash in her eyes that Miss Sarabeth found she didn't care for at all, especially because it became clearer and clearer that Bett wasn't trying to hide it. Worse still, Lillie began to behave the same way, flashing the same cross look Bett did. It would be there only for an instant, but Miss Sarabeth knew her friend's face, and she didn't like what it told her. The last time the two of them visited the cabin, Miss Sarabeth didn't feel welcome at all, as Bett and Lillie chattered and baked and she sat sourly at the eating table, picking at the bread when it was done and wanting to be anywhere else at all. After that, she decided that it probably wasn't fitting for her to be visiting Bett anymore. Soon, she stopped visiting Lillie too.

As Sarabeth had first approached the cabin today, the baking smell had seemed especially strong and she had drawn it in, feeling sadder than she expected to. She sometimes missed the bread and missed the warm old cabin where she used to enjoy it—even if she didn't miss the odd old woman who lived there. It was then that she heard the door open and turned to see Lillie emerge. Bett whispered something to her and the girl smiled and ran off to who knew where else. An uncertain smile crossed Sarabeth's face and she started to raise her hand in greeting, but neither Lillie nor Bett saw her. She had the strange feeling that even though everything around her as far as she could see belonged to her father and by rights to her too, she was tarrying somewhere she shouldn't be.

Sarabeth was surprised at the sense of melancholy that came over her. Still, she couldn't quite make out why Lillie would be there at all at this time of day, or what she and Bett had been whispering about. There was something going on that they didn't want anybody else to know about, and Sarabeth decided she did not like that. Her father looked after all these slaves, and if they were up to something improper, they were worse than disobedient, they were ungrateful. When Miss Sarabeth contemplated this, she did not feel quite as melancholy anymore. What she felt was cross and sour—and suspicious too.

Chapter Seven

CAL WAS ABOUT as happy as he'd ever been when he came to the tobacco field to do his work this morning. He believed he had plenty of cause to be so happy—but the truth was, he had plenty of cause to fear for his life.

In recent months, Cal—like all slave boys his age—had begun to chafe at the kind of work he'd been doing since he was small. Bird chasing, which once seemed like such fun, was for babies, and weed pulling—which was the job he'd been doing for the last two seasons—was for old ladies. Neither was fitting for a boy like him anymore. Already two other boys just a little older than Cal had begun working the fields with shovels and scythes, and before long would even try their hands behind a plow. Cal couldn't help but notice the swagger they'd been walking with ever since they'd been put to their new chores—nor the fact that the girls seemed to notice it too. None of them were of a mind to notice how many grown slaves would eventually be broken by such labors; that was something they would learn when they were older. For now, the work seemed only manly and thrilling.

For most of this season, it had appeared that Cal would have to wait until next year before he'd be given such serious chores, but this very morning it looked like all that had changed. Mr. Willis himself came to his cabin during breakfast and told Cal he'd finally decided to give him a chance to work the plow in the tobacco fields. Cal beamed at the news—and Nelly and George beamed to see him so happy. The boy had jumped past the scythe and shovel work the older boys were doing and gone straight to the labors of a full-grown man. If Mr. Willis had been cross about what happened with Bull, certainly this was proof that his anger had cooled and he might even value the boy's unexpected brass.

Mr. Willis allowed Cal to gulp down a mug of milk and two biscuits Nelly gave him, then escorted him personally to the spot where he'd be working today—the two of them attracting curious stares as they strolled along the grounds. When the man and the boy drew closer to the tobacco fields, Cal could see a few other, early-arriving slaves already at work, their heads and shoulders rising and falling above the tall leaves. Just at the edge of the field was a long patch of unplanted land that was known as the scrub strip, for its stony soil and bristly weeds. There'd been talk in recent months that the Master hoped to plant there next year. Though seeding season was months off, it would not be unusual for an uncultivated stretch of land like that to be cleared and turned in the early fall so it would have the winter to take in air and water. As Cal approached now, he was thrilled to see a large plow already standing in wait in the scrub strip with a black horse rigged to the front. The animal occasionally pawed the topsoil and tossed its mane, looking as impatient to set to work as Cal felt. Cal smiled broadly—but his expression quickly changed when he took a few more steps and saw just which horse it was that was waiting for him. He stopped and turned to Mr. Willis.

"That's Coal Mine," he said.

"Them's sharp eyes," Willis answered. "Coal Mine's who it is."

That was a very bad turn. Coal Mine was one of the biggest horses at Greenfog and easily the orneriest, a beast so ill-tempered it snorted and bit even when it was in a good frame of mind. The horse had been given its name on account of its deep, black coat, but none of the slaves ever addressed him that way, since—unlike any horse they'd ever seen—Coal Mine seemed to grow angrier at the very sound of his name. The safest way to address him was usually just "you horse!"—at least until he took offense to that too.

Cal slowly approached the field, stopping when he was

still a good fifteen feet away from the horse and the plow. Willis looked at him with a small, mean smile.

"The matter, boy?" he asked. "You ain't scared, are you?"

"No, sir," Cal said.

"You don't wanna go back to bird chasin', do you?"

"No, sir."

"Then get yourself in harness and get behind that animal," Willis instructed.

Cal nodded but didn't move.

"Now," the man said.

Cal circled nervously around Coal Mine and stepped toward the harness laid out along the ground. He lifted the heavy leather shoulder straps, jostling them as little as possible. Coal Mine snorted menacingly.

"Faster, boy!" Willis snapped. "Morning's half gone already."

Cal slipped the rest of the way into the harness, took hold of the reins, then snapped them and clicked his tongue the way he'd seen the grown slaves do. To his surprise, Coal Mine started to move. Even Mr. Willis looked like he hadn't expected that and grunted in what was either approval or annoyance. After a few moments of watching Cal at work, he turned to go back to the tobacco fields, warning Cal before he left that he'd be back to check on him and, if he saw him slacking, would whip him soundly. "Unless I don't jes' feed you to that horse," he added with a laugh.

For a little while after Mr. Willis left, Cal and Coal Mine got on passably well, but their work was not easy. The plow would never go more than a few feet before coming up against a slab of stone so big that the clank of the blade would vibrate right through the rigging and into the boy and the horse themselves, causing both to jump. Cal would then have to creep forward and clear away the obstacle before he could go any farther—always keeping low so as to dodge a hoof if it came his way. After enough clangs and enough delays, Coal Mine had had enough, stopping cold in the field and refusing to move. Cal clicked his tongue and the horse did nothing; he snapped the reins, and the horse kicked out. He tried doing both at once and Coal Mine first reared up and then kicked back, doing both so furiously that Cal was convinced the animal was going to tip the plow and rip the riggings.

"Ain't seen no one handle this horse so poor before," Mr. Willis's voice called out as he breasted back through the tobacco plants, nodding his head in mock disappointment. "I guess two beasts as thick as the pair of you just wasn't meant to be together."

"We was fine for a time, sir," Cal said, "but I can't make him do nothin' now."

"You best try harder," Willis snapped. "You push on him yet?"

"*Push* on him, sir?"

"You got mud in your ears, boy?"

"Mr. Willis, I touch that horse, and he'll kill me sure."

"You don't touch him, and I'll kill you sure. Stand off to the side and push him from there if you're so afraid. He kicks then, you might just dodge them hooves."

Cal looked at Willis warily, then at Coal Mine, and concluded he stood a better chance with the animal than with the man. He dropped the reins and harness, crept toward Coal Mine's left flank, and placed his hands on the hindquarters. The horse felt bristly and hot and, to Cal's surprise, did not react to his touch. Cal pushed gently, and Coal Mine snorted loudly.

"More!" Willis commanded.

Cal pushed Coal Mine harder and the animal snorted louder.

"More!" Willis shouted, snapping his whip loudly.

Cal drew a breath, closed his eyes and did as he was told, shoving Coal Mine hard enough to tell even the dimmest horse it had to move. "You horse!" he shouted for extra measure.

At that, Coal Mine produced a sound Cal had never heard from a horse before—less a snort than a roar. He lashed back with his hooves once, and then again, and still again.

On that last one, he twisted his body as he kicked, whipped a hind leg around and clipped Cal hard on the side of the head. The hoof and shoe met scalp and skull and the world seemed to explode in a burst of blackness and sparkles, accompanied by a pain so great it passed beyond pain altogether. Cal felt himself flying through the air and then hitting the ground with a hard, blind thump that shook all his bones and snapped his head back even more violently than the kick had. Cal heard nothing, saw nothing and lay completely still, reckoning with a strange sort of calm that this was probably the end of him and that, with his head and bones all likely broke, that just might be a good thing. After a time—there was no telling how long—the blackness began to part and he heard Mr. Willis's voice, muffled and thick as if it were coming through molasses.

"Get up, boy," it sounded like the voice was saying.

Cal could not move.

"Get up," the voice repeated.

Cal opened his eyes and saw the overseer standing above him. The man was bent over and squinting at him hard, with an unfamiliar expression on his face. The expression would have passed for concern if Cal had been a white child, but was likelier an expression of worry that one piece of the Master's property might have been broken beyond repair by another piece and that Willis himself might have to pay for the damage.

"You're fine," Willis said, and Cal now heard him more clearly. "That animal only nicked you. He'da hit you square, you'd be dead now."

Lifting himself on his elbows, Cal looked dizzily about and saw other slaves running toward him. Racing through their legs was Plato and behind him, his mama. Plato had been watching Cal admiringly as he worked Coal Mine along the plow line; the moment the horse kicked out, the boy took off.

"Is he gonna die, Mama?" Plato cried. "Is he gonna die?"

"Stand back!" Willis commanded. Plato kept running and when he came within reach, Willis shoved him away hard.

"Come to me, child!" Mama commanded. "This ain't your affair!"

"Hold that boy 'fore I decide not to wait for the appraiser and just sell him off today!" Willis yelled. Mama grabbed Plato and held him close

Cal sat the rest of the way up, feeling dizzy enough to lose his breakfast. His eyes seemed to be loose in their sockets. His face was sticky with blood flowing from a cut where the horse's hoof had hit. In the ground was an impression as deep as a bowl where his head had struck and sunk.

"I ain't gonna die," Cal said dully to Plato. His own voice sounded odd and echolike to him.

Two slave men stepped forward to help Cal to his feet and Willis glared at them. "The boy's gonna get up on his own," he said.

The men stepped back and Cal rose slowly to a crouch, steadied himself and stood up cautiously. He wiped the blood from his cheek and then, absently, wiped his hand on his shirt. He turned to Plato, flashed a weak smile—and then winked. Plato beamed.

"Somethin' funny to you?" Willis shouted at Cal.

"No, sir," Cal answered.

"To you?" he yelled even more fiercely at Plato.

Plato shook his head in a terrified no.

"You ready to get back behind that plow?" Willis barked at Cal.

Cal hesitated. "Yes, sir," he answered, his head throbbing with the mere effort of speaking.

"Louder!"

"Yes, sir."

"Again!"

"Yes, sir!" Cal shouted this time, wincing with the jolt of pain that seemed to go through his brain.

"Once more!" Willis screamed, snapping his whip at the ground next to Cal. "Answer me, boy, and answer me loud!"

"Yes, sir!" Cal now shouted as loudly as he could. "Yes sir, yes sir, yes sir!"

With that, Cal's eyes widened and his nostrils flared, and the people in the crowd looked at him and froze. In that instant, they could see, Cal was about to do the most dangerous thing any slave could do: He was about to forget who he was. He was no longer just the property of the Master doing the bidding of the overseer. He was a blameless boy being tormented by a small, cruel man with a whip. A slave who let himself think that way was a slave getting set to scream or curse or even strike out, and to earn himself a whipping so severe it would cut the flesh from his bones. In Willis's eyes there was a quick, cold spark as he braced for the blow—a blow, it was suddenly clear, he'd been hoping for all morning. In a flash, the two slave men who'd tried to help Cal before leapt forward and grabbed him hard. One of them pinned the boy's arms by his side, while the other slapped him hard across the face.

"Don't do it, boy," the one holding him hissed into his ear. "Don't do it."

Willis glared furiously at the men, then turned to Cal and fixed him with a poisonous look. "You're no good, boy!" he shouted, his pasty skin turning an angry crimson and a small, wormlike vein bulging in his forehead. "No good even for a slave. I'd whip you till there weren't nothing left to whip if the Master didn't think he could make a coin offa you. You best just hope he sells you before I kill you—

because that's what I aims to do! Now get back in that plow harness! The rest of you, back to work!"

The slaves edged away slowly, dispersing back into the field. The two men who had hold of Cal carried him bodily back to the plow and waited there until he had himself back in harness. Plato stood staring, and Mama turned him around by his shoulders and ordered him back to the fields. When the boy was gone, Mama approached Cal, touched his cheek and turned his head so she could examine him. The blood was oozing from a lump the size of an egg and Mama winced at the sight of it. Mr. Willis had been right; if that horse had kicked him square, Cal would be dead. She looked him in the eye.

"Keep hold of yourself, son," she said. "He means what he says."

Chapter Eight

MAMA WAS NOT happy when Lillie told her she'd be traveling to Bluffton with Bett. News like this was not the kind of thing that would have pleased Mama on any day, but having already seen Cal get kicked by the horse as the morning was just beginning, she had about had her fill of the kinds of trouble children their age could cook up for themselves.

"Are you tryin' to get yourselves sold?" Mama asked when Lillie told her about her plans.

"But, Mama," Lillie said, "Bett almost always takes a child with her when she goes to Bluffton."

"A small child," Mama said. "Girls as old as you got work to do right here."

The matter would have ended there, but Lillie's eyes looked so bright at the idea of leaving the grounds—brighter than they'd looked at any time since Papa died—that Mama couldn't bring herself to say no. The world could be tiny for any slave, especially one with the restless spirit of a child. If the plantation's gates opened even a little, it would be flat cruel not to let Lillie go through them. Mama swallowed her worries and said yes.

It was, as Bett had promised, just two mornings later that she and Lillie set out on their journey. Mama and Plato accompanied Lillie to the stable, where the wagon would be getting readied for the trip. The girl's breath quickened with each step that took her farther away from the cabin. Plato noticed her rising excitement and looked at his sister enviously.

"How come I can't go too, Mama?" he said.

"Hush, boy," Mama answered. "I can't have the both of you to worry about."

When the three of them rounded the path that led to the stables, they could see that the horse and wagon were already waiting and Bett had settled into one of the seats behind Samuel, the old wagon driver. Samuel had spent much of his life on the plantation and had never done any job but tending the horses and driving the Master or the other slaves. A tall, broad man with large, powerful hands, Samuel would once have been considered good protection for a woman and a girl traveling by themselves. But he was now past sixty—very old for a slave and even for many white men—and sometimes he seemed barely able to look after himself anymore. Mama regarded him uneasily.

Lillie pulled free of Mama's hand, which she had been

holding since they left the cabin, and sprinted ahead. She hopped up lightly into the seat beside Bett and kissed the old woman on the cheek. Bett patted her hand. Mama and Plato trotted up after her.

"You have your traveling pass?" Mama asked Samuel. The old man smiled and patted his breast pocket, then looked alarmed. He groped in his jacket for the paper that was the only thing that would protect them from slave catchers if they left the plantation without a white adult accompanying them. The paper was not there.

"Samuel!" Mama cried.

"Phibbi," Bett said evenly, "quit your worryin'. I got it here." She patted her apron pocket and Mama could see the edge of the precious paper poking from the top. "Samuel gave it to me already; he just forgot." Samuel looked embarrassed, and Lillie and Bett smiled. Mama didn't.

"All right, then," Mama said, waving her hands impatiently. "If you're gonna go, go. Soonest you leave is the soonest you come back."

"Yes, Miss Phibbi," Samuel said. He turned to Bett. "All right, Miss Bett?"

Bett nodded and Samuel snapped the reins. The wagon jerked into motion, and as it did, so did Lillie's heart, pounding in anticipation behind her breastbone. She waved excitedly to Plato—who waved back sulkily—and blew a kiss to Mama; then she watched them dwindle behind her as the horse clopped away. When Lillie could see them no more, she turned ahead, looking all about herself as the wagon bounced past the slave cabins, circled around the side of the Big House and headed for the long, tree-lined drive that led past the plantation gate and into the swirling world beyond.

For more than a quarter hour, Lillie sat with her back straight and her head swiveling from one side to the other, taking in the strange roads and fields and fences as they passed—roads and fields and fences that were no different from the ones on the grounds of Greenfog, but utterly different all the same. After a while, her neck began to ache and Bett pulled her gently back.

"Long trip and a lot to do when we get there," she said. "Don't work yourself up too much now."

Lillie nodded and settled back. Bett was right, she knew. Collecting baking supplies was not the only reason she was on this trip, nor even the one that concerned her much. She was really here to look for Henry, the one-legged slave who fought alongside Papa. Bluffton was a big place to go searching for someone—the biggest place Lillie had ever seen—and how a single person would go about finding a single other person there was beyond her. As Lillie thought of that, a feeling of worry came over her and she dropped her eyes. Her gaze fell on the traveling pass in Bett's pocket and Bett noticed her staring at it. The old woman looked at her, then carefully removed the paper and—as was the slave's habit even when no one was looking—glanced cautiously about herself. Then she handed the folded sheet to Lillie, who took it excitedly and unfolded it. She looked down at the curly writing on the page, trying to focus her eyes on the small fancy letters as the wagon bounced and bumped. Slowly, sometimes moving her lips, Lillie did something extraordinary: She read to herself.

"Know all men by this instrument: The slave man Samuel, the slave woman Bett and the slave girl Lillie have leave to journey from the Greenfog Estate to the town of Bluffton on plantation business on this Twelfth day of September, Eighteen Hundred and Sixty-Three. Please lend all assistance and offer no delay to their passage as they are under charge and order to return before nightfall of this day."

It was signed by the Master in letters even harder to read than those that filled the rest of the paper. Under his name were the words "Planter and Owner."

Lillie felt the pride she always experienced when she read, along with the thrill that came from doing something that was strictly forbidden and harshly punishable. No one was certain how many slaves on all the plantations of the South were able to read so much as a word, but the guessing was that it was not five in a hundred. Lillie had learned from her papa, who himself had learned as a boy, when he would carry his Master's son's books to school and then wait outside in the sun so that he could carry them home in the late afternoon. With nothing to do during those long hours, he found himself listening through the window as the white children got their lessons and slowly learning the letters himself. Oftentimes he'd even get to practice what he'd learned when the white boys would bring picture books and adventure journals to school—things their parents forbade them to read—and leave them with their slave boys to hold.

Papa taught Lillie's mama to read shortly after they wed, and he began teaching Lillie and Plato as soon as they could talk. He decided what he wanted to call Plato even before the boy was born, after he'd been summoned to the Master's library to fix a leaky ceiling and had secretly flipped through a book written by a man of the same name. Papa never had a chance to read more than a few scraps of sentences in those pages, but the little he did see had stayed with him. He told Plato that he'd given him the name to remind both of his children of the kinds of grand thoughts all people could think—whether they lived forever as slaves or one day tasted freedom.

Lillie carefully returned the traveling pass to Bett, then sat quietly for the rest of the hour-and-a-half-long journey to Bluffton. When they finally arrived, there was no mistaking where they were. Buildings rose up on either side of the hard dirt street, some of them three stories tall. The building fronts were a splash of colorful awnings and signs describing the businesses conducted inside—DRY GOODS,

HABERDASHER, HAY & FEED, TELEGRAPH OFFICE—but Lillie dared not linger on them, lest she reveal herself as being able to make sense of the letters.

People seemed to be milling everywhere—black people and white people alike, though it was mostly the whites who were on the planked sidewalks or inside the stores. The slaves kept largely to the streets, loading and unloading wagons and dodging the horses and rigs that clattered by. Lillie thought she recognized some of the black faces from visits those slaves had paid to Greenfog when they were running errands or driving their masters. None of the white people looked familiar.

"Stay close by me, girl," Bett said. "It won't do for you to get lost."

"Yes'm," Lillie said, not needing to be reminded of such a thing.

Samuel brought the wagon as close as he could to a store marked GROCER—PURE MILK, FOODS & NECESSITIES and reined the horse to a halt. Lillie hopped down from the wagon and helped Bett ease herself out of her seat and into the road. They left Samuel to mind the horse, dodged the puddles and wheel ruts underfoot, climbed the sidewalk and entered the store. With the sun not yet high, it was poorly lit inside, but as Lillie's eyes began to adjust, she gaped at the bounty on the shelves and tables that filled the big room.

There were bags of rice and grains, jars of beans and peas, baskets of apples and squash, jugs of milk still foaming at the top, dried fruits wrapped in brown paper and jars of preserves put up on shelves. There were whole salted fish and dried flanks of pork, wheels of cheese covered in wax and barrels of nuts, barley, coffee and cocoa. There were also large sacks of sugar and flour and salt, which were the things they had come here today to buy.

Lillie and Bett were the only shoppers in the store save for a white man in coveralls, and they stood to the side while the proprietor tended to him. As they waited, a young white mother and her small, toddling boy entered. The proprietor turned to them when he'd finished with his first customer, seeming not to notice Lillie and Bett at all. He smiled agreeably at the mother, inquired if she wasn't finding it warm for September and offered the boy a licorice stick from a large glass jar he kept on the counter. He filled the woman's order—a long shopping list of what seemed to be no end of items—and helped her out to her wagon with her bundles. It was only after the mother and child had left and the proprietor had sorted through some receipts on his counter and poured himself a cup of coffee from a pot he kept on a black iron stove, that he turned to Bett and Lillie.

"Traveling pass," he said brusquely. Bett stepped forward and handed the man the folded paper; he scanned it quickly and handed it back to Bett. "Greenfog," he said with a snort, as if this was somehow bad news. "Tell me what you're needin' and scat."

Bett told the man what they had come for and he gathered up the items quickly and wordlessly. Slaves were not allowed to carry money and the purchase would thus be billed to the Master. The shopkeeper made a note of the amount and carried the heavy sacks out to the sidewalk—less to be courteous, Lillie suspected, than to be done with her and Bett. Samuel spotted them and ran over. The man waved Lillie and Bett off the sidewalk and away from the front of his store.

"Your man can do your liftin'," he said. "You two wait in the street meantime. And tell your Master he's owin' me for two months of goods; I'll be expectin' payment soon."

Lillie went a little cold at that. The emptier the Master's purse grew, the more he'd need the money he could raise selling his slaves. The two hundred dollars the appraiser said he'd get in exchange for Plato would settle a lot of debts. Bett seemed to know what Lillie was thinking and squeezed her hand, and the two of them stepped off the sidewalk as Samuel began to hoist the sacks and load them into the wagon. Lillie tried to help, wrapping her arms around what looked to be the lightest one and feeling its scratchy burlap against her face and arms. She heaved with all her strength and while she got it off the ground, she staggered under the weight of it. Samuel took it from her with one hand and flipped it into the wagon bed. Bett then pulled Lillie aside, looked about herself and leaned toward her. She spoke in a low voice.

"We done with what I come here to do today, and the smart thing now is just to go home," she said.

Lillie nodded.

"You still mean to look for that man what can speak for your papa?"

"I do."

"You understand the trouble you can fetch yourself messin' in affairs like that?"

"I do."

Bett looked at her thoughtfully. "I reckon you do know," she said. "You best go do it, then, 'fore you lose your nerve." She waved Lillie off the way the shopkeeper had just shooed both of them. Lillie stayed where she was.

"You ain't comin' with me?" she asked.

"I'm old, child," Bett said. "I can't go chasin' around a town this size. And Samuel can't leave the wagon." She pointed Lillie toward the tall tower that crowned the top of the Bluffton town hall. A great clock with fancy hands looked down at them. "You read time as good as you can read words?" she asked.

Lillie nodded. "It's quarter past ten," she said.

"You got till quarter past four," Bett said. "That travelin' pass says we don't got to be home till sundown, but we don't dare get back a minute later. Keep that clock in sight and be here on time, lest we got to leave you behind." Bett pointed to a stand of sycamore trees that was casting a shade big enough for a wagon. "Samuel and I brought water and a bite o' bread. We'll be there waitin'."

Lillie looked slowly around herself at the busy town with the milling people and swallowed hard. Then she looked back at Bett.

"Go, little Ibo," the old woman said. "Do what you got to do."

Chapter Nine

MINERVY WASN'T the kind of girl inclined to use a curse word. That was good, since even at age thirteen, she hadn't yet learned one. Her mama was very strict on the matter of curse words and made that clear from the time Minervy was old enough to speak.

"There's words what are poison berries and words what are sweet berries," she'd say. "Put too many bad ones on your tongue and you quit tastin' the good ones."

That made sense to Minervy, and she'd always prided herself on never having uttered so much as a single word too nasty to say in polite company. She dearly wished she had at least one at her command, however, the day Lillie told her she'd be going off to Bluffton and leaving her to tend the nursery cabin on her own.

Lillie had mentioned nothing about the Bluffton trip until the very afternoon before she went, reckoning that every hour a nervous girl like Minervy knew about what lay ahead was another hour she'd fret about it. Best to give them both fewer of those hours to abide. When Lillie finally did reveal her plans, Minervy indeed became a tangle of worry.

"But what if somethin' happens when you're gone?" she asked.

"Somethin' like what?" Lillie responded.

"S'pose a baby gets sick or a mama gets cross?"

"That happens every day."

"S'pose all the littlest ones takes to squawlin' at once?"

"That happens too," Lillie answered. "And it's always you what sets things right."

Minervy was not convinced and passed the rest of the day clucking her tongue worriedly and looking at Lillie crossly. But when the next morning came, she handled the nursery cabin as well as Lillie had predicted she would, collecting the babies and shooing away the mamas with so little fuss that most of them didn't even seem to notice that Lillie was gone. Still, when the last of the mamas had left, Minervy closed the door in relief, knowing that it would not be until mid-morning that she'd see any of them again and looking forward to a quiet hour or two with no more noise in the nursery cabin than the sound of the sleeping babies. She was thus both surprised and cross when, not long after all the mamas were supposed to be at work, there was a rap at the door. Minervy snapped her eyes to the slumbering babies, who stirred slightly but did not awaken. The knock sounded again, and the door creaked open. Minervy rose and hurried over, hoping to stop whichever mama it was before she entered and created a disturbance.

"Babies is sleepin'!" she hissed in a tone she never took with any adult, much less with the mamas. "If you wakes 'em all up, I'll—"

Before she could continue her thought, the door opened the rest of the way and the words choked in her throat. Standing on the other side wasn't a slave mama at all, but Miss Sarabeth, the Master's daughter.

Sarabeth regarded Minervy with a cool expression and a small nod of the head and at first said nothing. She wore a frilly strolling dress and a large-brimmed hat with a little flurry of light green ribbons streaming from it. She carried a closed parasol that she could open to catch any stray beam of sunlight that might get past the oversized hat. At the moment, the morning sun was still low, lighting up Sarabeth from behind in such a way that she appeared to be less a true girl than a shadowed shape inside a cloud of luminous clothes. Minervy squinted to make out her face, and Sarabeth squinted back into the shadowy cabin.

"Miss Sarabeth!" Minervy burbled, still holding her voice to a whisper. "I didn't know it was you! I wouldn't've sassed you otherwise."

"That's all right," Sarabeth said, waving off the thought as if she hadn't quite heard it. She craned her head into the cabin and squinted again to see. "I didn't expect the babies would be so quiet this early."

"They usually isn't," Minervy said. "They usually wait till afternoon to go still."

Miss Sarabeth, of course, knew that. Until only a few months ago, she would stop by the nursery cabin almost every day. At first she'd come by around five o'clock when the mamas were picking up the babies, so that when the last one was gone she and Lillie could go off together. Later, she took to coming at other times too, to coo at the newest babies and play with the bigger ones and sometimes even help Lillie and Minervy put them to sleep. As a rule, the Master and the Missus didn't object, reckoning it was good practice for when Sarabeth grew up and had babies of her own.

"In the North, the girls only got doll babies to teach 'em," the Master would say. "In the South, they got slave babies."

But it had been a long time since Sarabeth had last come by. It was thus a particular shock to see her here this morning, and an even bigger shock to see how she'd changed. The Sarabeth who was standing in the doorway now was a starched and stiff young woman, looking more like the plantation Missus than a plantation child. Minervy much preferred the girl as she'd once been, and she addressed this new Sarabeth with unaccustomed awkwardness.

"Did you come by to see Lillie, Miss?" she asked.

"Is Lillie here?" Sarabeth asked in return, with a tone that suggested she knew the answer.

"No, she ain't."

"I expect I can't see her, then," Sarabeth said.

"No'm," Minervy said, "but she'll be back tonight. Went off to Bluffton with Bett and Samuel to fetch bakin' supplies."

"Yes," Miss Sarabeth said. "My daddy told me when he signed the traveling papers. Lillie doesn't tell me such things anymore. I wonder why Bett didn't take one of the younger children like she usually does."

Minervy fidgeted nervously. She had asked Lillie the same thing yesterday, and Lillie had answered in a way that wasn't quite an answer, saying simply that that was what Bett wanted and that that was how it would be.

"I wouldn't know about such things, Miss," Minervy now said.

"Strange too that they'd leave you here alone."

"I wouldn't know about that neither, Miss." Minervy struggled to make her frightened eyes meet the other girl's, but they'd hold still for only a moment before skittering off to something else.

"You're certain you don't know any other reason they went?" Miss Sarabeth pressed. Minervy said nothing. "Minervy?" Sarabeth added in a harder tone. She now not only looked like the plantation Missus but sounded like her too.

"No'm," Minervy said, "I don't know." A baby started to fuss behind her, and Minervy glanced over her shoulder. One fussing baby would quickly mean another fussing baby, and soon the whole cabinful of them would be crying. And it would be Miss Sarabeth, who knew better than to disturb them during a nap, who would be to blame. Minervy now turned back to her and spoke in a voice that had an uncommon sharpness to it, one that she had not expected, and neither had Sarabeth—at least judging by the look on her face. "Lillie ain't here, Miss, just as I said she ain't."

This time Minervy held Sarabeth's eyes as she spoke, and this time it was Sarabeth who broke the gaze and looked away. For an instant, she no longer looked like the Missus at all, but more like the girl she'd always been—a girl like Minervy herself, one wearing a grown-up's clothes and practicing a grown-up's manner, but a child all the same. Minervy's feelings softened, and her tone did too.

"Was you wantin' to play with Lillie and the babies?" she asked. "Is that why you come? We'll all be here tomorrow, and the babies is here now."

Miss Sarabeth looked at Minervy, and her expression wavered from stern to sad, then back again. Before she could speak, the fussing baby—a fat little boy named Charles—

began to cry loudly. Immediately Sarabeth flicked her gaze past Minervy, straining for another look inside the cabin.

Minervy turned and hurried over to the boy's sleeping mat. She picked him up and patted his bottom and was relieved to feel that it was dry. Charles needed only to be held, not to be cleaned. Minervy pressed his pillowy cheek against her own and began to hum a quiet song. She turned back toward the door and started to speak.

"Miss Sarabeth, would you like to—"

She stopped before she could finished her thought. The doorway was empty and Miss Sarabeth was gone, quick as if she'd never been there at all. Minervy bounced Charles gently in her arms and, after a moment, padded to the door and shut out the hard morning sun. It was only then that she realized with unease that she still had no idea why Miss Sarabeth had come around at all.

Chapter Ten

THERE WERE A LOT of reasons Lillie wouldn't have an easy time finding Henry, and one of them was his name. In recent years, masters had started having fun with what they called their slaves, giving boys fancy names like Caesar and Cassius and girls equally fussy ones like Messalina and Agrippina. Caesar and Cassius were names usually given to horses, and Messalina and Agrippina were what the white girls liked to call their cats. All the names, so the older slaves said, came from long ago in the land of Rome. In a place like Beaufort County in 1863, a name like Patsy or George would serve most slaves better.

Things were a little easier for slaves as old as Henry, who were born before masters started having such sport with names. It sometimes seemed to Lillie that every other slave man around her papa's age went by one of just three or four very plain names—and Henry was the plainest and most popular of all. Asking after a black man with such a name in Bluffton would therefore not do her much good. Asking after a black man named Henry who also had just one leg ought to have made matters less complicated, but as it turned out, it didn't.

Approaching white folks was not something Lillie dared do—lest they ask for her traveling papers, which Samuel and Bett still had. Most black folks were easier to talk to, but they couldn't help very much either. Lillie knew not to bother visiting slaves loading plantation wagons, since they wouldn't be any more familiar with the people who lived in town than she was, and besides, an overseer or slave driver who happened to be nearby might take a whip to a farm slave who stopped to talk. But there were plenty of other slaves who actually lived in Bluffton, working for merchants and sleeping in tiny cabins behind the shops, and these Lillie did approach.

"I seen a one-legged black man now and then," answered a slave woman sweeping up in front of the Bluffton bank.

"Is his name Henry?" Lillie asked excitedly.

"Can't say."

"Do you know where he lives?"

"Can't say," the woman repeated. "You's right about the leg, though; he's only got the one."

Lillie heard pretty much the same thing again from a slave boy sweeping out the blacksmith and saddlery barn, and again from a nervous young slave girl, perhaps three years older than Lillie, who was cleaning the windows of the big dry goods store while the old white man who owned the business glared at her from inside. Some had never seen Henry, some had; none of them knew where he could be found.

"He does keep to himself," the nervous girl said. "Never talks to nobody and don't come out much. When he does, he hobbles about like a man in pain." She said nothing else and quickly returned to her work, as the old man inside picked up a whipping stick with his right hand and began slapping it menacingly into the palm of his left.

Lillie turned away, feeling frustrated as well as hot, hungry and increasingly thirsty. The morning sun had now given way to high sun, and keeping the clock tower in sight, Lillie could see that it was now close to two in the afternoon. She'd had nothing to eat and not a sip to drink since breakfast early this morning, and while there were public water barrels and dippers in front of many of the stores in Bluffton, a black child dared not touch them with her hands or—worse—her lips. It was a footrace to see whether her hope or her strength would give out first, but whichever one failed her, it seemed less and less likely that she'd find the man she'd come to see in the two and a quarter hours she had remaining. When she left Bluffton today, it could be years before she'd ever have permission to come back.

As Lillie's mind was filling with these dark thoughts,

she once again scanned up and down the streets and this time saw something she hadn't expected at all: a familiar face. Leaning wearily against a hitching post next to an old, gray-muzzled horse was an equally old slave named Abner, who'd once worked the barns at the Bingham Woods plantation. Abner was one of those people who looked like they were meant to be old—as if they'd never been young. "Hatched from an old egg," was how Mama put it, and to Lillie that seemed about right.

When Lillie was little, Abner would sometimes visit Greenfog on business with his master, and when he came down to the slave cabins for food and water, he seemed to take special pleasure in playing with the children. He never could keep any of their names straight, and so he called all the boys either Edward or John, after his own sons who'd been sold off when they were small. He called all the girls either Eliza or Lillie—and though Lillie herself knew he was likely thinking of two girls from long ago who happened to have those names, she liked to think that maybe he'd taken a special shine to her.

If Abner never looked especially well to Lillie, he looked even worse now—thin, with little left of the crop of white hair he'd once had. He also appeared, even from a distance, to be down to his last few teeth. Still, the man was Abner if he was anyone, and Lillie hurried over to him.

"Abner?" she asked. He looked up and squinted at her.

His eyes were red and rheumy, and his face was covered with white stubble—not the kind that came from a face not having been shaved in a week or two, but the kind that came from skin that was so old it just didn't have the strength to push out true whiskers anymore. "Abner Bingham?" she asked, guessing she'd better use the last name all the slaves on his plantation were given. The man shook his head no.

"Beg pardon," Lillie said, flustered. "I thought you was someone I knew."

"I *was* someone you knew," the man answered. "Used to be Abner Bingham. Now I'm Abner Blue." He read Lillie's look of confusion. "I was manumitted, sugar."

The word, as always, carried a thrilling jolt. Manumitted meant freed, and while Lillie had met a few such remarkable slaves in her life, she hadn't met many—mostly because there just weren't many around. Most freed slaves had earned their manumission papers by performing some heroic act like saving their master's life. A few had been industrious enough and frugal enough to work extra jobs for which some masters offered pay, and purchased their freedom with their earnings. Fewer still had been freed after fighting in the war. Abner was too old to fight or to save anyone's life, and the master of Bingham Woods was known as a man who guarded his coins and rarely extended his slaves any special rewards.

"How'd you get loose?" she asked. "I didn't think anyone got manumitted where you was."

"Most don't, but the old ones sometimes do," Abner said. "Leastways the very old ones. Master Bingham likes to work his slaves till they can't work no more, then work 'em a couple years past that. Them what are finally no good for any labor at all, he frees. We gets one suit of clothes, one pair of shoes, and we gets driven here and left. Costs him less than feedin' us till we finally passes on, I reckon."

"How do you eat then?" Lillie asked.

"Take odd jobs when they's about. Get paid in coin or food."

"Where do you sleep?"

Abner smiled a smile that didn't really look like a smile and inclined his head in a manner that took in the whole town. "Any place the dogs ain't claimed."

Lillie's mind filled with a picture of Bett—who was younger than Abner but not by much—living the same life, and her eyes welled up. Abner noticed and offered a smile that looked like the genuine thing.

"You cryin' for me, sugar?" he asked. "No, no, I cry for you. You is still a slave." He squared his thin shoulders as much as he could. "I is a free man. Took the name Blue— Abner Blue—to remind me of the big, wide sky."

Lillie blinked her tears away, forced a smile and tried to

say something, but before she could, a cross-looking white man emerged from the nearby stable and began striding toward them. Abner saw him coming, sighed and moved away from the hitching post.

"A good thing you come off that post," the man called out.

"Yessir," Abner answered wearily.

"Free man or no, you got no business disturbing the horses," the man said. "Now you shoo, and take that little girl with you. She don't look like no freedchild to me, and I'll set the law on her if she don't show me she's busy with something."

Abner placed a reassuring hand on Lillie's shoulder. "She's busy, sir," he said. "We both is." He nudged Lillie toward the town square and the two began walking away, as the white man stood angrily near the hitching post with his fists on his hips.

"I got the whole day to pass the time with you," Abner said. "But it don't do for you to get in trouble. So s'pose you tells me what you come for?"

"I'm lookin' for a man," Lillie said. "A man named Henry. Used to be a slave, but he ain't no more."

Abner nodded. "Used to have two legs, but he don't no more neither?"

"You know him?" Lillie asked, this time trying not to let her hopes climb too high.

"There ain't but two free black men in this town, and there ain't but one who's short a leg."

"Where does he live?"

"Don't know for sure," Abner said, and Lillie slumped. "But I been told he got himself a job cuttin' wood and makin' chairs and tables. Likely sleeps in a shed 'round back of the furniture maker's store."

"Is he there now?"

"Oughta be. I don't see him 'round the streets but one or two times a month."

Lillie spun around toward the square and looked at the clock tower. It was twenty past two; she now had less than two hours to find Henry, conduct her business and get back to the wagon before Bett and Samuel would have to leave without her. "Can you tell me how to get there?" she asked Abner.

"It's a long run," he said. "All the way back to the spot where the road you drove in on meets the town. Fork right—not left—and go just a short piece past that." He glanced back over his shoulder at the square. "If that clock up there is pressin' on you, you'd best go."

Lillie wanted to do just that, but she could not help looking Abner up and down one last time, filling with sorrow at the used-up look of the old man. "What about you?" Lillie asked. "Ain't you hungry? We got bread and water back in our wagon."

"I done told you I'm fine," Abner said. "Now, you go do what you come here for." Lillie stayed where she was. "Go, Lillie, child," Abner insisted.

Lillie beamed. "You remembered who I am!" she exclaimed.

"Of course I do," Abner said and smiled at her. Then the smile faltered and his expression seemed to go cloudy. "You're the one what's called Eliza." He shooed her away once more, and this time Lillie turned and sprinted off as fast as she could, hoping he didn't see the tears that sprang once more to her eyes.

The run to the furniture store was indeed a long, hot one, and by the time Lillie got there, she was badly parched. The dry dirt of the town's roads swirled up as she ran, and her face and lips felt gritty with the stuff. When she reached the yard in front of the stable-like furniture store, she staggered to a stop, breathing heavily. The building was marked with a sign painted in red: A. A. KILE'S FINE FURNITURE & CABINETRY—PIECES MADE & MEASURED.

The wide front door was flung open on a large workshop, and Lillie could see a variety of furniture in various stages of completion standing next to low piles of smooth-cut lumber. Though no one was in sight inside, a few tools and a sweat rag rested atop a sawhorse; the tools would not be left about where anyone could snatch them unless the person using them was nearby.

"Hello?" Lillie called out in a voice too timid to be heard. There was no answer, and she tried again, this time louder. "Hello!" she said.

Again there was no response, but Lillie did hear something—a sort of step-scrape sound coming from around the back of the building. The sound drew closer, though slowly, as if whoever was making it could move only so fast. Lillie had no doubt who that person was and she called once more. "Is anyone there?" she asked.

From around the side of the building, Henry at last emerged. He looked to be about her papa's age, though not as tall and far more beaten down than Papa had been the last time Lillie saw him. He labored across the uneven ground, his one foot and his heavy crutch leaving twin trails in the dirt behind him. His empty right trouser leg was folded back and held fast with a heavy pin, and Lillie could see that the leg was missing from just about where the knee ought to be. It occurred to her that until that moment she had never thought about what a one-legged man would do with his two-legged trousers.

"You need somethin'?" Henry asked, barely glancing up before looking back down at the loose, pebbly soil, where his purchase seemed uncertain.

"Let me help you," Lillie said, hurrying toward him.

"Don't need no help," Henry said without looking at her. He spoke neither kindly nor unkindly. "You here for the nightstand? It ain't done yet, and Mr. Kile ain't here to take payment anyway."

"I ain't here for no nightstand," Lillie said. "I'm here to talk to you."

Henry finally stopped and looked up. The sun was in his eyes and he had to squint at Lillie. He raised his free hand to his forehead so that a shadow fell across his face. He looked at Lillie unrecognizingly at first—and then his expression softened.

"I expect you can help me after all, girl," Henry said. "How about you fetch two small sittin' boxes from inside that workshop and set them up over here in the shade?"

Before the man could change his mind, Lillie ran into the furniture barn, grabbed two crates that looked to be about the right size, and carried them to where he had indicated, under the canopy of a leafy magnolia tree. She approached him and tried to take hold of his arm and to her surprise, this time he allowed it. She walked him to one of the boxes and eased him down.

"Now why don't you fetch us a drink of water too?" he said, pointing to a rain barrel with a dipper hooked to its edge. Lillie ran over to it gratefully, scooped out some water and started to drink, then stopped herself and offered it to Henry first. He smiled and waved it off. "I don't really need it, but you do," he said. "You got road dust over most your face."

Lillie drained the dipper thirstily, then scooped another and drank that off too. "Thank you," she said, a little out of breath from the gulping she'd done. She hooked the dipper back on the edge of the barrel, wiped her face with her arm, and then sat down on the crate near Henry.

"I know why you come, girl," Henry said.

"You do?" Lillie asked.

"It's 'bout your papa."

Lillie nodded.

"About the way he died," Henry added.

Lillie looked at him wonderingly. "How did you know?"

"I'd wanna know too if I was his child. And with that face o' yours, there ain't no other man's girl you could be."

Lillie reached up and touched her face. As always, she had to fight back tears at just the mention of Papa.

"He said you looked like him, 'cept I didn't reckon how much."

Lillie's voice felt choked. "He talked about me?"

"All the time. Talked about all of you. Your mama, your baby brother—boy with a funny name. Ploto."

"Plato," Lillie said. She laughed slightly and blinked her wet eyes.

"He said you was called Lillie, but he said he give you another name too—one he said was more suited to you."

"Quashee?" Lillie asked, her throat choking.

Henry nodded. "Child born on a Sunday," he said. Lillie

merely nodded, not trusting herself to speak. "So what do you reckon I can do for you, Quashee, girl?"

"You can help us get free before the slave traders come to take my brother," Lillie answered plainly. "We was s'posed to be freed no matter whether Papa come back from the war or not. But now they say we can't cause o' some lie about a bag o' coins he had when he died. The Master has 'em now and he aims to keep 'em—and keep us too."

"It weren't no lie," Henry said softly.

"Papa didn't steal no coins!" Lillie snapped.

"I didn't say he stole coins. But he *had* coins. Went off to a farmhouse about two or three miles from the battlefield to fetch bandages one day; come back with a purse full o' Yankee money. He showed it to me plain and admitted he got it from the farmer; wouldn't never tell me how."

"So he didn't say he took it?" Lillie said.

"Some things don't need sayin'."

"That woulda."

"You think a Southern farmer gonna give a slave man a bag o' gold?"

"My papa weren't no thief!" Lillie repeated.

"All right, then," Henry said, spreading his hands. "Ain't no way o' knowing anyhow, seein' as your papa's dead."

"But there is a way."

"How?"

"You could ask the farmer."

"The farmer's in Mississippi," Henry said. "We's in South Carolina. I don't got a wagon, and I ain't gonna hop there on my one good leg."

"You could send him a telegraph!" Lillie said. "I seen the office."

"Ain't none but white folks allowed to talk by telegraph," Henry said. "Even free blacks ain't allowed. Besides, it costs dear, and I don't got enough money."

"You could write him a letter, then."

Henry gave off with a rueful laugh. "I was a slave till this summer, girl," he said. "I can't read nor write."

"I can!" Lillie exclaimed, then glanced around and lowered her voice. "I can," she whispered. "Do you know the farmer's name?"

"Everyone knew it. A man name of Appleton, in Warren County just outside o' Vicksburg. We was stationed near his land for three months; took regular runs over there for water and firewood and all manner o' things."

"Name and county's enough address to get a letter to him."

"The mails ain't runnin' regular anywhere in the South," Henry said. "The worse the fightin' goes, the more the roads get cut off. And the routes that is good are full o' thieves what steal the mailbags lookin' for money."

"I still gotta try."

"Even tryin's trouble. You get caught writin' a letter—

never mind sendin' it to a white man—you'll get whipped and sold."

"Maybe," Lillie said. "But you're a free man. You can do what you want. S'pose I write the letter but we put your name to it? You can send it from here and say you're thinkin' about a friend what died in the war and you won't sleep easy till you know if he done wrong."

"I do a fraud like that, and I could be called for helpin' you escape. How you reckon I'd do back on a plantation or tossed in prison with just the one leg?"

Lillie felt herself go hot. "But you got your freedom!" she cried. "We's still slaves and we ain't s'posed to be, and you got your freedom! This here's our only chance to get what's ours before my brother gets sold off!"

Henry regarded Lillie thoughtfully, and then sat back and rubbed his eyes. He looked tired—tired from his wound and tired from the war and tired, Lillie reckoned, from the things he'd seen there. She reflected that if her papa were alive, this was the way he'd look too. At length, Henry raised his eyes back to her and smiled wanly.

"Your papa was right," he said, "you is small, but you is a bull. All right, child, I'll help you." Lillie started to leap up and hug him, but Henry held up his hand. "Hear me, though. There's somethin' you got to do for me in return." Lillie sat back down. "I got a family on the Orchard Hill plantation—wife and a boy about ten years old. I ain't seen neither of 'em since before the war, and they think I died in the fightin'. You got to tell 'em otherwise."

"They wasn't freed with you?"

"They wasn't even livin' with me. We was once all together on a farm not far from here, but they got sold off 'bout a year before I went to war. That freedom rule don't hold for split-up families."

"Why'd you go fight, then?"

"I reckoned I could come home and earn some money and buy 'em free. Before I went to fight, I asked their master and he said yes. But when I got back from the war and went to tell 'em I weren't killed, the Master met me with a shotgun. Said I couldn't never see 'em till I had the money to buy 'em both. He told 'em I was dead and won't tell 'em otherwise in case they try to escape and join me."

"You think he'd let me talk to 'em for you?" Lillie asked.

"Course not. But if you was there on an errand, you could get to 'em easy enough."

"Dangerous business, sneakin' around like that," Lillie said.

"So's sending a letter I didn't even write," Henry answered.

He smiled and shrugged, and Lillie had to smile back. Henry was a smart man, and it was a fair deal he was offering, even if it was risky for both of them. She stood up and extended her hand for a shake the way she often saw adults do. Henry looked surprised and shook her hand with a laugh.

"I'll be back," Lillie said with a serious expression that made her feel grown-up. "When I am, I'll have word from your family and a letter for you to mail."

She sealed the bargain with a nod, then spun around and lit out for the center of town. She'd be home at Greenfog well before dark, and she'd have work to do once she got there.

Chapter Eleven

PSST! LITTLE CAL!"

The voice jumped out from seemingly nowhere, and Cal himself jumped in response. The stables were a dark and quiet place after the sun went down, particularly on a night like tonight, when the moon was just a shaving of its full self, shedding little light even when there were no clouds in the sky to get in its way. Cal had been here many times after sundown and ought to have been accustomed to the complete stillness of the place. But all those times he was here with permission, having been sent by the overseer to shoo a raccoon that was spooking the horses or chase out a tomcat that was stalking a she cat. The business he was here on tonight was a whole different matter.

"Psst! Little Cal!" came the voice again.

Cal leapt once more, though less than before, and this time he frowned a little too. It was Cupit who was calling his name, but calling it in a way only he would. Cupit had been addressing him as Little Cal since long ago when they were both small, and back then that was a fair enough thing to call him. Cal was the younger of the pair by close to three years, and he was indeed a good deal smaller—short and feather light while Cupit was broad and stocky. In the last year, however, Cal had begun to grow fast, even if he still didn't have much bulk on his bones. Cupit nonetheless continued to call him Little Cal, sometimes seeming to punch the first word harder than he used to, as if reminding Cal that no matter how big he grew, he'd still be the younger of the two.

"Over here!" Cal now answered in a loud whisper that he hoped could be heard anywhere inside the stable but nowhere outside it. Swaddled in shadow the way he was, he couldn't tell exactly where he was standing, but from the powerful smell of leather and riggings, he reckoned he was close to the harness room, which was where he was supposed to be.

"Don't move, boy," Cupit said. "I'm comin' your way."

Cal reached out his hand, felt a rough-hewn post and leaned against it. His eyes were starting to accustom themselves to the darkness and from around one row of stalls he saw the shadow of Cupit approaching. The older boy moved through the darkness with far greater speed and ease than Cal had earlier—not a surprise, since Cupit had been working as a stable boy for years and was well familiar with the lay of the place. It was Cupit who'd recommended meeting here tonight, knowing from experience that it was one of the spots the slave drivers and overseer patrolled least after dark. Cupit trotted up to Cal and spoke in a whisper.

"Did anyone see you come?" he asked.

"No," Cal answered. "Slipped out of the cabin after the others was asleep." Cal had a few ways of referring to George and Nelly. "The others" was one of them. "The growns" was another. He never described them as his parents.

"Did you cut through the field like I told you to?" Cupit said.

"Yes. Kept low, kept quiet. Didn't run into nobody. But I didn't see Benjy, neither."

"He was supposed to be here first!"

"I know it," Cal said.

"I don't like it," Cupit answered.

Neither boy could have been completely sure that Benjy would be here on time tonight, but the fact that he wasn't was nonetheless a cause for worry. When Benjy was late, it was usually because he was in some kind of trouble. Benjy was the oldest of the three boys—seventeen or so by most people's reckoning. He'd been bought from a plantation in Louisiana just two years ago, and that was the third time his ownership papers had changed hands since he was born on a farm somewhere in Kentucky well before the war began. When slaves were bought and sold so much, their true ages often got lost. However old Benjy was, he was old enough not to need any adult slaves to look after him, and he generally bedded down in the cabin of whatever family was willing to take him in for a few weeks or months at a time. When none were, he'd sleep under the stars, in the toolshed or sometimes even with the horses.

The reason Benjy got sold so many times had to do with his temperament. He was a good-enough-natured boy when he wanted to be, which was most of the time. He worked well and he worked fast, and he always seemed happy to join other slaves in their chores when he was done with his own. It was Benjy, in fact, who'd done the most to help Cal get his wound bandaged the day he got kicked by Coal Mine. Even Cupit had hung back, too afraid of the overseer to move, until Benjy ordered him to lend a hand, lest Cal and Benjy not be there for him if he ever got hurt the same way.

But Benjy worked best when he wasn't being pushed. The less he was interfered with, the more he got done. Smart slave drivers learned to recognize which slaves had that trait and knew to stand aside and let them be. The problem was that smart was just what most of the slave drivers who'd had a whip-hand over Benjy had not been. Louis and Bull seemed the dimmest of all, and they never appeared quite as happy as when they were badgering Benjy about how he was working, telling him to do something one way, then the other, then deciding both were wrong and coming up with a third way. Eventually, Benjy would grow angry enough to talk out of turn or throw down his hoe and earn himself a field flogging for it—which Cal reckoned was the reason Bull and Louis bothered him in the first place. Many was the time he and Cupit tried to tell Benjy that if he really wanted to bother the slave drivers in return, the best way to do it was to hold his temper and deny them the chance to lash him. But Benjy never seemed to hear that, and it was generally believed that he'd been whipped more than any young slave who'd ever worked at Greenfog before.

"I knew he'd be trouble tonight," Cal said to Cupit, looking around the stable. "We shouldn't never have allowed him to come."

"It was all his plan," Cupit said. "He's the one what gets to say who's a part of it."

Before Cal could answer, there was a loud jiggling of the stable latch, followed by the sound of the door opening with a squeak and closing with a careless rattle. Cal and Cupit froze. The only people who'd be making such a racket would be the overseer—who didn't have to care who knew he was here—or Benjy, who ought to care but wouldn't bother if he was in a foul temper. Neither possibility pleased Cal.

"Anyone there?" a voice whispered. It was Benjy's.

"Over here!" Cupit whispered.

Benjy moved clumsily though the darkness, thumping and bumping things as he went, and finally joining the other two boys. He was out of breath as if he'd been running.

"Woulda got here sooner," he said, "but I nearly run into Bull. He looked drunk as a hound and sounded like one too, the way he was bayin' at the sky. I had to keep 'specially low so he wouldn't see me."

"You still didn't need to slam that door!" Cupit whispered fiercely. "We get caught here, there ain't no tellin' the trouble."

Benjy waved him off. "Won't have to worry about none o' that soon enough. We'll be done with this place and done with bein' slaves too."

Benjy smiled and looked at Cal and Cupit, expecting them to smile back. The other boys tried, but somehow couldn't manage. It was no secret why they were all here tonight, but until this moment, none of them had ever said it out loud in quite that way. The fact that Benjy did was both thrilling and terrifying.

For a long time, Benjy had been whispering to Cal and Cupit about what it would be like to run away from Greenfog. There were ways it could be done, he'd say, routes through the woods where the thickets were so heavy and the swamps so muddy that no man could track them and no hound could smell them. There were people along the way who would help runaways—free blacks and other slaves who knew the route north. There were even a few whites—ladies, mostly, who lived in the South but were partial to the Union and were happy when the war came if only so all the slaves could be set loose. Naturally, talk of escape was forbidden among slaves, and whole families would be broken up and sold off one by one as punishment if a single member so much as whispered about it.

But Benjy never seemed troubled by such things—or by most matters that caused other slaves worry. He had courage—dumb courage often enough, but courage all the same—and he knew how to talk a line. The way Benjy's voice quickened and his eyes brightened when he spoke of escaping—the way his words painted a picture of how easy it could be—made it hard to imagine why every slave didn't try it. Cal and Cupit knew the folly of the thing, but when Benjy was talking to them, they forgot all about it. Still, tonight, when it was more than just talk, Cal didn't feel so sure.

"You really reckon this is right?" he asked.

"Righter'n it's ever been," Benjy answered.

"Fall's settin' in hard," Cal said. "Frost weather's comin'."

"It ain't here yet."

"Rain's comin' too, though," Cupit said. "That cold, cuttin' kind of rain."

"That's just the kind the hounds don't like," Benjy answered. "They can't track for nothin' when they's wet and chilled."

Cupit nodded, guessing that had to be true, but not knowing for sure—which was often the way it was when Benjy was telling you something.

Benjy then turned his attention to Cal. He held the boy's eyes fast, and he let a second or two pass. "Besides," he said at last, "there's Mr. Willis."

Cal had half expected Benjy to say that, but the mention of the name made him feel sick all the same. It was the day after Coal Mine kicked Cal in the head that the boys' idle talk about running away had turned serious. Scary as the blow from the horse had been, the look on Lillie's mama's face had been worse. Mr. Willis had said he meant to kill Cal one day, but Mr. Willis said a lot of things when his temper was up, and often as not he forgot all about them. This time, though, Lillie's mama's face said something else. It said she heard something different in the overseer's voice—something deadly—and Cal, truth be told, heard it too. Now, in the darkness of the barn, Benjy looked into his eyes and seemed to know what the younger boy was thinking.

"You only thirteen, Cal," he said. "You got a life ahead. Mr. Willis gonna end that life sure as we're talkin' here.

And if he don't end it, he's gonna make you so miser'ble you'll wish he did. You know that. I know that."

Cal said nothing, but he nodded.

"He's right, Little Cal," Cupit added. "I seen Mr. Willis look like that only one time before, when he caught the fox what was killing the chickens after the Master made him pay for the lost birds. Proper way to kill a fox is with a pistol. Mr. Willis used a shovel—and he looked like he liked it."

Cal found his voice and spoke up hoarsely. "What about you?" he said to Cupit. "You ain't the one he wants to kill, so why you wanna run?"

Cupit shrugged. "My papa's dead, my mama's sickly. Don't got no other family. Soon enough I'll be old enough for soldierin', and if this war keeps goin' bad for the whites, they'll surely get all their slaves to fight it for 'em. I'm scared o' runnin' away, but I'm scared more o' war. Both can get me free, but both can get me killed; I reckon I stand a better chance runnin'."

"Then we's settled on it," Benjy said. "We go next week. There's gonna be a Saturday slave dance at Bingham Woods. Greenfog slaves is invited." He smiled at the other two boys. "Three of 'em ain't coming back."

Cal swallowed hard. In a fortnight he'd be free. It didn't seem possible—but when Benjy was saying it, it somehow did.

Chapter Twelve

IT HAD BEEN A long time since there had been a slave party at Greenfog, but Lillie and the others remembered it well. Slave parties came as often as once a month on plantations with generous masters and as rarely as never on plantations with miserly ones. Whenever they did come, they were grand affairs. The mamas and the older girls would be released from work early so that they could prepare the cornbread and spoon bread and greens and beans that would be served up in portions so generous even the hungriest slaves couldn't finish them. The Master would provide a hog or a bunch of chickens for a big roasting that would begin hours before the dancing and feasting. Some masters would even donate a jug or two of whiskey, which would be passed around during the evening to any slave who was of age—and many who weren't—while the overseer kept a close eye on them all to make sure no one got too loosened by the liquor to remember that at the end of the night they were all still slaves. Usually the slaves from another plantation would be invited to attend and both masters would share the expense.

With the hard times across the South, such an expense was becoming something that masters could afford only rarely. The Master of Greenfog—whose fortunes seemed to be falling even faster than the other masters'—hadn't allowed his slaves a party since just a week before Lillie's papa left, and she thought about that night all the time. The morning of the party, the other slaves decided to give Papa a farewell gift and agreed that he would be the one to roast the hog—a job all the men liked to do and many of them would even argue about or wrestle over. Papa let Lillie and Plato help him with the roasting, giving them each a big wooden ladle and showing them how to spoon the sticky barbecue sauce onto the pig as it turned on the spit. When the job was done, he called them over so that they could be the first to taste the spicy-smoky-sugary flavor of the still-sizzling flesh. Lillie guessed she was about as happy that night as she'd ever been, and later, in their cabin, she told her papa so.

"I wish every day was a slave party day," she said.

"No you don't," Papa answered, with a frown that surprised her.

"But they's the most fun we ever have," Lillie said.

"That's why I don't like 'em. A slave thinkin' 'bout a party is a slave forgettin' she's a slave," Papa said. "The masters don't give us nothin' they don't reckon they have to, child. Parties is one way they keep you where you is and stop you from wantin' to be somewhere else."

Lillie never did look at a slave party the same way after that—but she never quit feeling the thrill of them either. She learned about the Bingham Woods party the day after she returned from Bluffton, and even with thoughts of her visit there crowding her mind, her heart jumped at the news. At the last party, Cal had seemed close to asking her to dance, and Lillie reasoned that now that he had grown up a bit, he might find the spine to do it. Later that day, she ran across Cal near the slave cabins, talking to the boys Benjy and Cupit.

"Heard 'bout the dance?" she asked. She called it a dance rather than a party, reckoning that might put ideas in his head.

"Heard about it, yeah," he mumbled.

"You ain't gonna go?" she asked.

"Don't know," he said. "Maybe." Then, oddly, he looked toward Benjy. "Yeah, I guess we is," he answered finally.

"We's goin'," Benjy said quickly, and gave her a big smile. "We's all goin'. I expect we'll see you there too."

"I expect," Lillie said. She looked at Cal—who wouldn't meet her gaze—then she walked away shaking her head.

Just like boys, she thought. Nice as you please till they get around one another and start thinking they've got to act tough.

After that, the business of the slave dance went mostly out of Lillie's head, allowing the more serious business of her bargain with Henry to flood back. Henry himself might not have believed that any letter Lillie mailed to Mississippi could make it through Southern roads that were being torn up by the war, but she was still determined to try. The job of actually writing the letter, at least, would not be all that difficult a business.

Slaves were not allowed to possess paper or pens, but that didn't mean they didn't have them anyway. There was plenty of paper to be found on a plantation—from the coarse brown wrapping paper that was used to protect breakables when they were stored in trunks to the fine white rice paper that the house slaves would use when they wrapped the Missus's silks to the creamy, smooth writing paper the Missus herself would use and simply discard if she was composing a letter and the ink splattered from her pen. All the paper could be collected from the rubbish and saved by slaves who would use it to draw pictures or practice their letters. Pens were easy enough to make, simply by plucking goose quills or sharpening sticks and dipping them into ink made of blackberry or wildberry juice. Slaves who could draw—and the few who could write—kept plenty of used paper and berry ink on hand but hidden, and the white families themselves sometimes relied on the same inventiveness as the war prevented the delivery of good paper and India ink. More and more, the Confederate mail was filled with brown-paper letters penned in runny blue juice.

Lillie had long kept her own pen and supply of paper hidden away, and even made herself a dried mud ink-pot with a tight-fitting lid, about the size of a lady's rouge pot. The overseer would flog her fierce if he found such forbidden things, but no one had discovered her secret yet, and now she reckoned she could make good use of it.

More worrisome than the matter of the letter was the matter of honoring the other part of the bargain she'd struck with Henry—sneaking onto the Orchard Hill plantation to tell his family he was fine and free. In the excitement of having found him in Bluffton, she was ready to promise him anything at all, but even before she got home that day, she'd begun to wonder how she could manage such a thing. The trip from Greenfog to Orchard Hill was not a long one—provided you were going by carriage over open roads. But it took a good deal longer if you were making the same trip by foot, and longer still if you had to avoid the roads and pick your way through the woods, as any slave who was traveling somewhere she wasn't supposed to be traveling would have to do. The only way Lillie could make the journey safely would be if she were sent there on an errand. But no such errand existed, and even if it did, there was no reason to think she'd be the one chosen for it. Years had gone by between the only two trips she'd ever made to Bluffton—and that was a place a wagon from Greenfog visited all the time. Lillie could be an old woman before she'd ever see Orchard Hill.

It was only late that night when she was lying awake in bed that an answer came to her, and that answer was the slave party. The slaves were always taken to parties by three wagons—the children in one, the adults in the other two. Leaving Greenfog, they'd travel straight for a time until they reached a fork in the road. As Bett had mentioned on their trip to Bluffton when they passed the same fork, the left-hand road led to Bingham Woods, the right-hand one led to Orchard Hill. All she would have to do would be to climb aboard the children's wagons, slip out at the turnoff, and run the rest of the way to Orchard Hill on her own. If she stayed low and kept to the shadows, she just might get where she was going with nobody seeing her.

There were problems with the plan, of course—though the matter of jumping off the wagon was actually not one of them. The children's wagon would probably be the third in the line that night, as it usually was, which would make it easier for Lillie to slip off without any adults seeing her. The other children would be a different matter, but if Lillie could find some way to persuade them to stay quiet, no one else needed to know what she'd done.

The more serious problem was one of time. When the party began and the slaves from the two plantations mingled, it would be a while before Mama would notice Lillie missing, since the adults and the children went their own ways and did their own dancing, almost as if they were at two different parties. But Mama had a sharp eye and at some point in the evening would surely come looking for her. Somehow, Lillie would have to get to Orchard Hill, find Henry's family, tell them what she'd come to tell them and get back to Bingham Woods before anyone realized she'd been gone. If she arrived too late, she might miss the wagon home altogether. If that happened, she'd have a lot more than just Mama to worry about.

But there might, Lillie figured, be an answer to all that. It was true that she could run only so fast; and it was just as true that there were only a certain number of hours in any evening. But not every hour, she'd lately learned, had to unspool at the same speed as every other.

It was time, Lillie reckoned, to pay another call on Bett.

Chapter Thirteen

THE COMMOTION COMING from Bett's cabin could be heard halfway across the tobacco field. Lillie was the only one in the field at the time, this being a Saturday afternoon—exactly one week before the dance at Bingham Woods—and the field thus being empty of anyone else. Saturdays were workdays at Greenfog but, as on most plantations, the quitting horn sounded early, just after what was usually the lunch break. The slaves had the rest of the day and all Sunday free, and the plantation was usually a quiet place during that easy stretch. Now the peace was being broken by what sounded like men arguing—two of them, Lillie guessed, though there could have been more. They sounded angry enough to be close to blows.

Lillie had not yet had a chance to speak to Bett about her plans for the night of the slave party, and she had been hoping today would be the day. As soon as Mama let her leave the cabin that morning, she lit out as fast as she could.

When she heard the arguing coming from Bett's, she began to run even faster. All the slaves liked and minded Bett and would take care that no harm ever came to her if they could help it. While some believed she was a charm worker and others thought that was just Ibo foolishness, none were willing to test the point by crossing her. All the same, angry, shouting men could easily lose their heads, and if they broke into a fight, there was no telling who could get bumped in the brawling.

As Bett's cabin came into view, Lillie could see that there was a small crowd gathered, surrounding what was indeed a pair of men, squaring off against one another. The first man was Evers, a plow worker; the second was Nate, a hauler who baled and lifted cotton and tobacco. Both men were strong, with muscled arms that seemed ready to pop the stitches of their shirts and necks almost as wide as a horse's. Evers was the younger by what might be ten years. He had a temper on him, but he rarely showed it. Nate, on the other hand, could be flat mean. He knew his strength and was not afraid to use it to get what he wanted. When Evers or any other slave had been wronged, it was as fair a bet as any that Nate had done the wronging.

The two men stood face-to-face barely inches apart, shouting and pointing. Nate appeared to have something in his right hand, though Lillie couldn't quite make out what it was. Bett, standing in her doorway with her arms folded, watched along with the others. If she feared any danger from the two snorting men, she didn't show it. Lillie hurried up to the group and could at last make out what was being said.

"—made it myself!" Evers was shouting. "You don't think I recognize somethin' I worked with my own hands?"

"No proof you made it, 'cept your word," Nate shouted back.

"My word and Lucy's!"

"Lucy's your wife. Any woman'll lie for her man!"

"My wife ain't no liar!"

"And I ain't no thief!"

Lillie looked closer at what Nate had in his hand and could now see that it was a necklace—and a fine one too. It was made of strands of cotton cord dyed red and green and braided up prettily. Hanging from it was a shiny, coin-sized disk the color of rich honey. Lillie had seen these kinds of amulets before, though this appeared to be one of the finest. It was made from a peach pit, sanded down and rubbed smooth, then stained with oil and varnish. Lucy was known to own such a necklace, and Evers was known to be a handy man, one who would know how to make such a lovely thing. If Nate had a necklace like it in his hand, he might well have stolen it—but maybe not. When one slave man made a gift for his wife, others were likely to copy it, lest their wives grow cross that they weren't being treated as kindly. It was possible that Nate had made a peach jewel too—though with his clumsy hands and surly ways, he didn't seem the sort.

Evers and Nate kept circling and shouting, now moving so close that they sprayed spittle into each other's face with every angry word. Nate puffed up his chest and bumped Evers's; Evers puffed his chest and bumped back. They were sure to exchange swings any second, and other men in the circle began moving forward to pull them apart. Before they could, Bett spoke out in a surprisingly strong voice.

"Don't matter who's tellin' the truth if one o' you's dead inside o' the hour," she said. The men didn't respond, so she spoke even louder. "I said it don't matter who's tellin' the truth if one o' you's dead inside the hour."

That time the men heard, stopped and turned.

"What're you sayin', old woman?" Nate asked.

"I got a way to settle the question, but it'll kill one o' you sure—the one what's lyin'. The one speakin' true will be fine."

"Ain't nothin' that'll do such a thing," Nate said.

"But there is," Bett answered. "And I got it. It's an Ibo powder, from Africa. Mix it up in a mug with water drawn from a stream. A truth-tellin' man can drink as much as he wants and no harm'll come to him; a liar dies. I'll go fetch some."

Bett turned to enter her cabin, and all the slaves but Nate and Evers—who stood uncertainly where they were—crowded toward her to follow. She turned back and held up her hand and the crowd stepped back. Bett vanished inside and returned a moment later with a brown mug and a small bag about the size of a tobacco pouch. As the other slaves watched, she walked slowly to her stream, eased herself down to her knees and dipped the mug into the water. She held it up, looked at it disapprovingly and spilled the water onto the ground. She did the same thing twice more, as if the water wasn't quite right. Then she got a mugful that seemed to please her. She climbed back to her feet and returned to the group.

"Didn't never think I'd get it cool enough nor clear enough," she said. "Wrong kind o' water, and the powder won't work."

As the crowd stayed silent, Bett gestured toward Nate and Evers to step forward. They obeyed, Nate still holding the necklace in his hand, though now he held it absently by his side. Bett looked over the crowd, spotted Lillie and summoned her too.

"Hold the water, child," Bett said.

Lillie came forward, took the mug and Bett opened the bag. She tipped it over and shook it gently. A stream of white powder flowed into the water and instantly produced a hissing sound. The crowd jumped back, and Lillie felt a fine spray of mist on her face and her hand. She backed away too, holding the cup out in front of her.

"Stay still, child," Bett said. "It can't hurt you. Just take care not to drop it."

The mug began to fill with a white foam that rose to the lip and overflowed, spilling down over Lillie's hand. Several women in the crowd let out a scream; Lillie trembled, but held still. Bett turned to Evers and Nate, who now regarded the mug in open fear.

"You two has to drink it," she said. "Each of you, two big swallows."

Both men stood frozen, then Evers stepped forward. He held out a trembling hand, and Lillie passed him the mug. Quickly, before he could change his mind, he took two big gulps. He closed his eyes tight, then slowly opened them and lowered the mug. He broke into a wide grin with flecks of foam covering his lips, which he wiped clean with his sleeve. Then he extended the mug to Nate, who stared at it. For long seconds, Nate stood absolutely still and then, seemingly to his own surprise, he broke.

"And what if I did take that necklace?" he shouted. "Ain't nothin' but a peach pit! I reckon I could make it just as good if I cared to!" He threw the necklace to the ground.

"Fool old woman!" he snapped at Bett. Then he wheeled around and stalked off.

The people in the crowd burst into laughter and closed around Evers, clapping his back. He scooped up the peach gem, blew the dirt off it and shined it against his shirt. Bett smiled and then forced her face to turn stern.

"Now, shoo!" she said to the crowd. "Shoo, the mess o' you, before Mr. Willis sets his whip boys on you."

The slaves, laughing and chattering, dispersed, and Lillie stood uncertainly, not sure if she should leave as well. Bett caught her eye and nodded for her to stay. When the last of the crowd had gone off, the old woman turned to go back inside, laughing to herself.

"Shoot," she said. "Weren't nothin' in that cup but bakin' soda." She turned to Lillie and winked. "That's an old Ibo trick too." Bett climbed the two small steps into the cabin, and Lillie followed her there.

After the shouting and shoving of a moment ago, the one small room that was Bett's small world seemed sleepy and subdued—and Bett, for that matter, did too. With her baking work done for the week, she would spend today the way she spent most Saturdays—napping and strolling and keeping to herself unless someone paid a visit. She eased herself down at her eating table and rubbed her eyes wearily, and Lillie suddenly felt ashamed that she'd come to bother her with her own problems.

"Trouble outside's over, and you ought to have your peace," Lillie said. "I expect I should go."

"You go and whatever you come here to get done will stay undone," Bett answered. "And judging by that face you're wearin', it's somethin' important."

Lillie hadn't realized she was showing any expression at all, but now that Bett called her attention to it, she could feel the way the whole of her face was stretched like a drum. She tried to let her eyes and mouth ease into a smile, but it was a counterfeit thing and Bett laughed kindly.

"Give me a smile when you got a real one," she said. "Why not just say what you come to say."

"It's Henry," Lillie said. "I got to go see his family, and I got to do it soon."

Bett nodded. On the way back from Bluffton, Lillie had described the conversation she'd had with Henry and the deal the two of them had struck, and Bett had seemed troubled by the plan. Henry was right, Bett had warned, that the worse the war grew, the less the South could count on the mails. And the other part of the agreement—Lillie going to Orchard Hill—seemed to Bett to be the worst kind of folly. But Lillie had repeated her decision that she aimed to try anyway. Bett said nothing after that, and Lillie had not known whether that meant she'd been convinced that the idea was a good one or simply decided that Lillie had made up her mind anyway so there was no point arguing. Lillie hadn't wanted to ask, lest she get an answer she didn't like.

"What plantation you say they live on?" was all Bett asked now.

"Orchard Hill."

"The Master give you leave to go there?"

"No'm."

"The overseer?"

"No'm."

"I reckon you ain't goin', then."

"I got to go," Lillie protested. "I got to tell his kin he's alive—otherwise, he ain't gonna send my letter!"

"I know that, child," Bett answered, "but you can't rightly explain that kind o' thing to Mr. Willis. And if you try runnin' without askin', he'll catch you, beat you and sell you sure."

"Maybe I don't got to ask, nor get caught," Lillie said. She leaned in close and lowered her voice to a whisper, though the two of them were alone in the cabin. "There's a slave party at Bingham Woods next Saturday. I can jump out o' Samuel's wagon on the way, get myself to Orchard Hill and get back before anyone knows—even Mama."

Bett pursed her lips. "It's a long way to Orchard Hill by foot. Too long for a slave child sneakin' by night."

"Maybe," Lillie said. "Or maybe not."

She cast her eyes over at Bett's cooking supplies and then at the stove, which was cold and dark. Bett followed her gaze and looked back at her, shaking her head.

"It don't do for you to mess with that," Bett said. "That ain't a bakin' soda trick; that's real. I tol' you I don't want to use no oven charms 'less we don't got no other choice."

"But I *don't* got no other choice."

"You do got a choice, but it's a hard one. You can stop thinkin' 'bout your papa. You can pay mind to where you is and what's left o' your family. That's what a slave does."

"But I ain't a slave!" Lillie cried. "I ain't supposed to be! My papa weren't no thief! That's the stone truth and no one's gonna hold my family nor sell my brother on account of a lie! No one!" At that, the frustration and the fear and the sorrow got the better of her, and she erupted in tears, burying her face in her hands and giving way to all that seemed to weigh down on her. Bett slowly rose, put her hand on Lillie's back, then took her head and cradled it against her hip. Lillie wept softly into Bett's apron.

"All right, girl, all right," Bett said softly, stroking Lillie's hair. She took Lillie's face in her hands and turned it up to her, then ran her thumb across the girl's cheek, rubbing away a tear. "I expect we can try a little bakin' this mornin'."

Lillie beamed but Bett held up her hand. "But this is work. It ain't play. And it can't be my bakin'; it's got to be yours—leastways, if you want the magic to do what it needs to do."

Wordlessly, Bett went to her oven, picked up a few pieces of firewood and a few sticks of kindling, stacked them inside and set them afire. Lillie watched as the flame popped and grew, and drew a breath as Bett's particular wood in her particular oven gave off a smell she'd long since learned to know meant fine baking was coming.

"We got to wait for that to heat proper," Bett said. "Meantime, you tell me what you want to do with this charm we're workin'."

"I don't know," Lillie said. "I reckon I wanna slow down the slave party at Bingham Woods so's I can get to Orchard Hill and back in time."

Bett shook her head no. "Can't do that."

"Why not?" Lillie asked.

"Your business is at both places. Can't slow down one without slowing down the other. It'd be like two legs walkin' different ways."

"Then slow them both."

"Can't do that neither," Bett said. "Not enough charmin' in the world to slow down even one whole plantation, never mind two of 'em."

"So there ain't no point," Lillie said, her shoulders slumping.

"There is," Bett answered. "Long as we quit thinkin' 'bout gettin' other people movin' slower and instead get you movin' quicker."

Lillie hadn't thought of that, but Bett had told her it was possible to do such a thing. Bake firm, Bett had said, and things slow down. Bake loose, and they speed up. All at once, Lillie felt uneasy. It was one thing to think of sending magic somewhere else; it was another thing to imagine conjuring it up and taking it on herself. But if that was what Bett said she had to do, she had to do it. She swallowed hard and squared off her shoulders.

"I'm ready," she said.

Bett laughed. "Not so fast, little Ibo. That's a bread we can't bake till just before we needs it. Meantime, if you're the one what's sending this charm, we got to see what kind o' magic you got in you first. We'll try some simple slow-bakin' today, and we'll start with somethin' easy like a cake."

Bett stood and went to her shelves, where she took down her mixing bowls and measures. She summoned Lillie and instructed her to open the bags of flour and other ingredients, then handed her scoops and told her how much to take from each bag. Bett let Lillie do the measuring and pouring, instructed her in the beating and folding, and let her manage that too. It was tiring work, and Lillie found herself feeling grateful that Bett had decided against a bread, which would have required a lot of hard kneading. When the batter was done, Bett allowed Lillie to dip her finger in and sample it. It tasted fine, and Lillie gazed into the bowl with more pride than she'd imagined she'd feel.

"Now spit in it," Bett instructed.

"What?" Lillie asked.

"Spit," Bett repeated. "It don't have to be a lot."

"That's our cake!" Lillie protested.

"And until you spit into it, a cake's all it's gonna be. You want it to be more'n that, you'll spit like I tell you."

Lillie sighed, then leaned over the bowl. She regarded the batter she'd worked so hard to whip up—and spat square in the center of it.

"Now stir it up," Bett said, and Lillie did that too.

"The thing about fooling with how time runs," Bett explained as Lillie wiped away a bit of spittle that had clung to her chin, "is that them Africa stones in the oven ain't always enough. I didn't know it myself till a few years back when I was tendin' a baby for one of the mamas who was workin' late. I was holdin' him on my hip with one hand and stirrin' my batter with the other, when he let go some dribble right into the bowl. It weren't much and the batter was good, so I baked it up anyway. By the time I was ready to take it out of the oven, them bees outside my window was movin' so slow you'da thought they was hung on strings. One o' the most powerful charms I ever sent."

"I can't reckon how spit can do that," Lillie said.

"This ain't regular spit; it's the sugar spit. Children got it, grown-ups lose it."

"I thought spit was spit."

"It ain't," Bett said. "Never bothers you wipin' off the wet chin of a baby, does it?"

Lillie shook her head. "Done it plenty o' times in the nursery cabin."

"How about the chin of an old lady? Old as me, say."

Lillie didn't want to give offense, but wrinkled up her nose all the same.

"Just so," Bett said. "That's the sugar spit at work. When I wanna cast a particular strong charm, I gotta have one o' the small children taste the batter first, so's I can save some o' their spit on the spoon."

"But I ain't a baby no more," Lillie said.

Bett shrugged. "Give me a peck right here," she said, indicating her lips. Lillie bent forward and gave Bett a small kiss, then straightened back up. Bett licked her lips thoughtfully. "You got it, child," she said. "You got it still. Probably not for much longer, but for a while yet you do."

Bett slid the batter into the oven and turned back to Lillie. "Now we got one more thing to do," she said. Wordlessly, she filled a small pot with water, poured a large scoop of sugar into it, and picked a handful of red berries from a bowl. She mashed the berries in a cup and scraped them into the pot. Finally she placed the pot on the stove above the oven flame and waited until the water came to a boil. She then stirred up the mixture—which was now a sticky red juice—and motioned to Lillie to follow her outside, where she placed the pot on the forked branch of a tree to cool.

"What's that for?" Lillie asked.

"To call the hummingbirds."

Bett and Lillie reentered the cabin and spent the better part of a peaceful hour drawing in the sweet fragrance of the small, rising cake and looking out the window at the pot in the tree. At almost the moment that the smell of the cake became so powerful Lillie's mouth began to water, two tiny green hummingbirds flashed into view outside. Lillie caught her breath. She'd always found hummingbirds enchanting—almost magical—and sometimes fancied that they were fairies, the living, winged wishes of small boys and girls who were taken by a sickness when they were very young and were rewarded with an eternity of lightness and flight. She watched the small, iridescent birds as they hovered about the pot, their wings moving so fast they were almost invisible as they darted toward the sugar water and back from it, dipping their long, slender beaks in for a drink.

But all at once, the hummingbirds weren't darting so quickly, their wings weren't beating invisibly. They seemed now as if they were moving in a dream, drifting to and from the pot at a creep, their slow, graceful wings pumping once, then twice, then three times at the air. Lillie gasped and turned to Bett, then turned back to look outside. Just as she did, she saw something else—something large and black and ugly darting through the air. It was followed by an angry call, one that Lillie had heard before.

"A shrike!" Lillie said—and as she said it, a black bird, far larger than the hummingbirds, dove into view, having arrived too late for the charm to take hold of it. It vanished once more and then dove once more, and this time headed straight for the hummingbirds, which were still imprisoned by the charm.

"No!" Lillie screamed, but she was too late. The shrike speared one of the hummingbirds on its beak, tossed its head angrily, and threw the tiny creature to the ground. Then it swooped down, grabbed the small green body in its talons and flew off. Bett spun around, grabbed a broomstick, and swung it into the oven, smashing the cake. Instantly, the remaining hummingbird was freed from the magic and darted safely away. Lillie dropped her head into her hands, too horrified to look anymore. Bett came up behind her and rested what felt like a trembling hand on her hair.

"Charms is powerful, child," she said. "They's also dangerous. I guess it's best you know that now."

Chapter Fourteen

SARABETH HAD biscuits, ham and red-eye gravy for breakfast on the day the slaves were going to have their dance at Bingham Woods. She didn't particularly care for biscuits and never really had, though you couldn't have gravy without having something to soak it up. The ham was good—not too smoky like it had been the last time. She'd asked her mother to tell the kitchen slaves not to leave it in the smoke as long as they had before, and judging by the way the ham tasted this morning, it seemed like they had obeyed. There had also been grits— which Sarabeth's father had urged her to eat but which she had simply pushed around her plate—and sweet tea, which had not been sweet enough and which Sarabeth had thus let stand as well. Her little brother, Cody, who never seemed to mind what he ate, finished what was on his plate and in his glass and then began eating and drinking from Sarabeth's as well. The Master scolded him and instructed the parlor maid to serve the boy properly. Then he scolded the parlor maid for not filling the boy's plate and glass in time and causing his breach of manners in the first place.

None of this put Sarabeth in a good frame of mind, but the fact was, she'd been in a cross temper from the moment she'd come downstairs this morning. A disagreeable breakfast was bad enough, but on a day like today, lunch and dinner did not seem likely to be much better. With the dance on all the slaves' minds, her mother would allow most of the house servants to go back to their cabins even earlier than usual for a Saturday to prepare for the evening. Only the two older kitchen slaves would be left in the Big House, where they would be minding the slave children who were too small to go to the party. As was the custom, the kitchen slaves would cook up a fancy little dinner of honey cakes and pork for the children, so that they wouldn't fuss too much about being left behind. Often, the children were even told to wear their own fine party clothes if they had them, which made the dinner all the more special.

Sarabeth's father thought the little dinners were a nuisance, but Sarabeth's mother looked forward to them. She liked to think of herself as a good Missus, and she thought most highly of herself when she felt she was pampering the slave children. "They're so pretty when they're small," she'd say. "I wonder if their parents see it." Often on the day of a party, the Missus herself would spend the afternoon in the kitchen, directing the two old slaves as they prepared for the children's meal.

What all this meant for Sarabeth was that the kitchen slaves would be busy all day, her mother would be working alongside them and both lunch and dinner would be simple, hurried affairs. In the evening, in fact, she'd probably dine entirely alone. Her father would be going off to Bingham Woods to drink and smoke with the Master of the plantation, as well as with masters of other nearby plantations who would come to enjoy the cigars and the whiskey and would return the courtesy by bringing along their own whip men, who would help keep order among the slaves. Cody would be staying home, but he'd be eating with the slave children, occupying the chair at the head of the kitchen table, just like the Master he'd one day be. The Missus invited Sarabeth to join them all in the kitchen, but she wanted no part of such childish affairs.

"Little children are little beasts," she'd said. "I'm too old to dine with them."

It was, of course, at just such a dinner years ago that Sarabeth and Lillie had become good friends, with Sarabeth seated at the head of the table and Lillie, after a time, always seated at her right. The Missus would allow Lillie to arrive before the other children so that she could go upstairs to Sarabeth's room and help her dress. When they had grown and Lillie was old enough to attend slave dances herself, Sarabeth would be the one doing the helping, visiting Lillie's cabin to tie ribbons in her hair and admire her as she spun in her only fancy dress. Eventually, the Master and the Missus told Sarabeth to stop, since it was a slave girl's job to dress the Young Mistress, not the Mistress's job to dress the slave girl. The two girls played less and less after that, until the day came that they didn't play at all.

Now, as the Young Mistress sat at the breakfast table, glowering down at her disappointing plate and looking glumly ahead to the day that faced her, she began to feel cross—just as she had the day she saw Lillie sneaking to see Bett. She'd done Lillie a favor by playing with her for so many years. It had been a mark of her kindness—even of her pity for the girl. Now that kindness was not being repaid. Lillie would be going to a party tonight, perhaps dancing with boys, perhaps even kissing one. She was obviously a spoiled slave, and the more Sarabeth thought about it, the more she decided that Lillie was a bit peculiar too—spending so much time with that baker woman, who only encouraged her to put on airs. Now the old baker had Lillie's loyalty, Sarabeth had lost it, and tonight Lillie would be having fun, while Sarabeth—the daughter of the planter who owned all the acreage around them for as far as anyone living on Greenfog could see—would be staying home.

The world had turned upside down, and Sarabeth all at once decided that tonight she'd set it right.

"Papa," she said, folding her napkin, pushing away from the table and rising to her feet, "I would like to accompany you to Bingham Woods tonight. Other planters' children will be there, and I think I'm old enough."

She smoothed her dress and lifted her head in a way that made her feel both stern and ladylike and her father looked at her, trying to contain a smile. He cast his eyes to the Missus, who smiled the same way.

"You're certain you want to come?" he asked Sarabeth. "It might not be a very exciting evening for a child."

"For a child, no," Sarabeth said. "But for a lady it will be fine."

Her father smiled again. "Yes, that's true," he said. "A lady is mature enough to enjoy such things." He glanced at the Missus, who nodded. "All right, then," the Master said formally. "You may be my escort for the evening."

Sarabeth nodded her thanks, and her father broke into a laugh, pulled her toward him and kissed her on the forehead. She turned, left the room and went upstairs to begin considering what she should wear. Tonight would indeed be a stuffy affair, with all the white folks closed up in the Big House while somewhere outside the slaves would be singing and celebrating. But Sarabeth's long-ago playmate, Lillie, would be there too, and that held a dark sort of appeal. Sarabeth did not know what she would say or do if she saw her disloyal friend tonight—but something, she was certain, would occur to her.

Lillie had an even worse start to her day than Sarabeth did, having passed a frightful night. Her mind had been filled with thoughts of the dangers she would face at the slave dance this evening—dangers that left her fretting and tossing and barely able to close her eyes. The little sleep she did get was filled with images of hounds and whips and the darkened woods. Lillie was at the center of it all, with the Bingham Woods plantation off to the west, Orchard Hill to the east and the safety of her cabin at Greenfog far, far behind her. When Mama finally tried to roust her from bed shortly before dawn, Lillie waved her off and buried her face in her thin, scratchy mattress.

"Up, child, up," Mama said.

"Later, Mama."

"Later is too late, 'less you want to explain to the overseer why you didn't show up to tend the babies."

The party tonight did not free the slaves from their Saturday morning responsibilities, and that meant that Lillie had to be in the nursery cabin by the time the work horn sounded, just as if it were any other day. Mama got the family out of bed especially early so that the children could try on their fancy clothes for the evening to make sure they still fit. As it turned out, Lillie's dress did crowd her too much on top. Mama opened up some seams in the sides of the dress and sewed them out rounder, allowing the girl to breathe and her shape to show itself. Lillie felt pleased by that at first and then embarrassed, especially after Plato noticed what was happening, covered his mouth and snickered.

"You quit that laughin', Plato," Mama said, "'less you want me to take that suit offa you and send you to that dinner in nothin' but your skin." Now it was Lillie's turn to snicker and Plato's to turn away grumpily.

Lillie did make it to the nursery cabin on time—just barely—and the morning, as she'd feared, passed slowly. After the terrible thing that happened to the hummingbird a week before, Lillie had lingered in Bett's cabin, while Bett explained what the two of them would have to do to make tonight's charm work properly. The most important thing, Bett had said, was that Lillie should come to her cabin as soon as she could today, and that she should bring Plato with her. Bett assured her that the boy would face no danger if the charm went wrong, and Lillie believed her, but that did not free her of worry entirely. When the quitting horn finally sounded about midday today, Lillie sprinted out of the nursery cabin and sped to the tobacco field, where

Mama would be finishing up the morning's weeding and Plato would be busy with his bird chasing. When she arrived, Mama was surprised to see her, especially as out of breath as she was.

"What are you about, girl?" she asked suspiciously. "You in some kind o' trouble?"

"No, Mama, no trouble. I just come to fetch Plato."

"On what business?"

"No business, just playin'. We got the afternoon free. Ain't it all right for me to play with my little brother?"

Plato brightened and bounded to Lillie. "Hen fox!" he said. "We can play hen fox!"

Lillie grinned. "That's just what I was thinkin'."

Hen fox was a game their papa used to play with them that involved not much more than hiding in the tobacco plants and leaping out to scare each other—the one doing the scaring being the fox, the one who got scared being the hen. For a time after Papa died, Lillie had tried to continue the game so that Plato wouldn't miss it too much. He always enjoyed it, but it usually made Lillie want to cry and she soon had to give it up.

"You ain't played hen fox in months," Mama said. "What are you up to, child?"

Lillie looked at Mama and worked to make her face appear as honest as she could. "The boy's gonna be all alone tonight," she said in a half whisper, as if she were a mama herself. "I don't want him to miss us too much."

Mama looked at her skeptically, but finally nodded her agreement. Plato leapt up and began bounding through the fields. Lillie chased after him, feeling both relieved and a bit ashamed for fooling Mama so.

"I'm the fox!" Plato shouted when he'd run barely twenty yards. He dove into the sod around the tobacco plants.

Lillie dove after him, wrestling with him and tickling him as the boy laughed delightedly. Then she whispered into his ear. "I've got somethin' better to do!"

"What?" Plato asked, still giggling and squirming.

"It's a surprise," Lillie answered, "but if you come with me, you may get some cake!"

Plato brightened. "Cake? Now?"

"Soon. But we got to bake it first. And for that, we gotta go see Bett!" Lillie tickled Plato again, saying, "Get up, get up!" The boy wriggled to his feet and the two of them ran ahead.

It seemed like barely a minute before they arrived at Bett's cabin and as they were approaching, Lillie could smell the fragrance of baking. She scanned ahead to see if the slowbees were about, but this baking seemed to be ordinary baking; any charm connected to it was too weak to show itself. That was good, since while Plato had never asked why things behaved so peculiarly around Bett's cabin, the time was surely approaching when he would. Bett must have heard them coming, because she appeared in her doorway and waved them toward her. They raced the rest of the way to the cabin and came to a skidding stop at the door.

"All that runnin'," Bett said. "You'll get yourselves hungry. I expect I can take care o' that, though."

Bett stepped aside and Lillie and Plato entered the cabin, where the rich smell from the oven was everywhere. Both children looked around to see what Bett was preparing, but when Plato looked toward the table and saw a fresh, warm tray of biscuits, his face fell.

"That ain't cake," he sulked. "You said we'd have cake."

"Plato!" Lillie scolded. "That ain't polite!" She glanced at Bett, who laughed it off.

"Cake is comin'," she said. "You'll have biscuits and milk first." Bett selected two big biscuits and poured two cups of milk for Lillie and Plato, and the children sat down and ate hungrily. Before Lillie was finished, Bett waved her over to the worktable near the oven. "You and I have business," she said quietly. "Finish your food later."

While Plato ate—gobbling down his biscuit and starting on Lillie's—Bett laid out the ingredients for a cake batter and told Lillie exactly how much of each one she'd need to scoop and pour. Lillie set to work, with Bett watching closely. When the girl needed help, Bett would explain what she had to do, but would step away with her hands clasped behind her back as she did, resisting the temptation to do the work for her. When Lillie looked like her mind was wandering, Bett cautioned her, "Think hard about the baking, child. And think hard about what you want it to do. That's the only way to make it work." Even before Lillie was done with the mixing, Bett looked in the bowl and smiled in approval at what she was seeing. Then she turned to Plato.

"You want to help your sister and me, child?" she asked. Plato looked up from his plate, his mouth covered with biscuit crumbs, and nodded. "Good, then run to my stream and fetch us some water. Not just any water; it's got to be extra cold and extra clear. You understand?"

"Yes'm," Plato said, jumping up. Bett pointed to a bucket near the hearth, Plato snatched it up, and vanished out the door. When he was gone, Lillie looked toward Bett questioningly.

"Don't need no water," Bett said. "But he's a boy. He gets to playing with a stream full o' fish, and he won't be back till we're ready for him." Her face then turned serious and she took Lillie by the shoulders. "You think hard while you was workin' like I told you to?"

"Yes'm," Lillie answered.

Bett nodded. "Listen good, then. I'll light my oven fires before the wagons load tonight and set this batter to bake as soon as I hear you all goin' off to Bingham Woods. It don't take long to short-bake a cake, but it ought to be enough for you to reach the fork in the road that'll take you to Orchard Hill instead. Soon as I pull the batter out o' the oven, you jump outta that wagon."

"How will I know you pulled it out?" Lillie asked.

"You'll smell the bakin', child. You and no one else. You smell it, you jump. You understand?"

Lillie nodded. "How will I know the charm's workin' after that? How will I know it's quickenin' me up?"

Bett smiled a smile Lillie couldn't quite read. "You'll know. Don't worry 'bout that. But remember, the charm will carry you, but it don't last long. Once you get to Orchard Hill, it'll be done. You got to do your work there quick, 'cause you'll have nothin' but your own legs to carry you back to Bingham Woods. That's a lot o' hard runnin' for a grown person—more for a child." Lillie nodded her understanding and Bett pointed to the bowl. "Now," she said, "finish up that mixing and spit in it." Lillie mixed hurriedly, then leaned over the bowl and spat.

"We need the boy's spit too," Bett said. "A powerful charm calls for powerful sugar, and he's young enough his spit oughta be sweet as plums. Later tonight, I'll bake him a proper cake what ain't short-cooked or spat in, so's we don't lie to him."

Bett stuck her head out the door and called to Plato,

who ran back inside. As Bett had suspected, the bucket was empty and his clothes were soaked from playing in the stream. She steered him to the worktable, crouched down in front of him and held the batter bowl out to him.

"Boy," she said, "you got to spit in the cake."

"Why?" Plato asked.

"It's your cake, ain't it?" Bett asked.

Plato nodded.

"Then we gotta make sure you're the only one what eats it," Bett said. "Ain't nobody gonna touch it if you tells 'em it's got your spit."

Plato beamed, spat messily into the bowl and laughed delightedly at what he'd just done. Lillie looked at him with mingled feelings. In one afternoon, she'd lied first to her mama and then to her brother. She reckoned she felt low about that, but she reckoned too that she had no choice.

Chapter Fifteen

THE WAGONS LOADED for the Saturday party at what would normally have been the dinner hour at Greenfog. Some of the slaves, particularly the ones Lillie's age, ate a light supper in their cabins first so that they wouldn't get too hungry on the ride to Bingham Woods. Most of the adults ate nothing at all—the women not wanting to grow too full for the dancing, the men wanting to save room both for the roasted hog they knew they would eat and the whiskey they hoped they would drink. Lillie, like the adults, ate nothing—though for her it was worry that claimed her appetite. Even if she did try to force down some food, her jumping stomach would probably not let her hold on to it.

Perhaps, she thought, this was a fool idea after all. Perhaps there were other ways. Hadn't Bett said that her oven and its black stone could work more magic than just the kind she'd told her about? Maybe that magic was too dangerous, but could it be more dangerous than a slave girl running alone on a dark road at night? With effort, Lillie pushed those thoughts from her head. She and Bett had come up with a plan for tonight, and that plan had seemed like a good one. It was no surprise that it wouldn't seem as good now, when the time was coming close that it would be more than just planning. But that, Lillie reckoned, was fear talking. "The charm will carry you," Bett had said, and Lillie would have to trust that it would.

The three wagons that would be carrying the thirty or so slaves to Bingham Woods lined up on the dirt path not far from the cabins. The overseer and the slave drivers were there too and would be traveling to the party as well. Louis was given the first wagon to mind—the one that carried the mamas and the oldest girls. Slave women on the way to a slave party liked to use the ride to laugh and gossip in private, usually about the men. The overseer never imagined they'd cause any trouble and thus set only one whip man to watch them. The second wagon carried the men, and both Mr. Willis and Bull were seated with them. Give a wagonful of slave men a smell of the world, the overseer feared, and there was no telling what thoughts of running it would give them. Best to have two whips handy just to be safe.

The last wagon—as always—would carry the slave children, and nobody believed they needed to be guarded. No child on any plantation had tried to escape in as long as anyone in Beaufort County could remember. Most were spooked enough on a country road late at night that they'd huddle together for the entire ride, no likelier to jump from the wagon than from the roof of the Big House itself.

Lillie, Plato and Mama dressed in their party finery shortly before it was time to board the wagons, and they made a handsome group. The last time they'd all dressed so prettily, Papa had been with them. When Lillie thought of that, she felt a wave of sadness come over her, but she pushed it away. Mama was surely feeling the same thing, but Mama wasn't showing it, lest she spoil the family's fun. Lillie guessed she could contain her feelings just the same.

The three of them left the cabin and stepped out into the late-summer crispness, hand in hand. Mama enjoyed promenading with her smart and well turned-out family and couldn't resist looking this way and that to see if any other slaves were noticing them. They'd all gone no more than a few yards, however, before their good spirits froze up hard. Coming toward them through the lowering shadows was Mr. Willis. The family stopped where they were, and as the overseer drew near, he looked them up and down with the appraising eye of a slave buyer at auction.

"Awful pretty family, Franny," he said to Mama. Then, with a leer that made Lillie feel ill, he looked Mama up and down an extra time and added, "And an awful fine-lookin' mama too."

"Thank you, sir," Mama said. "Just tryin' not to be late for the wagons."

"Wagons ain't goin' nowhere without me," Mr. Willis answered. His gaze stayed on Mama, then it shifted to Lillie. The hungry, smirking expression he wore didn't change. "I expect I'll see you ladies doin' some fine dancin' tonight."

Lillie started to say something, but Mama answered for her. "Child's too young for dancin'," she said. "She might take a turn with the other girls, but that's all."

Willis laughed unpleasantly. "A girl growin' up as ripe as this one don't look too young for dancin' to me," he said. "Course, she ain't never gonna be as much of a picture as her mama. Looks more like the papa—taller, bonier."

Lillie, despite her fear of the man, looked up at him with a glare she could barely control. Willis didn't notice. Instead, he turned his attention to Plato.

"You best protect these ladies tonight, boy," he directed. "Keep 'em from forgettin' how to behave themselves with so much dancin' and liquor around."

Plato shrank against Mama, and Mama held him by the shoulder. "The boy ain't comin' tonight. I'm takin' him to the Big House kitchen now."

"Too bad, son," the overseer said. "No dances for you this year, and by next year . . ." He allowed his words to trail off, leaving only their meaning behind. By next year, those unsaid words were saying, Plato would be gone.

Willis turned and walked off and Mama stood staring at him, her face rock-still but a twitch playing about her mouth. Lillie watched the little man striding away and felt nothing but a cold, clear loathing. It was a frightening feeling, if only because it was so big and so sudden—a feeling that seemed like it could get away from her if she wasn't careful.

"He don't think I'll be big enough for the dances next year, Mama?" Plato asked.

Mama collected herself before speaking. "That silly man don't know what he's talkin' about," she said with a shaky laugh. "By next year you'll be big enough to look down at the top o' that pink head o' his." Plato laughed and Mama turned to Lillie and spoke seriously. "I'm takin' the boy to the Big House. You go straight to them wagons, and I'll join you there presently. Don't get in no trouble on the way."

Lillie nodded and gave Plato a kiss on his forehead, then ran off toward the wagons. When she arrived, she was pleased to see that the children's wagon was indeed last in line—and that Samuel was at the reins. As the oldest and slowest of the rig-drivers, he was considered the best choice to drive the wagon that wouldn't need much minding. With his fading eyesight and wandering thinking, Samuel had to pay such close attention to the road that it was unlikely he'd notice her jumping quietly out of the back.

The wagon was mostly full by now, but there was still a spot or two at the back, which was where Lillie needed to be if she was going to hop off with a minimum of fuss. She frowned when she saw that Cal was seated far at the front. She knew that it would not have been a good idea for her to ride directly beside Cal tonight, since she found it hard to imagine that a boy like him could watch her jump down into the road and run off into the darkness without taking it into his head to light out after her just for the sport of the thing. Still, the idea of sitting close to him in the bouncing wagon had been playing in her mind for the past few days.

The last time the young slaves had been taken to a party, she'd indeed sat directly next to Cal and in the middle of the ride, the wagon suddenly hit a rut and jumped. He grabbed her arm to keep her from losing her seat and held it fast till the bouncing stopped, continuing to talk the whole while and never seeming to notice what he was doing. Lillie guessed that was the most mannerly thing a boy had ever done for her. Tonight Cal was sitting with the slave boys Benjy and Cupit, the three of them bunched together, talking low and close, just as they had been when Lillie caught them near the cabins more than a week earlier. She didn't like the look of that, but with her mind so full of worries of her own, she pushed the thought aside.

Finally, Lillie looked for one more face and found Minervy also seated near the back, though she was wedged between two other girls. That was a problem, but it couldn't be helped. When Lillie hopped aboard, she squeezed herself next to Minervy, pushing away another girl, who glared at her. Minervy herself seemed pleased that Lillie wanted to sit beside her and shimmied over to make room.

Tonight, Lillie noticed, Minervy looked prettier than she had ever seen her, with green and red bows in her hair and a white cotton dress, hemmed clean and straight with no tatters Lillie could see. The dress was too big for Minervy, which meant her mama had made it only recently and expected it to last her two or three years. What Lillie noticed even more than Minervy's pretty clothes and hair was her face. There were none of the usual fret lines on her forehead or worry crinkles about her eyes. Her face looked like the face of a child—which is how it ought to look, but almost never did.

"Didn't eat so much as a nibble tonight," Minervy said brightly. "My papa said the Bingham Woods slaves make a hog as sweet as cane, and I aim to have some."

"Fine hog," Lillie answered, trying to muster something else to say but feeling too jumpy and distracted. She looked about herself nervously, taking the measure of her surroundings—the nearness of the other wagons, the darkness of the night, the height of the jump from her seat to the ground. None of them brought her much comfort.

"My mama said she didn't want me doin' no dancin',

least not with boys," Minervy went on, whispering now and sidling up to Lillie. "What'd your mama say?"

"Same," Lillie answered. "No boy dancin'."

"Mamas ain't watchin' the whole time, though, is they?" Minervy said, giggling.

Lillie looked at her. "Watchin' what?" she said. "Who ain't watchin'?"

"The mamas! Lillie, are you listenin' to me?"

"Yes," Lillie said, her mind buzzing. "No. I don't know." She shook her head to clear it. "No, Minervy, I ain't listenin'. I need to talk to you."

"What'd you do?" Minervy asked immediately. She looked at Lillie anxiously, her smooth face crinkling right back up. "What'd you do wrong?"

"Didn't do nothin'," Lillie whispered as low as she could. "But I'm gonna do somethin', and you gotta know 'cause you gotta help."

"What are you on about?"

"I'm gonna jump, girl. Soonest we get to the fork in the road, I'm gonna slip off, go take care o' some business, and come back. No one gots to know, 'specially no white folks nor grown slaves."

"Lillie!" Minervy hissed. "You're thinkin' wild."

"I'm thinkin' straight. Straight as I ever thought."

"You'll get caught for sure!"

"I won't get caught."

"Can't no slave travel roads like this at night, least of all a child slave."

"I can."

"How?"

"Never mind. I got ways."

"But what for? Ain't no business worth gettin' caught, flogged and sold off."

"Mine is," Lillie said. "And I'm gonna go do it." She looked at Minervy hard and straight, her tone flat. "I'm doin' this and ain't nothin' gonna tell me otherwise. But I still need your help, else I won't get away."

Minervy studied Lillie's face. Lillie thought she'd turn away, but Minervy didn't. The girl had a keen sense for how to avoid trouble, and along the way had taught herself to manage it when it came anyway. There was no doubt in Minervy's mind that Lillie meant what she said about jumping. That would lead either to terrible things or not so terrible things—depending on whether Lillie got caught. And it was Minervy who could make the difference.

"What can I do?" she asked simply.

Lillie leaned into her. "You got a way about you, girl. I see it when you talk to the little ones. I tell 'em to shush, they don't shush. You tell 'em—with that voice and that face and that no-foolin' way—they shush." She gestured to the other children in the wagon. "When I jump, you got to do the same with them."

"These ain't babies, Lillie. Some of 'em's older'n me."

"Don't matter. They still ain't grown, which means they got children's ways. You, girl, you got a mama's ways."

Minervy started to protest, but stopped herself. Lillie was right, and they both knew it.

"But what about Samuel?" Minervy asked. "He ain't a child."

"He also can't hardly hear nor see. The whole lot of us could jump out 'fore he'd notice."

Minervy, despite herself, laughed. Then she took Lillie's hand and squeezed it hard. "I'll do what you need," she said at last. "I don't like it, but I will. You just come back."

Lillie said nothing and looked away, her heart starting to pound. At that moment, she saw Mama, without Plato, hurrying toward the wagons. Lillie raised her hand and smiled to show she was where she was supposed to be. Mama waved back, then climbed aboard the women's wagon. Lillie was seized with the terrible fear that she'd just waved good-bye to her mama forever. Before she could go further with that dark thought, all three wagons jerked into motion.

As the grand evening at last began, all the slaves began talking happily. And at almost the same moment, a rhythmic clapping began in the second wagon. The slaves fell silent as quickly as they'd started speaking and turned to the sound in delight and surprise. It was the juba patters—

four of them, seated in the middle of the wagon—practicing their music before the party began.

Patting juba was a skill the slaves had been passing down to one another for generations, from the moment they were captured in Africa and brought to America. The masters forbade most slaves to have musical instruments, fearing that drums could be used to pass coded signals from plantation to plantation, and other kinds of music-making were simply not in keeping with the hard work that always needed to get done. In recent decades, most masters had relaxed these rules, but by then many of the slaves didn't care, having long since taught themselves to make music with the only instruments nobody could take away from them— their hands and feet—clapping, stomping and patting their thighs, bellies, chests and cheeks. Four or five good juba players could turn out as much fine music as a whole parlor full of instruments.

The juba players in the second wagon began their patting slowly this evening, with a light slapping of thighs and clapping of hands, while the horses plodded off the plantation and onto the shadowy, tree-canopied roads. As the road darkened and the horses quickened, the players quickened too, adding their toes, then their heels, then the whole hard flat of their feet against the floorboards of the wagons. The rhythm picked up and the drumming grew louder, the players striking their broad barrel chests with the flats of their hands and letting out the occasional deep whoop. The men played for a long while, and the music they produced seemed to swirl around the slaves, rising up, rustling the very leaves of the overhanging trees, and pouring back down. The horses' hooves and the rattling wheels themselves fell into the rhythm, driven by the fast-flying hands and rat-a-tat feet of the four juba men.

Lillie closed her eyes and began to feel enveloped by the music, almost as if she were being gathered up and held aloft. Minervy looked at her, noticing her face and her pose and the distant look in her eyes, then turned back toward the rest of the wagon. Whatever was going to happen, she reckoned, was going to happen now.

"Pssst!" Minervy hissed, in a sound that caused all the children to turn. "Psst!" she repeated. She fixed the children with the same strong eyes and stern face she used on the squawling babies, and to her surprise, the children did just what the babies did: They looked back, grew still and kept their own eyes directly on her.

Somewhere, as if from a distance, Minervy's hiss reached Lillie too. And at that moment, Lillie became aware of one more thing beyond the silence of the children and the drumming of the juba and the pounding of her own anxious heart: It was the smell of baking—Bett's baking, the rich scent of a cake mixed by Lillie's own hand and sweetened by her baby brother's sugar spit. Without thinking, she drew a breath and let herself go slack. Then she rolled as if drunk from the back of the wagon, down to the hard and rutted road below.

A tumble like that at the speed the horses were moving could have been the end of Lillie, but she fell in a way she'd never fallen before—less like a girl than like a cat, spinning in the air and finding her feet, then landing on them as light and sure as if she'd hopped out of bed. She heard a skid that she reckoned was her heels finding their purchase in the dirt, but she didn't feel it. Instead, she felt light, almost dreamy, and more than anything else, quick.

Standing in the road, she watched, untroubled, as the wagon pulled away from her and she saw it swerve left on the fork to Bingham Woods. That meant Orchard Hill lay to the right. Without needing to think, she began running, first straight and then a sharp right turn. Lillie could still smell the baking, stronger than ever in fact, and more remarkably, she could still hear the juba drumming, the music growing louder even as the wagon carrying the players retreated farther behind her. She ran down the road lightly, effortlessly, her legs pounding, almost whirling, along with the music. Her heartbeat was strong and steady, and her breath came deep and calm. It was not at all the urgent breathing and trip-hammer heart that ought to come with running, but it was all she felt she needed.

A near full moon hung in the sky, which cast a helpful

shimmer of light, and the more Lillie's eyes grew adjusted to the night, the better she could see. She glanced around at a world that looked oddly different from any she'd seen before. As the juba grew louder and quicker and she moved faster and faster, everything else appeared to go slower and slower. The leaves in the trees seemed not so much to be rustling in the wind as waving, swinging, with a gentle, liquid motion. She glanced down and saw that the spray of dust her feet were kicking up rose like slow smoke; the pebbles that flew along with it floated up and settled back down like slips of paper on the wind. She looked ahead and, to her surprise, saw a tiny, dark-eyed tree bat flying toward her. Ordinarily, she'd drop and scream when one of the hateful things approached. Now she simply sidestepped it, having more than enough time to avoid the little beast, which slowly flapped its way into the night behind her.

Distantly, Lillie heard what sounded like voices—white men's voices. She turned toward the sound and in the woods saw the light of two torches. These were the night patrols, men who walked the boundaries of the plantations, looking for runaways and other slaves who weren't where they ought to be. The sight of the men should have been many times more terrifying than the sight of the bat, but again, Lillie felt no fear. The night patrollers, instead, were likely fearing her. They could not see her, she was certain of that, and they could not hear the juba either. If anything, they would have heard a windy, whooshing sound in the road, turned toward it and seen only a shadow flitting by. Perhaps it was a wolf, perhaps it was a ghost—whatever it was, it was a creature of the night, one that they feared could do them much more harm than they could do it. Lillie was a night creature now, and when she thought of the fright she was causing the men, she felt only strength.

The baking smell, the juba music and Lillie's own fleet feet carried her along for a good distance more, until she at last saw cabin lights and a clearing ahead. Beyond them, she saw the warm, golden windows of a plantation Big House. She had arrived at Orchard Hill, at the edge of the thick stand of trees and brush that opened onto the slave cabins. This was where the very family she'd come to visit surely lived. At the sight of that, Lillie's feet began to slow and her heart and breath began to calm. The smell of the baking and sound of the juba music at last began to fade, depositing her here like the hand of a giant placing her gently down.

Chapter Sixteen

THE GRASS AROUND the slave cabins at Orchard Hill was surprisingly thick and surprisingly damp. It seemed that a drizzle had fallen here but not at Greenfog, an idea that was new to Lillie since she had rarely traveled far enough to think about where weather started and where it stopped. She was tempted to pull her shoes off and walk through the grass barefoot, since now that the charm had quit, her feet were just ordinary feet again, and with the kind of running she'd just done, they felt like they'd been worn to nubs. She kept her shoes on, however, in case she had to make a quick escape.

The lush grass around the cabins was a sign of a prosperous plantation—a rare thing lately—since most masters would buy just enough grass seed for the grounds around the Big House and no more. Only those who didn't have to worry about the expense would buy so much seed they could scatter some to their slaves. Lillie also noticed the fragrance of freshly cut wood—another sign of wealth. A smell like that in the vicinity of the slave cabins likely meant that new cabins had recently been built. That either meant that new slaves had recently been bought or that the Master had allowed the ones he owned already to rebuild their little homes. Either way, there'd been no such money spent at Greenfog in a long while.

Lillie stood as still as she could, twenty or so yards from the closest cabin. She could hear voices coming softly from some of them and could see lantern light in the windows of most. It was not quite time for the children to go to sleep and not nearly bedtime for the grown-ups. That was good, since had she gotten here any later, most of the parents would have come outside, where they could smoke and talk in quiet tones to allow the children inside to fall asleep. A stranger like Lillie bursting out of the woods would have surely caused screams.

Stepping through the grass, she scanned the cabins, wondering how she could figure out which one was home to Henry's wife and son without knocking on all the doors and creating a disturbance that might fetch the Orchard Hill overseer. She hadn't considered that problem until this very moment, but now, confronted with cabin after cabin, all of which looked more or less the same, she wished she'd remembered to ask Henry for some way to pick his family's home from all the others. She scanned the cabins anxiously, aware that time was once again passing at its ordinary, uncharmed pace and she'd have to make the run back to Bingham Woods at her ordinary, uncharmed speed. She took another quiet step when suddenly she heard a voice.

"Here!" it whispered loudly from off to Lillie's left. "Over here!"

Lillie's breath stopped cold in her chest, and a fear so big ran through her that she felt she'd swoon. She managed to keep her head and stay on her feet, and the voice spoke again.

"No," it said in a louder whisper. "Here! Here!"

The voice sounded like it belonged to a girl, one who was older than Lillie but not by much. The girl's call was answered not by another voice, but by the sound of running footsteps, and now Lillie reckoned she was caught for certain. This time she dared not simply stay where she was and instead took a few bounding leaps toward the closest tree, hoping that the sound of the other footsteps would mask her own. She ducked behind the tree's thick trunk, banging her elbow hard against it and feeling the rough bark scrape away a portion of skin. She sealed her lips to prevent herself from crying out.

In the weak lamplight spilling from the window of one of the cabins, Lillie could now see a boy, perhaps seventeen years old, running lightly in the direction of the girl's voice. He was tall and lean like many boys his age, but with the beginnings of muscles that said he'd already spent a season in the fields. He stopped and flattened himself against the wall of the cabin, and from around the side a girl emerged. Even from a distance, Lillie could see how pretty she was, and even from here she could see that the girl had taken the trouble to comb out her hair and put on a dress that was too fine for wearing around the cabins just before bedtime.

"I didn't think you was comin'," the girl whispered.

"I didn't neither," the boy said. "I couldn't get left alone long enough to get away."

He looked at the girl for a moment and then, with a suddenness that caused Lillie to jump, took hold of her fast and hard. Lillie thought that the girl would scream, but the girl didn't scream. Instead she grabbed the boy in return, and they fell into a long kiss. The boy's arms wrapped easily around the girl's back, and her arms held him tight. Lillie's eyes went wide and she emerged a bit from behind the tree, forgetting herself entirely. She watched the boy and the girl, whose kiss went on longer than she had known a kiss could—forgetting for a moment that every second it did go on took her a second further away from finding Henry's family, and brought her a second closer to getting caught, flogged and sold. The boy and girl broke once for a breath, exchanged a whispered word Lillie couldn't hear, followed by a giggle, and then kissed some more.

There was no telling how long they would have gone on

like that if a door hadn't suddenly banged open two cabins away. The sound of the thing made all three of them jump, and the wedge of low light it threw across the grass seemed as startling as daylight. Lillie turned toward the sound and the light and then turned back to the boy and the girl. The boy was already gone, vanishing as completely as if he'd never been there at all. The girl lingered against the cabin wall, smoothing her hair and her clothes and catching her breath. Then she disappeared back around the side of the cabin. There was a second little wedge of light as she creaked the door open and slipped back inside.

Lillie herself still could not move, and she felt a wave of panic, suddenly imagining herself having to hide behind this tree all night until tomorrow morning when the sun finally rose and she was exposed. She shook off the thought and turned back to the other cabin, where the door still stood wide. A little boy who appeared to be about three years old appeared, hopping anxiously on one foot and then the other and looking back over his shoulder. Lillie recognized that hop from just a few years ago, when Plato was learning to get through the night without wetting his bed and would sometimes wait too long before realizing how badly he needed to use the privy. Behind the boy, a papa now appeared.

"Go, boy, go," he said. "B'fore you do your business here."

"It's dark, Papa," the boy said, looking fearfully out at the tiny privy house, which stood perhaps thirty yards away, but might as well have been in another county to a child of three.

"It's night; it's s'posed to be dark," the papa said. "And you're near four; you're s'posed to be able to do this on your own." He reached down and swatted the boy gently on the bottom. "Go," he said again.

The boy hesitated a second more, then put his head down and sprinted across the grass. Lillie heard the privy door swing open and shut as the boy vanished inside. A few moments later, it swung open again, and the boy sprinted back across the grass.

"I did it! I did it! I did it!" he said. He ran to his papa, who stood in the doorway and scooped him up in his arms. He kissed the child, went back inside and closed the door.

Lillie stood staring in the darkness, her mind suddenly filled with memories of how she and Papa and Mama would take turns standing guard in just the same way while Plato would pluck up his courage to dash through the night, and Papa would wait to pick him up and swing him about happily when he finished in the privy and came running back. She forced the thought out of her head and squinted back into the dark, her eyes still holding a ghost image of the wedge of gold light and the faint, illuminated shapes of the trees and other cabins standing nearby. She was surprised at how well the picture still lingered. And as she thought of that, she clapped her hand over her mouth and her eyes once again went wide. On the door of the very next cabin there was a large scrap of black cloth. It was knotted up in such a way that it appeared it was once a bow, but the wind and rain had caused it to go limp and undone. Nonetheless, there was no doubt what its meaning had once been: It was a mourning ribbon, just like the one that had been on Lillie's family's cabin. Someone who'd lived here was dead—had died a few months ago from the look of the bow, or just about the time her papa had died. That was also the time that Henry's family would have been given the news that he wasn't coming home—but not been given the news that it was because he'd been wounded and freed, not killed.

Lillie stepped out from the protection of the tree, crossed the soft, wet grass and approached the cabin. The light coming from the window was almost too faint to see, but just enough to guide her. She climbed the tiny plank porch of the house, knocked once and then again, her hand rustling the black cloth as she did. The door opened. A woman about Lillie's mama's age stood there. A boy who looked to be about ten years old stood peering out from behind her. The woman looked at Lillie's unfamiliar face, and her own face showed fear.

"Who are you?" she asked.

Lillie didn't answer that question. "I seen Henry," she said instead.

"What?" the woman asked, barely able to get out the word.

"I seen him," Lillie said. "He's alive."

The woman fainted where she stood.

"Mama!" her boy exclaimed.

Chapter Seventeen

THE AIR INSIDE the parlor of the Bingham Woods Big House was warm and suffocating—much warmer and more suffocating than Sarabeth had thought it would be. The windows were closed against the mosquitoes outside, and her autumn party clothes, while suited to the month, were not suited to the actual weather, which was still summery. Sarabeth's mother liked to tell her that ladies don't sweat, and while Sarabeth had often tried to abide by that rule, she'd never had much luck at it. She certainly wasn't having any this evening.

As difficult as it was to tolerate the heat, it was harder still to take the boredom. Sarabeth had known she wouldn't be invited into the library with the masters tonight, but she'd thought at least she'd be visiting with the plantation Missus, eating cakes and sipping teas and touring the Big House rooms—the kind of social call that never looked like a great deal of fun when her mother did it, but at least felt grown-up. The Missus herself, however, didn't consider

Sarabeth quite grown-up enough and wanted no part of having to spend her evening entertaining a thirteen-year-old child.

What made things even worse was that Sarabeth was not the only child visiting the grand home tonight. The Master of Bingham Woods had decided that as long as he'd be hosting the Master of Greenfog this evening, he might as well invite the families from some of the other surrounding plantations too. This would give the men a chance to smoke and drink, the women a chance to tour the rooms and the children—including Sarabeth—a chance to play together, an opportunity they did not get often enough.

All the children—Sarabeth included—were thus instructed to spend the evening in the parlor in the care of a plantation nanny. They were not permitted to wander the house lest they break things, nor wander the grounds, lest they interfere with the slave party and distract the whip men trying to keep order. The door to the parlor was kept closed, and what made that confinement especially cruel for Sarabeth was that most of the children imprisoned inside with her were boys and the few who were girls appeared to be no older than five. The boys were wild little creatures—wrestling, racing, fighting, tumbling, ignoring the toy carriages, wooden horses and piles of building logs the nanny gave them to play with, except when one of them would take it into his head to throw them at another. Sarabeth could always abide Cody, but Cody was her little brother and he adored her. She had often wondered if she could bear a small boy whose savage nature wasn't softened in such a way. Now she knew: she couldn't.

The nanny, who was a slave about Sarabeth's mother's age, was working hard keeping the boys well fed on cakes and other treats and appeared to be trying to get them so stuffed they'd grow sleepy and doze off. Sarabeth declined the food, hoping to make it as clear as possible that while she was held in the room with the dreadful children, she was certainly not to be counted as one of them.

At length, Sarabeth decided she could take no more of the heat and the tedium and the noise of the boys. She rose from the settee and walked to the window. The nanny—who was busy picking up a small, round table and a heavy crystal snifter the boys had just knocked over—did not notice her. Sarabeth flung open the window and poked her head outside. The light nighttime breeze was far fresher than the thick, cottony air filling the room, and she longed to be outside where she could feel it better. She cocked her head and could just make out the voices of the slaves and that music they made by slapping themselves and stamping their feet. It sounded strange and dangerous—and oddly exciting. It was certainly better than the din of the parlor. She listened for a moment longer and frowned. The slaves were enjoying themselves, the fathers were enjoying themselves, even the horrible boys in the parlor were enjoying themselves. Sarabeth was the only one who wasn't enjoying herself tonight. She turned and strode to the parlor door, and with that, the nanny at last noticed her.

"Miss Sarabeth, Miss Sarabeth," she said, hurrying over with a piece of broken toy in her hand. "Is there somethin' I can git you?"

"Nothing," Sarabeth said.

"Does you need to use the house privy?"

"I'll look after myself if I need to use the privy," Sarabeth said. "I just need a walk."

"Your daddy said you wasn't to leave the house."

"I'll stay inside and tour the rooms."

"Your daddy said you wasn't to leave *this* room."

"Well, my daddy isn't the one talking to you now, is he?" Sarabeth snapped.

"No'm."

"Do you want to ask him? Do you want to walk in there and disturb the masters?" Sarabeth gestured past the closed door in the direction of the library.

"No'm."

"And you can't very well chase after me and leave the children alone if I go."

"No'm," the nanny said. A loud bang sounded behind her as the boys once again knocked over the table and snifter. The nanny flinched.

"Very well, then," Sarabeth said, smoothing her dress and tossing her hair. "I will take a walk then—outside the house if I choose to—and I will return shortly." She reached for the door.

"Miss Sarabeth!" the nanny cried, loudly enough to startle her.

"What is it?" Sarabeth snapped back.

"At least take your wrap, Miss." She hurried over to the settee where Sarabeth had been sitting and snatched up the silk shoulder covering that her mother had made her bring with her against the night chill. The nanny brought it back and Sarabeth put it on. Then she opened the door, walked out and shut it smartly behind her.

Standing in the hallway, Sarabeth could now hear the voices of the fathers coming from the library across the hall and smell the tobacco smoke seeping out from under the door. She wondered if it had been such a good idea to close the parlor door as loudly as she had. If her father came out to see what the disturbance was, the grand airs that had worked so well with the nanny would be of no use to her at all. She slipped out the front door as quietly as she could.

On the porch of the great white Big House, Sarabeth looked around herself and inhaled the early autumn air. She could smell the heavy scent of barbecue from somewhere off to her left and could hear the music flowing toward her even more clearly. To her right, she could detect the subtler smell of freshly cut crops—a telltale sign that the first part of the harvest had begun. From one direction was the faint scent produced by the slaves' labor; from the other was the richer scent produced by their joy. She stepped off the porch and turned toward the joy.

Sarabeth approached the party cautiously, realizing she had no business being there. The slaves would react awkwardly and formally to her, as they did more and more the older she got. The whip men would react quickly, hurrying over to her and insisting that she return to the Big House straightaway, if only for her own safety. Sarabeth knew these things would happen, but nonetheless felt irresistibly drawn to the dance—the music and the smells and the laughing voices seeming to hook her and reel her toward them. She picked up her pace and felt the urge to kick off her tightly laced shoes, and she might have too if she hadn't known she'd soil her stockings in the grass and dirt. Instead she bounded clumsily ahead, trying as best she could to hold her balance and stay upright. Finally, she drew close enough to the party that she could actually make out the faces of the slaves—distinguishing between the familiar ones of Greenfog and the unfamiliar ones of Bingham Woods.

For all of her thirteen years, the Greenfog slaves had

worked for Sarabeth's family, served her family, obeyed her family—and Sarabeth had pitied them their lot. But tonight, she pitied herself. The lives the slaves were living may have been terrible, but she did envy them this evening. Without another thought, she tossed off her scarf and ran even faster toward the party.

Chapter Eighteen

ILLIE'S VISIT WITH Henry's family was a brief one. The slave cabins were closely watched at Orchard Hill, and while families were free to mingle and talk after the children went to sleep, the overseer conducted regular patrols to make sure no drinking or other forbidden activity was going on. There was nothing more strictly forbidden than harboring a runaway from another plantation, and a slave who broke that rule would be severely flogged and likely sold. No matter how big or wonderful the news was that Lillie was bringing, she thus had to share it quickly, whisper it quietly and then leave as soon as she could.

Lillie did not know how Henry's wife and boy would react to what she came to tell them, but once the moment was over, she knew she'd never forget it: how they didn't believe Henry was alive at first; how they wept with happiness when they did come to believe it; how they asked and asked when they could see him; how they wept again when they thought of the suffering he'd endured.

"Does it hurt him—the place the leg was?" the wife kept asking.

"No, it don't," Lillie answered, having no idea if that were true or not, but sparing the woman more cause for tears.

"Does he think about us?"

"He don't seem to think 'bout nothin' else."

Even as Lillie was bringing them such joy, she felt a familiar sadness rising inside her. What Henry's family was feeling, after all, was a happiness she and Mama and Plato would never know. Papa was dead—well and forever dead—and no strange slave girl was going to come knocking on their door late one night to tell them otherwise. When Henry's wife was done with her questions and told Lillie she'd best go, she felt strangely relieved. The two of them exchanged a long, teary hug, then Henry's wife peered out the window to make sure no one was prowling and opened the door a crack.

"Go," she said. "Go fast—and be safe!" Lillie slipped outside, looked around and made a quick sprint through the soft grass and into the cover of the woods.

With the magic of the oven and the stone now gone and nothing but her own legs to carry her back to Bingham Woods, Lillie suddenly felt all the fear she'd been spared during her charmed run to Orchard Hill. The road between the plantations was filled with the same bats and slave catchers and chilling darkness as before, but she could no longer outrun or sidestep or breeze past them. She was just an ordinary slave girl, out at night when she wasn't supposed to be—a runaway child who was breaking the law and would pay dearly if she was caught.

Picking through the thin patch of dark woods, she quickly came back upon the road and looked far down it in the direction of Bingham Woods—or as far down it as the black of the night would allow. She took a few steps and winced at the sound her feet made against the dirt and stones. When she was running here under the spell of the baking, she had made no such noise. She had felt as if she were practically flying—as if little more than her toe-tips were grazing the road. Now that she heard how loud a road it could be when you truly trod on it, she reckoned she had been correct.

All the same, Lillie had to run, and she set off as fast and as light-footedly as she could. Her legs, she noticed, ached terribly, surely from the hard work they'd done bringing her here. At the same time, they had an odd tingliness about them—a little like the crackle in the wind that could make her hair stand up before a lightning storm. She liked the feeling and idly wondered if it would last—if maybe it was something the charm had left with her forever.

Lillie was beginning to make good speed. When she looked down, the light of the moon revealed streaks and scattered pebbles in the soil below her feet, which she reckoned were the tracks she'd left as she was coming in the other direction. It made her smile and reassured her that she was going the right way. All at once, however, she snapped her head to the right and her blood ran icy. She was sure she'd seen a flicker of light deep in the woods—the same light she'd seen from the torches of the slave catchers earlier. She stopped cold, almost losing her footing and risking making even more noise as she fell into the road, but she caught her balance and held her ground.

She scanned about, with her breath catching. The woods in these parts were full of fireflies, Lillie told herself. She'd seen them; she and Plato had even hunted them. That was surely all she had noticed. Then, with a deep sense of relief, she saw the unmistakable cool blue light of one of the little creatures hovering right in front of her. She allowed herself a nervous laugh; she'd been a fool girl after all! No sooner had she thought that, however, than her laugh stopped cold in her throat. Further away, deep among the trees, she saw the equally unmistakable orange-yellow light of a fire. And it was a fire that moved in the bobbing way of a torch being carried by a person. Behind it was a second fire, moving the same way. It was indeed the slave catchers—and they were on the move. Lillie felt fit to swoon, but stayed collected and bounded over to the far side of the road, where she threw herself down in the dirt.

"Whazzat?" she heard a man's distant voice say from somewhere in the direction of the torches. She was surprised and alarmed at how far the voice carried on the cool night air.

"What's what?" another man responded.

"That noise."

"Didn't hear no noise. Maybe some night critter."

Lillie held her breath. The men said nothing and she dared peek up slightly. The torchlights were still in the distance and had moved no closer—but neither had they moved farther away.

"That ain't the sound a night critter makes," the first voice said at length.

"It don't do to chase everything you think you hear."

"It don't do not to."

To Lillie's horror, she now heard the sound of the men's footsteps crunching through underbrush, and she peeked back up to see that the torches were once again bobbing. She also, for the first time, heard panting. The men had a dog—a slave hound surely, a small, ugly breed of beast that was not good for much at all except for smelling fear. Lillie had no doubt that just such a smell was coming off her powerfully now. She reckoned the hound was not yet close enough to pick up her scent, but when it was, she'd be done for. The animal was known both for its fleet speed and its powerful bite, and once it had hold of a slave, it never let go. A tiny whimper escaped Lillie, and she immediately silenced herself—but too late.

"Over there!" one of the men said. Immediately, the speed of their footsteps picked up and an excited yip came from the dog. A wave of helplessness overcame Lillie. Her wits may have dreamed up the plan that brought her here tonight and her courage may have carried her this far, but her fear—the fear of a child—had finally betrayed her.

But Lillie wasn't just a child. Lying by the road, feeling her heart pound, knowing that that heart was sending out a drumbeat of scent to the slave hound's nose, she thought of her papa. Papa was Ibo; Papa's papa had been Ibo too. And that meant Lillie was Ibo. She was part of a tribe whose girls hunted alongside the boys, whose women went to war alongside the men. Lillie might be nothing but a slave child in South Carolina, but she was an Ibo warrior too—and no laws or slave-catchers or cruel, fool dogs could ever change what was in her blood. And with that thought, she felt her heart slow. And with her heart slowing, she felt her breath grow even. And with that, she sprang to her feet.

"Again!" one of the men's voices cried. "I heard it again!"

Lillie lit out down the road again and heard the slave catcher's footsteps pursuing her as fast as they could and the crashing sound of the dog racing along with them. But as surely as she knew anything, she knew that the dog was running blind. If she'd left a fear scent before, it was now gone. The animal would be fighting through the blackness of the night just like the men were. And the men—carrying their torches and still stumbling through the woods—would not be moving fast until they reached the clear running of the road. This was a fair race, Lillie reckoned—and one she could win if she kept her wits.

She held that thought in her head, thinking only of the safety of the slave dance that lay far ahead and not the danger that approached from behind. As she did, she felt calmer still, stronger still, charmed now not by the workings of an old woman's magic but by her own renewed courage. If she didn't shake off the slave catchers, she knew, she might at least beat them back to Bingham Woods, where she could rejoin the party and get lost among the other slaves. The whip men there wouldn't care for men from another plantation stumbling in and causing a disturbance as they chased after a shadow they and their dog hadn't even seen.

Finally, far ahead, Lillie saw another light—the warm sky-brightening orange of lanterns and a large cook fire. Faintly, she could hear music, and more faintly still, voices. She had the length of about three plow rows ahead of her before she could break through the woods and be back at Bingham Woods. Soon it was two lengths, then just one, and then she plunged into the thick stand of trees that bordered the plantation and at last was on the grounds. In front of her was a dancing, laughing swirl of slaves and everywhere around her was the sweet smell of roasting meat. She ran even faster toward the crowd—head down, feet pounding—when suddenly, off to her left, someone who was running just as fast in the same direction collided with her hard.

Lillie was shoved to the ground, her head striking the soil and her vision filling with flashes and stars. The wind was knocked entirely out of her, preventing her from crying out. She felt a weight on top of her and realized that she was pinned to the ground. The road men had caught her! They had doubled back, circled the plantation and hit her from the other side! Any moment she would be feeling the terrible pain of the slave hound's bite. But then she heard a voice, and it was not the voice of a slave catcher at all.

"Lillie!" it said. "Lillie! What is this about?"

Lillie tried to make her eyes line up properly, but they were loose and swoony from the fall. She sat up and closed one eye to focus better on the face in front of her. It was, to her astonishment, Miss Sarabeth, looking back at her crossly.

"Lillie!" she repeated. "What's the meaning of this?"

"Miss Sarabeth," Lillie said. "Why . . . why did you hit me?"

"I didn't hit you!" Sarabeth answered. "You hit me!"

The two girls got clumsily to their feet and began to straighten their clothes and collect themselves. "Look at this, Lillie," Sarabeth moaned, holding out a handful of her skirt that was stained green with grass and brown with dirt. "There'll be no explaining this to my mother when she catches sight of it."

"I'm sorry, Miss Sarabeth. I am," Lillie said. "I can help you try to clean it."

"There's nothing we can do for it here," Sarabeth answered, giving up on the dress and turning back to Lillie. "What were you doing running like that anyway? There isn't anything over there but the woods."

Lillie looked at Sarabeth, broke the gaze, then looked nervously back at the woods—half expecting the slave catchers and the hound to burst through at any second. "Weren't doin' nothin'," she said. "I just needed the privy."

"Isn't there a slave privy near the cabins?"

"It was busy," Lillie answered. "I had to use the woods."

"Then why were you running back?"

Lillie kept her eyes fixed on the ground and took a moment to respond—a moment that said that whatever her answer was, it wasn't going to be a truthful one. "I was afraid." She shrugged. "Woods are dark; no tellin' what animals are about."

Sarabeth scowled disbelievingly and scanned Lillie

up and down. Her clothes were rumpled; her hair was undone; even now, she didn't seem fully to have caught her
breath. Sarabeth took all that in, and her mouth dropped
open as she realized what it must mean. She craned her
neck around Lillie toward the woods.

"Lillie, you wicked girl!" she said. "Is there a boy out
there?"

Lillie looked up, this time meeting Sarabeth's eyes
square.

"No! No, there's not! My mama would flog me herself if
I did such a thing."

"You don't get your clothes all tangled and leaves in your
hair from using the privy," Sarabeth said.

Lillie reached up and felt her hair. There was a scrap of
leaf clinging to it, and she plucked it away. "Miss Sarabeth,
you has to believe me. I'm not a girl what would behave like
that."

"Then what were you doing?"

Lillie said nothing and Sarabeth studied her closely once
more. This time, her gaze settled on the slave girl's shoes.
They were covered with fresh dust, road dust, and so, for
that matter, were Lillie's legs. Sarabeth snapped her gaze
back up.

"You ran off!" she said. "You went somewhere."

"No!" Lillie stammered. "I didn't. I wouldn't!"

"Don't lie to me!"

"I ain't lyin'!"

"Do you know what happens to runaway slaves?"

"I ain't no runaway!"

"They get sold off is what happens. They never see their families again."

"But I'm here now, Miss Sarabeth! How could I be a runaway?"

"Maybe you got lost. Maybe you got scared of the roads. But you were doing something you're not supposed to do."

"Miss Sarabeth," Lillie implored, "whatever I done I had to do, and I come straightly back. Please don't tell nobody!"

"If I stay quiet, Lillie, then I'm doing something *I'm* not supposed to do. There's strict rules about reporting runaways."

Lillie's face now showed true fear and she frantically shook her head no. "Miss Sarabeth, we ain't never done nothin' to hurt each other before," Lillie said. "You're my friend."

"I was your friend," Sarabeth answered. "You don't want that anymore."

"But I do, I do! Just don't tell nobody I'm a runaway, 'cause I ain't!"

Lillie looked at the other girl beseechingly. Sarabeth's expression began to soften, though she kept her eyes narrow and her arms folded. As the girls stood there, fixed on one another's faces, a voice called out.

"Lillie!" it said.

Both girls turned. From the crowd of dancing and feasting slaves, they could see an arm waving. It belonged to Lillie's mama, who was standing on tiptoes to see over the crowd. The part of the evening had now arrived when the grown slaves and the child slaves would mix for family dances, and all the mamas and papas would be looking for their boys and girls.

"Lillie," Mama called again, "come here 'fore I have to fetch you."

Lillie waved back and nodded a big yes that her mama would be sure to see, then turned back toward Sarabeth.

"Go," Sarabeth said flatly. "Before you get yourself in even more trouble."

Lillie struggled for something to say, but before she could, the Master's daughter turned on her heel and walked away. From deep in the woods, Lillie faintly heard the barking of an angry hound, but it was too far away to do her any harm.

Chapter Nineteen

IT WASN'T UNTIL Sunday morning that anyone at Greenfog realized Benjy and Cupit were missing. Benjy had no parents, so no one paid much mind when he didn't turn up after the slave dance. Cupit did have a mama, but she was sickly and didn't go to the dance and was asleep when Cupit was supposed to have come home.

Cal did come home when he was supposed to, but he stayed mostly out of Nelly and George's sight during the family dances and later as he boarded the wagon back to Greenfog. Once he got to the cabin, he slipped into bed right away. That was good, since otherwise he would surely have given away the fact that he was injured—that his right ankle had swelled to half again its usual size and his foot looked almost twice as big as that, puffed up so much it barely looked like a foot at all. Cal might have kept the problem a secret all night long had the foot not hurt him so much he began moaning with pain while he slept. Eventually, Nelly and George pulled back the blanket and saw what had happened to the boy.

Lillie, like the rest of the slaves, had no reason to think there was anything amiss with Cal or Benjy or Cupit until the morning. On the ride back to Greenfog, she had too much on her mind to notice which children were and weren't seated around her. She did look for Minervy—who was relieved to see that Lillie had made it safely back but was smart enough merely to nod to her and let it go at that. Some of the other slave children who had seen Lillie roll off the back of the slave wagon tried to ask her where she'd been and what she'd done, but Minervy, seeing that Lillie was lost in thought, hushed them in the same way she had before—and the children obeyed the same way. Lillie was grateful for that. Her accidental meeting with Sarabeth troubled her terribly. With the Master still of a mind to sell off some of his slaves, a single word that she'd been misbehaving in any way might be enough to have her packed up and sent off to who knew where. Even if Miss Sarabeth never mentioned anything to her father, she could still see to it that word of what Lillie had done got back to Mama—and then she would be in a whole different kind of trouble.

But that wasn't all that was on Lillie's mind. Now that she'd kept her part of the bargain she and Henry had struck, it was time for him to keep his part and mail Lillie's letter to the farmer named Appleton in Warren County, Mississippi. It would not be an easy letter to compose. She'd have to write it as if she were Henry, using the words of a soldier and freedman, not the words of a slave and a girl. She would have to work on it in secret, since any kind of writing could get her whipped, and even Mama, while proud that her children could read and write, took close notice anytime they put ink to paper, lest they be up to the very kinds of mischief Lillie was up to now. Most important, Lillie would have to write the letter fast. The sooner she got it to Bluffton for Henry to mail, the sooner it would get to Mississippi, and the sooner an answer would come back clearing her papa's name and freeing the family. Every day she waited was one day closer to the time the slave appraiser would come and take Plato away forever.

Lillie did not have to wait long to find the private time to write. Plato had stuffed himself full at the kitchen dinner on Saturday night and fell into a deep slumber from which he seemed unlikely to stir till well past dawn. Mama too had eaten well and had danced long at the slave party, and slept the kind of deep sleep she hadn't enjoyed since before Papa died—the kind that had her snoring low and steady. Papa used to say that when Mama snored like that she'd sleep "for a weekend plus a Monday" if he let her. Lillie lay awake listening to the steady breathing that came from them both, then crept out of her bed, lit a dim lantern at the eating table and pulled out her paper, ink pot and sharpened goose quill.

Sitting down at the table, she stared at the paper, which stared back at her blankly. She'd never written anything for anyone else's eyes before, and the fact that this letter would not just be read, but read closely—by an educated man who'd likely be able to spot a fraud—set her hand shaking so much she wasn't certain she'd be able to form any letters at all. What's more, unlike the Missus of Greenfog, she didn't have sheet after sheet of creamy white paper she could simply throw away if she didn't like the way her writing was turning out. She'd have to do her work well on the very first try, since that would be the only try she'd have.

After a long, long while spent thinking hard and chewing the nib of the quill, she at last set ink to paper:

To the onnerable Master of the appleton farm—

I am a Free man name henry and use to be a slave. i was a Solder in the army but don't have both legs anymore. it got lost in fighting at viks Burg. My friend died there and he had money. the money was Gold and they sed he stole it from you but i dont think so. now they give it all to his

Master cause they cood not find you. Pleese tell
me if my frend stole the money so i can know if
he was a Theef but I dont think so.

from henry
I am at the Firnitur stor in bluffton. thats in
charlston Countee and in south Carolina

When Lillie was done, she sat back reading and reread-
ing the letter. She'd been proud of other things she'd done
in her life, but nothing had ever puffed her up like this. She
wasn't completely certain of all the words she'd chosen.
Papa had used the word *honorable* in a story once, and while
he never told her precisely what it meant, she was sure it
was suited to the way she'd used it. She wasn't sure of all
her spellings either, but she read the words carefully and
sounded them out the way Papa had taught her and she was
certain that even if the way she had spelled them wasn't the
right way, it was so good that it ought to be. She folded the
letter carefully, wrapped it in another piece of paper and
carefully printed out "Appleton farm" and "Warren Countee, Missisippy." She spelled *Mississippi* with a jumble of
s's and *p*'s and a *y* at the end, and that one she reckoned was
surely wrong—but reckoned too that even white folks found
it hard it get right.

Henry had promised her he would seal the letter with

a drop of wax and pay for the one-penny stamp from his earnings at the furniture store and mail it the moment she gave it to him. There was still the matter of the letter making its way through the fires of the war and the thieves swarming the roads leading south, but that, Lillie reckoned, was out of her control. She rubbed her tired eyes, tucked the letter under her mattress and climbed wearily back in bed. She tumbled immediately into a deep and satisfied sleep.

It was not a sleep that lasted long.

"Out of the cabins! Out of the cabins! Everybody out of the cabins!" came a booming man's voice from the other side of the door.

The cry rang out loudly up and down the cabin line, but so heavily was Lillie sleeping that at first it simply got rolled up into a dream—one in which an angry man or many angry men were screaming and pounding on drums or walls. The voice got louder and so did the pounding, and Lillie now began to stir.

"Out of the cabins! Out of the cabins!" the voice repeated, and all at once Mama was atop Lillie, shaking her hard.

"Lillie! Lillie! Get up! Get up 'fore you're whipped!" she shouted.

Lillie's eyes flew open. Early morning sun was coming through the window, and in it she could see Mama in her nightclothes leaning over her and Plato standing nearby wearing Papa's old shirt. Lillie could hear more men's voices outside and could now clearly make out that they belonged to Bull and Louis and Mr. Willis. She could hear the same pounding that had disturbed her sleep, only now it was farther away, rattling one slave cabin after another. It was a harder, sharper banging than a man's hand could make, and Lillie knew from experience that it was produced by a wooden whip handle being knocked against walls and doors.

"Mama, Mama!" Plato cried.

"Mama, what is it?" Lillie asked.

"Children, outside!" was all Mama said. She pulled Lillie's covers down, tugged her out of bed and pushed both children to the door and out into the morning.

Everywhere, from all the cabins, the slaves were staggering barefoot into the early light and chill. Most of them, like Lillie's family, were wearing their nightclothes. Bull and Louis were pacing in front of them all, snapping their whip tips impatiently in the soil, stirring up tiny tornadoes of dust. Mr. Willis was standing two steps behind them, his arms folded and his own whip still coiled—for now.

"Line up, line up, line up!" Bull roared.

"Line up!" Louis repeated in his higher, reedier voice.

Lillie scanned fearfully up and down the quickly forming line. She saw Minervy emerge with her parents and two older brothers. The brothers looked afraid, but Minervy looked flat terrified, holding her mother's arm even more tightly than Plato was holding Mama's. She saw the plow-man Evers and the hauler Nate emerge from their cabins with their families. Despite the men's size and muscles, they lined up as obediently as everyone else. Looking the other way, Lillie saw Nelly and George standing nervously in line, but she could not see Cal. She craned her neck out and then did spot him, standing between the two adults and leaning heavily on George's arm. Cal appeared to be favoring his right foot . . . actually he appeared not to be using it at all; he was standing entirely on his left and keeping his right knee bent. He hopped to keep his balance.

"I thought you got all your dancin' outta you last night!" Bull shouted at him.

"Hurt myself, sir," Cal answered.

"You'd best get well fast, then," Bull responded. "You slaves stand on your own feet, or I'll knock you off'n 'em."

George released Cal's arm, and Cal stood hopping as best he could. Lillie stared at him and tried to catch his eye, hoping for some signal that he was all right, but Cal was fighting so hard to remain upright he didn't notice her at all. When the slaves were all lined up, Willis stepped forward.

"Appears to me that some o' you don't want to live here no more," he began in an almost casual tone, pacing from left to right and back again. "I can't reckon why. You're fed well, ain't you?" Some of the slaves desultorily nodded, but most just looked at the ground. "You got good houses, don't you?" Again a few nods. "And them what don't like all that, well, the slave trader's comin' back soon enough, and you just might get lucky and get sold off."

At those words, Mama took a tighter hold of Plato. Lillie did the same.

"But that don't seem to make no difference to some o' you," Mr. Willis continued. Suddenly, the reasonable tone of his voice switched to something angry, ugly, cutting. "Some o' you decides to run off instead!"

Lillie felt a hot surge of terror run through her. He knew about last night! He knew about Orchard Hill! He knew about where she'd been and what she'd done! Miss Sarabeth had told her daddy!

"Some o' you take it into your heads to go where you want to," Willis went on, "to go *when* you want to. Like you was free! Like you was *white!*" He spat out the word *white* as if to say that there was nothing lower, more laughable than a slave thinking such a thing. His voice now rose to a furious pitch, and the pale, hairless top of his head flamed a bright red. "You are slaves!" he screamed. "You are property! No better than the Master's plow! No better than the Master's horse! You ain't even as good as the horse! The horse obeys the man what feeds it, and it don't run off!"

Now Mr. Willis uncoiled his whip and snapped it on the ground with an explosive noise that sounded like nothing short of a pistol shot. No whip crack from Bull had ever been so loud. Lillie braced for the next swing of the lash, which she was sure would be across her hide.

"The boy Benjy and the boy Cupit has run off," Willis announced. "I sent Louis and Bull around to do a bed check before light. 'Don't trust slaves what've been to a party,' I told 'em. 'They gets big heads about 'em.' And it turns out I was right! I already been to the Big House and told the Master, and he give me free hand to do what I gotta do to find out where them boys has gone!" Willis barked.

He stopped in front of Cupit's sickly mama. She always looked frail, and now she looked terrified too—a weak, worked-out scrap of a woman. She sobbed softly into her hands.

"The mama says she don't know, and I reckon she's speakin' true," Willis barked. "Just like a boy like Cupit to go off without tellin' his own mama." He wheeled toward the rest of the slaves and cracked his whip. "Any o' you others know where them boys is at?"

The slaves said nothing, none of them meeting the overseer's eyes. Lillie wanted to look at Cal, fearing that he knew something and just as afraid that he'd lose control of his tongue and say something he oughtn't. But she dared not even glance his way, lest she call attention to both of them.

Lillie had never seen Mr. Willis so angry—angrier than even a runaway slave ought to make him, and she reckoned she knew why. If Benjy and Cupit ran off from the slave party, the overseer and slave drivers should have known, because they should have done a count before the wagons returned to Greenfog. If they didn't, that had to mean they were drinking at the party and forgot. The Master would surely have figured that out when Mr. Willis told him the boys were missing and would now be as furious with his overseer as the overseer was with the slaves.

"It'll go hard on any of you what helped them boys go," Willis said, "but it'll go harder on those what helped and don't confess. Now, who wants to be first?"

The overseer began pacing the line, and Bull and Louis fell in behind him. They approached the hot-tempered Nate. The anger Nate had shown in his fight with Evers over the stolen peach jewel was nothing next to what he could show if he was taunted with a whip. He'd lost control of himself in such situations before and been savagely lashed for it. Lillie could feel the slaves along the line bracing for the same violence again.

"You know what happened to them boys?" Willis asked.

Nate kept his eyes down and muttered, "No, sir."

"I can't see your face, boy!" Willis shouted.

Nate did not move his head, but cast his eyes up to meet Willis's. "No, sir, I don't know nothin', sir."

"I still can't see you proper, boy!" Willis jabbed his whip handle under Nate's chin and lifted his head. Nate's jaw tightened and Lillie could see his fist clench by his side.

"Lemme see them eyes," Willis said. "Are they lyin' eyes or truth-tellin' eyes?"

"Truth-tellin' eyes, sir," Nate said through his teeth.

Willis stared at the man for a long moment—a moment in which the slaves could see that Nate was coming close to losing hold of himself and that Willis was daring him to do just that. No one breathed for several seconds, and then the overseer lowered the whip handle slightly, releasing Nate's chin. Nate snapped his head away.

"I reckon even a man like you can be trusted sometimes," Willis said. He wheeled to Evers. "What about you? You know anything?"

"No, sir," Evers said. "I surely don't."

Willis glared at Evers, then turned to walk the other way. As he did, Cal, who'd continued to fight for his balance, lost it again and fell against George. His bad foot struck the ground, and he cried out in pain. Willis flicked his eyes toward him.

"What's that noise down there?"

"N-nothing," Cal stammered, hanging on to George.

"It's nothing, sir," George said. "Boy just hurt his foot."

Willis narrowed his eyes. "And what about that 'zactly?" he asked, approaching. "How's a boy as strong as this one hurt a foot as bad as he done?"

"Dancin', sir," Cal answered.

"Dancin', eh?" Mr. Willis asked. He was now standing

directly in front of Cal. "Never seen a boy do himself so much damage from dancin'. Runnin', sure. Jumpin' over logs or gulleys in the woods at night, sure. Helpin' two other boys escape, maybe. You do any of that last night, boy?"

"No, sir," Cal said emphatically. "I wouldn't never do such a thing."

"That's what you say," Willis answered. "That foot o' yours says somethin' else. Better let me have a look at it." With that Willis turned to George. "Set the boy down on the ground," he ordered.

George said nothing, and Nelly stepped in front of Cal. "The boy's hurt, sir. He's talkin' truth; I seen him dancin' last night with my own eyes. Twisted up his foot somethin' terrible."

Willis let loose a small, sharp laugh. "Spoke like a real mama," he said. "Almost like you was one." Nelly looked as if she'd been slapped. "Now, set the boy down 'fore I shove him down!" Willis commanded.

Nelly and George took Cal by the elbows and lowered him gently to the ground, where he sat, staring up fearfully at Mr. Willis. He rubbed his injured foot in his hand, protecting it more than massaging it.

"Gimme that ankle, boy," Willis said.

Cal lifted his right leg and laid the foot in the overseer's palm. Willis turned it slightly this way and that, as Cal stared at him wide-eyed. Lillie looked on from far down the line, craning her neck out as far as she could. Bull noticed and flashed her a menacing look, and Mama pulled her back.

"Nasty," Willis said, regarding the foot as if he were a doctor, but one who enjoyed the pain of his patients. "Swolled up big as a melon. Does it hurt when I do this?" He pressed his thumb hard into the swelling; Cal cried out. "Yep, seems it does hurt," Willis said. "I reckon it ain't no better here." He pressed onto another spot, harder than before and much longer.

"Yes!" Cal cried. "Yes, yes, it hurts! It hurts!"

"And here?" Willis said, gripping the entirety of the ankle in one strong hand and squeezing until the veins and muscles stood out on his forearm.

"Yes, yes, yes!" Cal screamed. "Please stop!"

Lillie closed her eyes tightly and tried to cover her ears. Mama pulled her hands away lest she call the slave driver's attention again.

"You're gonna kill him sure," George pleaded. "The boy didn't do nothin'. He told you that."

"Boys lie!" Willis barked, giving Cal's ankle a hard twist and making him cry out again. "They lie and they lie and they lie!" He followed each repetition with another twist. "And this one lies most of all!"

"I ain't lyin', sir," Cal gasped, barely able to speak. "I wasn't runnin'. I was dancin'." His voice choked and his head drooped, as if he would faint clean away.

"That's what you say!" Willis answered. "And if it's the truth, that's what you'll keep sayin', even if I have to twist this foot clean off! Now for the last time, boy, where was you and where is them other two?"

Willis gave Cal's foot one more hard twist, and this time the scream that escaped the boy was so sharp and loud it cut into every slave standing along the line. Even Louis and Bull seemed surprised by the sound, and Lillie thought she saw a barely perceptible softening of their faces, a momentary flicker that for all the world appeared to be something like pity. Then it was gone as quick as a flint spark. Willis twisted the foot again, and again the scream poured from Cal. At last, Lillie could take no more.

"It's the truth, it's the truth, it's the truth!" she said, leaping from the line. "He was dancin'! He was dancin' with me! My mama said no dancin', but we did it anyhow! We danced and danced and he tripped on a rut and turned his ankle, and I fell on top of it and it near broke. Please, Mr. Willis, don't hurt him no more!" Lillie cried those words with a voice that came from deep in her belly, one she'd never used before because until this moment she never knew she had it.

Mama stared at Lillie in shock. Willis wheeled toward them with fire in his eyes and began striding in Lillie's direction. He gripped his whip tightly and twitched it menacingly. Bull and Louis followed, grinning. Mama stepped in front of Lillie, and Willis waved her out of the way, but Mama didn't move. Willis glanced toward Louis and Bull, who converged on Mama and pulled her away, pinning her arms behind her back. Mama screamed and Bull covered her mouth. Plato screamed, and Louis grabbed him with his free arm and covered his mouth too. Willis fixed his gaze on Lillie, his eyes glinting coldly. He moved closer and closer, raising his whip higher and higher, and cocking his arm to strike. Lillie closed her eyes, drew her breath and braced herself for a pain that had taunted her in her dreams for as long as she could remember but which she'd never before actually felt. Now she would feel it true and she reckoned it just might kill her.

"See here, Mr. Willis!" a voice suddenly called out. "What is all of this?"

The slaves, the slave drivers and the overseer turned. Lillie opened her eyes and did the same. They all saw the Master racing toward them. His hair was unbrushed and his shirt was untucked, and he looked like he'd not been ready to leave the house at all, but instead had just been preparing to eat his breakfast. He ran stiffly on short, stout legs and he looked cross.

"I told you to talk to the slaves and whip only if you had to!" he said.

"I do have to, sir," Willis said, lowering his arm. "They din't give me no other way to question 'em."

"It doesn't sound like you even tried to question them, it sounds like you're skinning them! I heard the screaming all the way from the house!" He waved his arm toward Cal. "What's this one doing on the ground? Did you do that to his foot?"

"No, sir," the overseer answered.

"I pay high coin for these slaves, Mr. Willis. Just like I pay high coin for my horses. The boy's just coming to working age, and this one"—he waved his hand to Lillie—"is just coming to baby age. You break 'em down or make 'em lame, and you're taking money out of my pocket."

"Yes, sir," Willis answered.

"If you'd done a count last night like you were supposed to, we'd all be having a quiet morning. This business is your fault from the start!"

"Yes, sir," Willis said, using a humble tone no slave had ever heard from him before.

"Maybe the reason you haven't gotten any answers from these slaves is because they don't have any answers. Meantime, the ones who did get away are just getting farther. Now, you take your drivers and see if you can't go find them."

"Yes, sir," Willis said. He tightened his jaw but did what

he was told, coiling his whip back up and stalking off. Bull and Louis followed.

"And you slaves get back to what you were doing!" the Master commanded. "You've got Sunday chores to do!"

The Master walked off, hiking up his pants and tucking in his shirt. Mama grabbed Lillie hard by the arm and fixed her a look that told her there would be a reckoning once they got back to the cabin. She pulled her along, and Plato followed. Lillie allowed herself to turn back once, looking toward Cal as Nelly and George helped him up. He looked back at her and nodded his thanks. Both children had just told terrible lies, and if there was pain to come from that, both of them would suffer it.

Chapter Twenty

LILLIE GOT A BEATING from Mama as soon as the family returned to the cabin after the slave lineup. It had been a long time since Mama had touched either child in anger, and Lillie had come to think that at thirteen, she might finally have grown too big for such punishment. Mama had other ideas.

A beating from Mama never amounted to much more than a few hard swats on the bottom, but Mama had field muscles, and even a single swat from her was a single swat too many. Any more than that, and it wouldn't pay for a child to sit on anything harder than loose hay or soft grass for the rest of the day.

"What was you thinking 'bout, girl?" Mama shouted at Lillie, pulling both children inside the cabin and slamming the door behind them. As Plato watched, she took Lillie by the arm, spun her around and began angrily delivering her paddling, scolding her all the while. "Did you *want* the overseer to whip you?" she said. "Do you *want* to be sold off? Do you want to get your *brother* sold?" Each time Mama landed a blow, it landed on a very particular word, and to Lillie it seemed like just the word Mama wanted her to hear most. Finally, Mama spun her back around and took her by the shoulders. "Was you really dancin' with that boy?" she asked.

That was the question Lillie least wanted to answer, since a yes meant she'd disobeyed Mama and a no meant she'd lied to the overseer. But she knew better than to cross Mama further—and she knew better than to lie anymore. "No, Mama," she mumbled. "Didn't do no dancin'."

"Then you was helpin' that boy run!" Mama said, lowering her voice to a furious whisper so that no one outside could hear her.

"No!" Lillie answered. "I didn't do that neither, and that's the truth! I just fibbed this mornin' so's Mr. Willis wouldn't hurt him no more."

"Fibbin' today is the same as helpin' him yesterday! To the overseer that makes you bad as a runaway yourself!"

Mama went on like this for a while, directing most of her wrath at Lillie, but now and then turning to Plato to remind him not to follow the example of his fool sister. Lillie stayed silent—even when Mama ran out of words and decided she needed a few more swats—and that was the smartest thing to do. She had told the truth as far as she could tell it. The entire truth, about her trip to Orchard Hill and the charm that got her there, was something no one could know.

It wasn't until later in the afternoon that Mama let Plato or Lillie venture out of her sight. She first made both of them clean the cabin from floorboards to beams, as well as shake out the sleeping blankets, scoop the ashes from the hearth, and weed the little vegetable garden out back. Mama would have had the children do chores on any Sunday, but today she was not inclined to give them an easy time of it—and Lillie was not inclined to argue with her.

When they were at last done and Mama let them go outside, Plato ran off to the tobacco fields, where he knew there would be birds to chase and other children to join him. Lillie ran off to Nelly and George's cabin, where she knew there would be a lying boy with a bad ankle who needed a talking-to.

Lillie had been hornet-mad at Cal since the moment he hobbled out to the lineup this morning. She'd known as soon as she'd seen him that he'd hurt himself doing something he wasn't supposed to do—and that anything he told the overseer about it would be a lie. Cal's fibs and mischief always seemed to tangle up other people, and today Lillie was the one who got caught. Her anger only grew greater as she strode to Nelly and George's, and when she got there, she was pleased to see that the door was open a crack. That spared her the courtesy of having to knock, which spared her the business of waiting to be invited inside. Instead, she simply swung the door open with a bang.

"What was you thinkin', boy?" she barked at Cal, echoing Mama's words without planning to. Cal was lying on his narrow bed, his melon of a foot propped up on a small sack of potatoes.

"Lillie!" Nelly cried, leaping up and bringing her hand to her heart. "You gave me a terrible fright!"

"What's your business here, child?" George demanded. "You shouldn't come burstin' in like that!"

"I'm sorry, Miss Nelly, Mr. George," Lillie said, immediately regretting startling the pair. They were not old people, but they weren't young, either, and they had enough worries looking after Cal without Lillie upsetting them further. "I didn't mean to spook you."

"But you did all the same," George said sternly. "What is it you want?"

"I come to talk to him," Lillie said, turning to face Cal, who avoided her gaze. "Come to ask him what he was doin' last night and how he busted up his foot."

"He was at Bingham Woods," Nelly said. "And he got hurt dancin' with you. Ain't that what you said?"

"It is."

"Weren't it the truth?"

"Truth enough for the overseer," Lillie said, "and lie

enough to get me whipped if I got caught for tellin' it. The true truth is somethin' else." She stepped to the edge of Cal's bed and stood directly in front of him. "Ain't it?" she asked.

Cal didn't answer.

"Boy," Nelly said, "what is she talkin' about?"

"Nothin'," Cal grumbled.

"It don't seem like nothin'," Nelly persisted.

"I said it's nothin'."

"Tell me, Cal," Nelly said.

"It's nothin'!" Cal snapped.

His tone was sharp, angry, not at all the tone he would dare use if Nelly were his true mama, and it took her by surprise. That, it seemed, was enough for George, who had had his fill of trouble for one day—particularly trouble that came from Cal.

"Boy!" George snapped. "This here woman is the person what looks after you, and you'll treat her like a mama even if she ain't. And I'm the person what looks after her, and you'll talk to me like I'm a papa. Now, you answer the questions what been put to you or I'll paddle you like a papa too!"

Cal mumbled something that was impossible to understand.

"What did you say?" George said.

"I said yes, sir," Cal answered.

"Now where was you last night?"

"I was at the dance," Cal said. George took a step toward

him. "Truth!" Cal said, raising his hand as if taking a pledge. He lowered his eyes. "And then I was runnin'."

Nelly gasped and covered her mouth. George and Lillie remained standing. Cal looked mournfully at all three of them; then he told his story. It was true, he confessed, that he'd tried to escape last night, and it was true that he ran with Benjy and Cupit. The three boys came to Bingham Woods dressed for the dance like everyone else, but they kept mostly to themselves, waiting until the whiskey got passed around. They reckoned that the overseers and slave drivers would help themselves to the drink and that while they were busy with the jugs, they'd likely take their eyes off the slaves. As soon as that happened, Cal, Benjy and Cupit began edging away from the clearing and toward the tree line. As soon as all the whip men were looking completely the other way, they plunged into the woods.

Benjy and Cupit, with their stronger legs and quicker strides, had promised not to let Cal fall behind, and for a little while, they made good on that—helping the younger boy over rocks and through tangles. But as the woods got darker and the tangles got thicker, it became so hard for any of the boys to keep their footing that it was all they could do to look after themselves. Before long, Cal began slipping back.

"Cal!" Benjy hissed into the darkness behind him once or twice.

"I'm all right," Cal hissed back, not meaning it but knowing the other boys might not be able to fight their way back to him even if they tried, making it likelier they'd all get caught.

"Cal!" Cupit called once or twice more from a greater distance, now barely audible.

"I said I'm fine," Cal answered. "Keep goin', I'll catch up!"

It was at that moment that Cal encountered the log or the rock or the short, hollow stump that caught the tip of his foot and held it fast, even as the speed of his tumbling run continued to carry him forward and to the side, wrenching his ankle with a violence that made it feel as if the very cords that held his foot to his leg were being stretched to the point of breaking. He collapsed in pain and grabbed the foot but pulled in his lips and bit them hard to prevent himself from screaming. For long moments, Cal lay that way, listening to his panting breath and pounding heart and then, when they had quieted enough, to the woods around him. There was no sound at all of the other boys' footsteps. They'd either heard him tell them to keep going or they hadn't, but in any event they'd gone. Behind him, he could faintly make out the distant sound of slave voices and juba music from the dance that now felt like it was a whole world away.

Cal struggled up on his one good foot and painfully hopped his way back to the party, falling again and again, but mindful of the fact that he had to get where he was going before the wagons returned to Greenfog and left him behind entirely. Finally, he reached the clearing at Bingham Woods and hid himself until the slave drivers weren't looking and he could brush himself clean of dirt and leaves. Then he rejoined the party but sat silently off to the side, as if he'd eaten his fill and danced too much and now only wanted to go home to his bed.

Cal finished his tale and hung his head, and Lillie, Nelly and George stood silently.

"Do you know where them other boys was goin'?" George asked at last.

"No," Cal answered. "And that's the truth. They wouldn't tell me. Said I should just follow them."

"They won't get far," George said. "They don't know the woods, not like the trackers."

"When will they catch them?" Lillie asked.

"Soon."

"What'll they do to them?"

"They'll flog them, maybe till they kill them—leastways Cupit. Benjy's bigger; he'll fetch more at sale."

"They can't kill Cupit!" Cal cried, looking up. "Master won't let 'em break his property!"

"Master's happy to break one slave if'n he thinks it'll keep the others in line," George said. "Either way, they's both gone—one to the slave trader, one to the grave." Cal stared at George with his eyes wide. George looked back at him coolly. "You shoulda knowed all this, son," he said. "And now you does."

Lillie looked at George and considered the terrible things he'd just said—and the equally terrible things he hadn't. It was true that Cupit would likely be flogged to his death; it was also true that before he died they'd try to make him tell how he'd planned his run. With the whip across his back, he'd surely mention Cal—which meant Cal himself would feel the lash too.

Even before Lillie got up this morning, she knew she had one more visit to make today. Now that visit was more important than ever.

Chapter Twenty-one

IT WAS BETT, OF COURSE, Lillie had to go see, though even as she was running there, she knew she shouldn't. The day had passed fast, what with her and Plato not having left the cabin until the middle of the afternoon. Now it would not be long before the long shadows of late day gave way to the full dark of evening. Plato was surely back from playing by now, and if Lillie didn't make it home soon too, Mama would turn cross all over again.

What's more, it was Sunday—the quietest day of the week for Bett, and the one she had told Lillie she enjoyed the most. At this hour, she would just be getting ready for a long stroll about the edges of the plantation and would then return for the small supper she'd make herself as the sun set over the fields. Lillie knew she would be disturbing the old woman's peace—and knew all the same that she had no choice.

"Bett!" she cried as she approached the cabin. "Bett!"

She got no response but could see the light of a lantern

in the window. She took the two little steps that led into the house at a single bound and opened the door without knocking. It occurred to her—fleetingly—that this was the second time today she'd been so rude, but she pushed the thought out of her head. Bett was bending over her stove and poking at a pot. She turned to Lillie and, unlike Nelly, did not seem startled by her sudden, noisy arrival.

"Lillie," Bett said evenly, as if the girl had been spending the whole day with her and had simply stepped outside for a moment to fetch some water, "ain't this late for you to be about?"

"I reckon it is," Lillie answered, catching her breath and closing the door behind her.

"Your mama will be cross if you ain't back before dark, 'specially after everything that happened today." As always, Bett was not required to be at the slave lineup, but word went around the plantation fast, and by now she would have been told about everything that had happened.

"It was terrible," Lillie said. "I ain't never seen the overseer like that."

"I know, child. I could hear the shoutin' and poundin' from here. And then there was all that screamin' from a child."

"Cal," Lillie said.

"Did he run?" Bett asked the question, but she looked as if she knew the answer already.

"He tried to—with two other boys."

"Benjy and Cupit," Bett guessed.

Lillie nodded.

"And they's still gone," Bett said, more to herself than to Lillie. "It'll go hard on 'em when they's caught; hard on Cal too."

"I know," Lillie said.

Bett now changed her tone slightly—to one that was just a tick brighter. "And what about the business you was doin' last night? You did some runnin' of your own, I expect."

Despite her worry over Cal, Lillie beamed at the mention of that. The wondrous memory of her run through the darkness under the charm of the bread had been pushed to the side of her thoughts since morning, but now it came pouring back.

"I did, I did!" she said. "It was wonderful!"

"Like you was floatin'," Bett said knowledgeably.

"Just like it."

"But you never got tired."

"Not a lick!"

"Good. You take care o' that matter you had to tend to at Orchard Hill?"

Lillie nodded. "Kept my promise to Henry jus' like I said I would. Now he's got to keep his."

She reached into the small pocket in the front of her dress and carefully withdrew the letter she'd worked so hard to write. She looked at it proudly and Bett held her hand out for it, but Lillie instead stepped to the table and laid it down carefully. She smoothed it with both hands and only then stood aside. Bett picked it up, regarded the printing on the envelope, then took out the letter and looked at it. She could not read a word of it. Lillie worried that it might embarrass Bett to be shown up by a child who could not only read but could fill up a page with such wonderful print. But Bett was long since past such vanities.

"That's fine writin', child," she said. "As fine as I ever seen." Bett slid the letter carefully back into the envelope. "You gonna need some wax to seal it."

"Henry said he'd tend to that," Lillie answered.

"You gonna need a stamp too."

"Henry said he'd pay for that."

"Then all you need is to get it into his hands so's he can mail it," Bett said as she laid the letter back down on the table. She spoke as if she knew that was the very reason Lillie had come to see her, and of course it was.

"Can you help me?" Lillie asked. "Can you go back to Bluffton?"

"I only just been there. My flour and such ain't nearly all gone."

Lillie's spirits sank. She hadn't considered that problem, but of course it was true. Bett was allowed to travel only when she had to, and from the look of the still-bulging bags of supplies near her work counter, that would be a while.

"How soon till they's all done?" Lillie asked.

"Not soon enough—weeks," Bett answered.

"But we ain't got weeks! There ain't no tellin' when that slave appraiser's gonna come for Plato!"

"I know that," Bett said, "but I don't think there's no help for it."

"There has to be!" Lillie said.

Bett looked thoughtful. "Maybe there is a way," she said. "I reckon if my supplies got ruined, we'd have to go to Bluffton as early as tomorrow."

"But they ain't ruined—are they?"

"How do they look to you?" Bett asked, gesturing toward the bags.

Lillie went to them, opened them up and peered inside. They looked and smelled fresh. "They's fine," she said dourly. "And there's plenty of 'em too."

Bett nodded and waved Lillie out of the way. She stepped to the bags, scooped out several cups' worth of flour, salt and cornmeal and set them aside. Then, she turned to her stove and picked up a large pot of water that she appeared to have used earlier for boiling. Bits of turnip or potato skin still floated on top. She lifted the pot with both hands and grunted with the effort—then emptied the water into the flour and cornmeal sacks. Lillie's mouth opened.

"They still look fine to you?" Bett asked. "Terrible accident, spillin' water like that. By tomorrow morning there oughta be so much mold growin' in those sacks, they'll both be spoiled. The Missus herself could see we needed to go fetch more."

"Bett . . . ," Lillie said, stunned at what the old woman had just done. Bett had spent her life tending her ovens and making her breads, and Lillie had never seen her waste a lick of food if she could help it, nor abide anyone who would. Now she had ruined a month's worth of eating. She started to speak, but Bett spoke first.

"If you gonna go free, girl, you gonna have to move fast," she said, slipping Lillie's letter into her apron pocket. Then she turned to the flour, salt and cornmeal she had set aside on the counter. "Meantime, why don't I bake up somethin' nice and see if I can't slow down them slave catchers goin' after them boys."

Chapter Twenty-two

THE MOOD IN THE Big House had been growing darker all day—ever since the overseer had knocked early in the morning to tell the Master that the two slave boys were gone. Sarabeth had not even been awake at the time, but soon enough, she had heard screaming from the slave cabins and her father storming out the front door to see what the commotion was. By the time he returned, he was angry and red-faced, and he spent much of the day that way, scolding the children, snapping at the house slaves and stomping out to the front porch, where he'd stand with his fists on his hips, waiting for Mr. Willis or one of the slave catchers to appear with the happy news that the runaways had been found.

That news did not come by the end of the morning, nor by the afternoon, nor by late in the day when the shadows were starting to grow long. Sarabeth knew that good slave catchers with good hounds could hunt at night, so she was hopeful as the dinner hour approached that the day might yet end well. But the dinner hour came and went, and dinner itself was a sour affair. She and Cody and their mother barely tasted their food, and the Master did not touch his at all, drumming his fingers on the table and snapping the cover of his pocket watch open and closed as he checked the time minute by minute.

Finally, shortly before nine o'clock, when Sarabeth was in her room preparing for bed, there was a knock on the front door. Cody was already asleep in his own bedroom and did not hear it, but Sarabeth threw on her dressing gown, hurried out of her bedroom and tiptoed down the great staircase of the house, stopping just at the point at which she could peek down at the front door but where nobody standing there would be likely to look back up and see her. Her father and mother hurried across the entry hall and opened the door wide. A slave catcher was standing there.

Slave catchers, in Sarabeth's experience, always looked dirty, but the one at the door tonight seemed especially so. His face was streaked with mud and soil, and his trousers were prickly with brambles and bits of twig. He looked like a man who'd been galloping through the woods but had spent as much time being tossed off his horse as riding it. He spoke quietly to the Master and Missus, his hat in his hands in front of him, and the Master answered him in low, angry tones. Sarabeth could not make out what the men were saying, but she could see the back of her father's neck reddening. Finally, he erupted at the man.

"I'm not paying you to lose those boys!" he shouted. "I'm paying you to catch them!"

"And we had 'em," the man protested, his own voice rising some. "The hounds smelled 'em, the men heard 'em. Even the horses knew we was close."

"And?" the Master barked.

"And then they was gone," the catcher answered meekly. "Boys can be quick—quick as rabbits, these ones, I guess."

"And boys can be caught! It shouldn't take a dozen of you to find two small slaves! Now take your men and your animals and go do what you were hired to do!"

"Can't, sir," the man answered, and now he seemed to shrink into himself, as if he feared the Master would strike him at what he had to say next. "Horses won't go."

"The . . . the *horses* won't go?" the Master spluttered.

"They seemed sluggish; hounds too," the slave catcher said, "like they couldn't get their speed up. After a time, they just got spooked and turned. Charged outta the woods and won't go back. Some of us was even throwed along the way."

The Master's neck turned crimson now, and he raised a hand as if he truly would attack the man. The Missus restrained him, and he settled for simply ordering the catcher to find fresh horses and dogs and not to come back from the woods until he had Benjy and Cupit trussed and chained and ready for the whipping post. Then he slammed the door with a bang that made the window panes rattle in their frames. After that, he retreated to his library, where he uncorked a bottle of brandy and began to drink. Spirits usually turned the Master's mood black, and this evening was no exception. Deep into the night, Sarabeth could hear him pacing back and forth behind the closed library door, cursing the war and the North and the disloyalty of his slaves—and the way all of them were working together to ruin his livelihood. The noise went on for what seemed to be hours until at last her father grew still. Sarabeth was relieved at the quiet. She hoped it was because he'd spent all his anger—but she feared it was simply because he'd drunk all his brandy.

The next morning never did bring the happy news Sarabeth and her family had been hoping for. The slave catcher visited once around breakfast and once more around lunch—both times promising that his men and his animals were still at work, but by now he didn't sound as if even he believed they'd ever find the runaway boys. Between his visits, the baker woman, Bett, came to the back door about some fool accident she'd had with her flour. No one dared disturb the Master with such a matter this morning, so the

Missus had to go down to the old woman's cabin herself to see what the problem was, then write out a traveling pass so that Bett and Samuel could go to Bluffton to buy more supplies that very day. The Master—as he often did after a night of heavy drink—kept to himself, working in his library and keeping the drapes drawn against the bright light of the day.

Sarabeth, even without any drink in her, felt nearly as poorly as her father did. She'd lain awake most of the night, fretting for him and feeling terrible about herself as well. Of all the people at Greenfog, she might have been the only one who had a clue of what the runaway boys were planning—and of who might have helped them. It was Sarabeth alone, after all, who'd spotted Lillie at the slave dance— Lillie, with her windblown look and her lying eyes, lurking near the very woods through which the boys had likely slipped to freedom. The minute Sarabeth saw that, it had been up to her to tell her father what she'd seen. Instead, she had thought only of herself—of how cross and jealous and childish she was feeling. And look what had happened. Well, the boys might be gone forever, but the disloyal slave who helped them was still here, and it was Sarabeth's responsibility to do the right thing now.

"Poppy?" she said softly, tapping on the library door late in the afternoon. There was no answer. "Poppy?" she repeated, tapping again.

She opened the door and saw her father sitting at his desk, his glasses low on his nose as he read through plantation correspondence. He looked tired and fretful with the cares he had to bear. He glanced up at her and managed a weak smile.

"What is it, child?" he asked.

"Poppy," she said, "I think I did something wrong."

"What did you do?"

"I think I know something about the runaways."

Her father looked at her thoughtfully and removed his reading glasses. "Come in," he said, "and close the door."

Chapter Twenty-three

PLATO USUALLY DID his best to avoid Mr. Willis, but that wasn't possible a few days after Benjy and Cupit were given up for lost. Early in the morning, the overseer was giving out the daily work assignments as he always did and announced that while the mamas would be doing their usual work in the tobacco or cotton fields, the bird-chasing boys and girls would be needed in a smaller patch of cropland where the Master had lately been trying to grow beets.

"Crows is eatin' up the seed as fast as we can plant it," he grumbled. "Master ain't gonna be pleased if we got no crop to show him next year."

The beets weren't something the slaves usually had to spend too much time tending, since the Master wasn't yet sure he could raise a good crop of them anyway. But the times being the times, the mamas reckoned he needed to make any money he could any way he could. That, at least, was what they told themselves when they watched their children being led away and called after them to mind the overseer and do what they were told.

Mr. Willis let the children chase the birds for a little while and then strode into the beet field, looking left and right. At first he showed no interest in Plato, calling out instead to a seven-year-old boy named Jordan, a small and often sickly child who mostly kept to himself and always seemed to have trouble catching his breath. Jordan trotted to the overseer when he was summoned, and the two of them disappeared up the hill near the beet field and vanished over the crest. Later they returned and Mr. Willis demanded to see Gadsby, a boy about Plato's age. Gadsby was a strong and good-natured child, but the slave drivers and even his own mama often grew short with him on account of the hard time he seemed to have understanding instructions when they were given to him, often needing to have them repeated again and again. Plato once tried to teach Gadsby to write the alphabet—a foolish thing to do since he could get flogged himself for knowing his letters—but Gadsby never got much past D, nor seemed much interested in trying to go further. Mr. Willis took Gadsby away and returned with him too a short while later. Finally, he called out to Plato.

"Boy!" he said. "Your turn. Come with me, and don't make me wait for you."

Plato hurried after the overseer, trying as best he could

to match his short strides to Mr. Willis's longer ones. He reckoned he ought to be afraid, but Gadsby and Jordan seemed fine when they came back—though Mr. Willis did send them to work a different part of the field, making it impossible for Plato to ask them what the overseer had wanted. He followed Mr. Willis all the way up the beet field hill, past the cotton field and at last around to the stables. They went inside and when they did, Plato saw Bull waiting for him. Now he was well and truly afraid.

"Mr. Willis, I ain't done nothin' wrong, did I?" he asked.

"You tell me, boy," the overseer answered, prodding Plato in the back with his whip handle and shoving him toward Bull. "Did you?"

"No, sir," Plato exclaimed. "I promise."

"Then you ain't got cause to be worried. Just do what I say and hop up there."

Mr. Willis pointed to where Bull was standing and Plato noticed a scale next to him, hanging from a ceiling beam. The scale was usually used for weighing foals after mama horses gave birth or weighing cotton bales before they were sent to market. Plato looked at the overseer quizzically.

"You hear Mr. Willis, boy?" Bull snapped. "Do like he said."

Plato approached the scale warily and tried to take its measure. The business end was a large pan suspended by chains from a weighing dial that looked like a clock face.

That, in turn, was hung from another chain attached to the beam. The pan was at the level of Plato's chin. He took hold of it and tried to swing his legs up, but the pan slipped away and he lost his grip, falling in the hay that covered the floor. Bull laughed.

"I seen new colts what could hop up there better'n that," he said.

Mr. Willis glowered. "Try it again, boy," he said.

Plato tried again and fell again and tried once more and fell once more. Finally, Bull scooped him up with one meaty arm and dropped him in the pan. Plato knocked his head on the metal rim and cried out in pain.

"Quiet, boy," Bull said. "Try to pretend you're a cotton bale."

Bull steadied the pan while Mr. Willis approached it and read the dial.

"Forty-eight pounds," he said disdainfully.

"That ain't enough?" Bull asked.

"Shy by five pounds, maybe more. Ain't no ship wants a deckhand that puny."

"Want me to fetch another one?" Bull said.

"Can't," Mr. Willis answered. "These is the only three the Master asked about, and he wants this one to go first." He lifted Plato out of the pan and set him roughly on his feet. Then he picked up a measuring stick leaning against a post and lined it up next to the boy. "Stand up straight!"

he snapped. Plato complied while the overseer squinted at the stick and seemed pleased. "Least he's proper height," he said.

"So sell 'im by the inch instead o' the pound," Bull said. "Either way, he gets sold."

Plato wheeled to the slave driver. "Sold?" he said. "But I don't wanna get sold! My mama said I don't have to!"

"Your mama did, eh?" Bull sneered. "I reckon we got to do what she says, then." Plato looked at him with a flash of hope on his face, and the slave driver barked out a laugh.

Willis shot a silencing glare at Bull. A crying child would be a nuisance right now, and the overseer had enough nuisances today already. "You ain't got nothin' to worry 'bout, boy," he said to Plato. He reached impatiently into his leather whip bag and groped about inside it. "Here," he said, pulling out a large square of cornbread wrapped in cloth. "Eat this up."

"I ain't hungry," Plato said.

"I didn't ask you if you was. I told you to eat it."

The overseer pushed the cornbread into Plato's hands, and the boy began reluctantly nibbling at it.

"Faster, boy!" Willis said. "I got another here when you're done with that one. Master wants you fatter, and fatter's what you'll be."

•   •   •

Lillie was at work in the nursery cabin when the overseer came to fetch Plato. She had no idea the boy was in danger, and she was thus free to busy her mind with the one thing that had been occupying it for the last week: whether her letter to Mississippi had arrived at its destination yet and whether the farmer named Appleton had sent Henry a response. No such thing was possible, of course, and Lillie knew that. Even in peacetime, it was hard to know how long it would take for a letter to travel from Charleston County all the way down to the deepest Southern states and an answer to come back.

Still, Lillie had lingered around the stables as the sun was setting on the day Bett went back to Bluffton to fetch new supplies, waiting for her and Samuel to return. When they did, she raced to Bett and asked about the letter, and Bett assured her she'd placed it safely in Henry's hand. He had promised that if he did receive an answer he would do his best to borrow a wagon to take him to Greenfog and bring the letter straight to Lillie. As a free man he had leave to travel wherever he wanted, and since Greenfog was not where his family lived, the Master might allow him on the grounds on a Sunday to visit with friends he knew from his own slaving days. But even if the Master did permit Henry such a social call, Bett reminded Lillie it wasn't coming any time soon.

"I told you 'bout patience, child," she would say each

time Lillie would drop by her cabin in the following days to ask if there'd been any word from Henry. "You'll wait as long as you gots to wait."

Now, that wait seemed like it would only grow longer. For much of the week, whispers had been going around the plantations that Yankee gunboats had been spotted approaching Charleston harbor. At first the talk was dismissed as nothing but rumors, but late yesterday, the Northern Navy had begun shelling the small harbor islands where the cannons that protected the city were mounted.

So far, Charleston itself was untouched, but the people who lived in the surrounding counties were having a hard go of it. Farmers, merchants and even unarmed ladies dared not venture out on any of the public roads for fear that their horses and wagons would be seized, either by rogue Yankees or by loyal Confederates who needed the goods and transport for the war. Those roads that weren't overrun had been shelled so badly that that wagons could no longer travel them. There was no telling when the fighting would end, but Lillie clung to the belief that even if commerce couldn't proceed as it usually did, the mail wagons could. Bett was less hopeful.

"Wagons is wagons, child," she said. "If they move, the soldiers want 'em."

"Then there ain't no hope," Lillie said mournfully.

"There's always hope, girl."

Lillie brightened slightly. "There's that other thing," she said.

"What other thing?" Bett asked.

"That other thing you said the oven stones could do. The one you said is too dangerous."

"I didn't say it turned less dangerous, did I?"

"But if the mail don't go, we got to try somethin'!" Lillie said. "There won't be no other way."

Bett nodded sadly, then reached out and laid her hands over Lillie's. "Little girl, I been a slave a lot longer than most folks' whole lives, and I reckon I know a thing or two about when there ain't no other way to do somethin'. You ain't there yet." She laughed a tiny laugh. "You's close, I give you that. But you got a scrap of a chance left. You got to trust me about that, you hear?"

Lillie nodded, but deep inside, she was thinking no.

It was that promise from Bett—the possibility that not all hope was gone—that Lillie was turning 'round and 'round in her head while she was working at the nursery cabin and Mr. Willis was weighing and measuring Plato. It was still on her mind that night when the family was back in the cabin. Plato had yet to make any mention of his visit to the barn and in fact had given little thought to it himself. As soon as he got back to the beet field, he and the other boys got caught up wrestling by the creek bank, getting their clothes and hair so covered with mud that at the end of the workday their mamas had to scrub them down. So much excitement knocked other matters completely out of his head. It wasn't until Mama noticed he was just picking at his supper and asked him why that his thoughts returned.

"It was the cornbread," Plato answered.

"What cornbread?" Mama asked. "You didn't eat no cornbread."

"Yes, I did; I ate two pieces. He made me."

"Who made you?"

"Mr. Willis."

"What are you talkin' about, boy?" Mama asked.

"Mr. Willis took me from the beet field and put me on the scale. I'm forty-eight pounds," Plato said proudly. "But he said no ship wants to buy no deckhand as puny as me, so he gave me the cornbread."

"What do you mean, buy?" Lillie asked in alarm. "Who said anything 'bout buyin'?"

"Sshh!" Mama hushed her, and then turned back to Plato. "Who said anything 'bout buyin'? Who said anything 'bout deckhands?"

"The Master wants to sell me to a ship, 'cept I'm not for sale 'cause you don't want me to go. That's what Bull said, so I reckon I ain't goin'. Still, they said I got to eat the cornbread every day so's I get big."

At that, Mama bolted up from her chair so fast and hard she knocked Plato's milk cup onto the floor. Plato and Lillie jumped, and Mama turned and tore out the door. The children looked at each other and then lit out after her.

"Mr. Willis!" Mama cried, running off into the descending dark. "Mr. Willis!" She looked behind her, saw Plato and Lillie following, and screamed at them. "Go back! Go back now!"

Paying no mind to where she was running, Mama caught her toe in a rut and stumbled to the ground. Plato and Lillie screamed and sped up to reach her, but Mama simply rolled with the fall and was up on her feet again, continuing to race toward the overseer's cabin. "Mr. Willis! Mr. Willis!" she cried.

Slaves in the stables poked their heads out of the door and others coming home late from the fields stopped and stared. But none followed the wild-looking mama and the two children trailing her, lest whatever trouble she was courting came to them too.

"Mr. Willis!" Mama screamed once more as she drew near the cabin. The overseer now emerged, wearing nothing but his trousers and his suspenders. His whip was in his hand, and he swayed on his feet. He'd been drinking—a lot, judging by the heavy-lidded look of his eyes and the drunk-man's snarl playing around his mouth. He spun his whip furiously over his head till it cut the air with a whistle that would have sent a hound howling, then cracked it on the ground.

"Stay where you is, Franny!" he roared. "You and them babies o' yours!" He snapped the whip again, and Mama came to a stop, stumbling to her knees. Plato and Lillie raced up next to her, dropped down and took hold of her. "What's your business here—all o' you!—disturbin' my supper this way?" the overseer demanded.

"Mr. Willis, Mr. Willis," Mama said. "What do you want with my boy? Why you troublin' him when he's workin' hard for the Master like he always done?"

"Boy talked, eh?" Willis said. "Too much cornbread, eh? Don't worry, Franny. I don't want nothin' with your boy. Don't reckon he's worth much at all."

Mama started to slump in relief, but the overseer went on.

"Can't say the same for them ship captains, though. They likes to get 'em young. Train 'em up right."

"He ain't but a child, Mr. Willis, a child," Mama pleaded. "He ain't no sailor!"

Willis swayed dizzily, then waved her off absently. "Course he ain't. Not yet anyways. But when he's fattened up, maybe. When he's taught right, maybe."

"No!" Mama wailed. "He can't go! He can't go!"

"Maybe the girl oughta thought o' that before she took

to helpin' runaways!" Willis roared, turning Lillie's way. "The Master knows 'bout that now! He knows it good!"

Mama looked at Lillie, not understanding what the overseer had said. Lillie looked back, not able to make full sense of it either. Plato clung to both of them, too terrified now to move or weep or even breathe.

Lillie took hold of Mama hard, her eyes filling with tears. "Mama, Mama," she whispered. "Mama, your babies is here."

Mama wheeled back to her and cried aloud. "For how long, child? For how long?" She spun back to the overseer. "There ain't nothin' left of our family but what you see here! We ain't got no man! Let me keep my children, please!"

The overseer looked at Mama, his face now curling in full disgust. He whirled his whip around his head again and lashed it out once more. The tip of it struck the ground and this time seemed to explode against the soil just inches in front of Mama, pelleting the family with pebbles and dirt.

"The boy's gone, Franny!" Mr. Willis shouted. "Appraiser's comin' back inside o' the week. You try to hide him, I'll find him. I'll find him, and I promise you, I'll kill him dead!" The drunken man then looked down at them all, and his face this time lifted in a wicked smile. "Besides, Franny," he said, running his eyes over her, "once you're free o' the boy, you'll have more time for other things."

With that, Willis turned around, staggered back into his cabin and slammed the door. Mama collapsed onto the ground, and Lillie and Plato held her tight.

Chapter Twenty-four

IN THE QUIET of the cabin later that night, Lillie came to accept that Plato was well and truly lost—and that she and Mama were partly to blame.

Mama knew better than to talk to Mr. Willis the way she had tonight, even if her fears for Plato made it impossible for her not to. There were few things that set Mr. Willis's mind firmer to something he was planning to do than someone's begging him not to do it. A slave about to receive ten lashes dared not plead for mercy, lest that ten become twenty. Twenty could easily become fifty the same way. Not long before Lillie was born, so the stories went, the Master ordered Mr. Willis to sell off four slaves and gave him leave to select which four. One of the slaves he chose was a strong boy who was the younger of a mama's two sons. The mama wept and sobbed and clung to Mr. Willis's leg when she learned what was to happen. Then she said the one thing she oughtn't have said.

"You're too kind a man to take my baby away," she cried.

It would not do, Mr. Willis believed, for any slave to think him too kind for anything—so he sold off both of the sons instead. The mama died within the year, killed by sorrow as much as by the sure knowledge that it was her own words that had doomed her child.

But Mama's hand in dooming Plato was nothing next to Lillie's. With all the noise and tears outside the overseer's cabin, Mama did not seem to have kept hold of what Mr. Willis had said about Lillie helping runaways. The overseer was drunk and he was angry, and Mama likely reckoned he was just remembering the whipping he wanted to give Lillie when she told her tale about hurting Cal's foot. But Lillie suspected there was more to it than that—and that Sarabeth was involved. More than once, her old friend had told her that there was nothing in the world she loved so finely and fiercely as her family—and no one in her family she loved so finely and fiercely as her father. If Sarabeth concluded that Lillie had had a hand in Benjy and Cupit's disappearance, as she surely would have when she caught her coming out of the woods, she would just as surely have carried that news back home. *The Master knows 'bout that now,* Mr. Willis had said. *He knows it good!* Lillie was certain she knew how he came to know.

Lillie turned her face into her thin, rough pillow and broke into quiet, helpless tears. The two people who loved Plato most had now also done the most to help send him away. Her tears came harder, and she covered her mouth to stifle her sobs and felt surely as if she might perish from the idea of what awaited the boy, and then—something broke clear in her mind.

She flipped over on her back and stared at the ceiling with eyes wide and her breath quick. All at once, she understood! She'd figured it out, the "something else" the stones and the oven could do! It was the only thing that made sense. It was the only thing it could be.

And with that, she also knew what she had to do. As she had on the night she wrote her letter to the farmer in Mississippi, she forced herself to lie awake until she could hear both Plato and Mama breathing steadily in their sleep. Then she climbed out of bed and crept to her dresser, silently cursing the floorboards of the cabin, which creaked with every step she took. She reached around in her bottom drawer until she felt what she was trying to find—an old dress she'd worn for much of last year and all the year before. The dress was too small for her now and was frayed around the hem and sleeves. But there was still some serviceable cloth in it, and Mama intended to save what she could for patches and scrap.

Lillie wadded up the dress, tiptoed to the cabin door and stepped outside in her nightshirt and bare feet. The ground was cold and wet, and she stayed on her toes to avoid the crawly feel of it. She crept twenty or thirty steps from the cabin—far enough, she hoped, that her work would not be overheard. Then she bent down and felt around on the ground, groping for a sharp rock. She found one she thought was right and held it up in the watery gray moonlight. It looked suited to the job, but Lillie hesitated before she could go further. Mama had worked hard to make that dress, and Lillie remembered well the night she finished it. She had sewn straight through the evening and gave it to Lillie to try on just before bed. Papa had smiled broadly when Lillie twirled before him in it, and he said he could all at once see the grown woman hiding inside his girl. He pronounced it the finest dress Mama had ever made. Mama had beamed and given him a kiss.

Lillie pushed that memory from her head and, with one quick move, slashed the dress with her rock. Carefully then, so as not to waste a bit of the fabric, she tore it into long ribbons, glancing nervously at the cabin to be sure the noise didn't wake Mama. When she was done, she gathered the ribbons up in her arms and tiptoed back inside—taking care to kick the soil off her feet first. Then she tucked the strips of the dress under her mattress and slipped quietly back into bed.

Day broke cold and drizzly, which Lillie noticed when she woke up and counted as a good thing. On rainy days, there were still chores for many slaves to do, but not for most fieldworkers, which meant the mamas would be staying around the cabins. If the mamas had the day free, they wouldn't be bringing their babies to the nursery cabin, which meant Lillie had the day free too.

The gray sky outside matched the grim mood inside the cabin as Lillie, Mama and Plato rose and had their breakfast. Mama's eyes looked heavy and red. Plato had not spoken much about the terrible things the overseer had said, and it was not certain he really understood them. But he remained so quiet this morning—and clung so close to Mama—he must surely have been feeling the danger he faced. All three picked disinterestedly at their breakfast and when the meal was done, Mama put the uneaten hoecakes away. She'd serve them up again, along with some greens, when lunchtime came around.

Mama did not press the children to do much cleaning, save sweeping the floors and washing out their breakfast plates and cups. Lillie did as she was told, waiting for a chance to be left alone. When, at last, Mama and Plato went outside to fetch some water, she hurried over to her bed and pulled the cloth strips from under the mattress. She hiked up her dress and tied them around her waist, pulling the dress back down and smoothing it out as much as she could. When all the work was done, a quiet Plato wanted only to climb into Mama's lap and listen to stories, and that suited

Mama too. When Lillie asked if she could go outside, Mama nodded, seeming to hear her only halfway. Lillie kissed her mother and her brother and left the cabin.

Outside, Lillie slipped around the back of the cabin where no one could see her, pulled her dress up again and untied the strips. Then she hurried off to Nelly and George's cabin.

The distance to the cabin was a short one, but Lillie ran it in a sprint, heedless of the puddles she stepped in along the way. When she arrived, she knocked on the door and once again entered before she was invited. Nelly, George and Cal were sitting at their eating table having their breakfast. Cal's injured foot was propped up on a box. George turned in Lillie's direction and rolled his eyes at the sight of her.

"Girl!" he snapped. "Do I have to talk to your mama 'bout you?"

"I'm sorry, I'm sorry," Lillie said hurriedly. "I forgot again."

"You're too old to forget such things."

"Yes, sir," Lillie said. "But I come to see Cal."

"On what business?" George asked.

"No business," Lillie said. "I was just hopin' he could come outside and play."

"Cal still can't walk proper," Nelly said. "He surely can't play."

Lillie looked at Cal's foot. It was still puffy, though it had begun to look much more like a proper foot again. "Maybe I can help," Lillie said.

She walked over to Cal, crouched down in front of him, and took the foot in her hand. Cal flinched and laughed at the tickle against the skin of his sole and pulled the foot away.

"What do you think you're doin', girl?" George asked, and then, noticing the dress ribbons for the first time, added, "And what do you mean to do with them strips?"

"Somethin' my mama did for me once when I hurt my own foot," Lillie said. She laid the ribbons on the floor, then put out her hand and waggled her fingers, instructing Cal to give the foot back to her.

"You ain't no doctor," he said. "Whatta you want with my foot?"

Lillie ignored him and waggled again, this time giving him a firm glance—and this time he obeyed. "Cal, you are a lazy boy," she clucked, taking his foot in her hand. "You ain't never gonna get better just sittin'."

She unrolled one of the ribbons and began to wind it around Cal's arch and instep. When Lillie was nine years old, she'd fallen from a tree and made the same mess of her foot as Cal had made of his. Mama had wound the foot in the same kind of ribbons Lillie had now, and while that didn't heal her up fully, it did take away much of the pain and allow her to walk and even run a bit. Lillie got good at winding and unwinding the ribbons each day and learned well how to do it, and she remembered it now. The most important thing, she recalled, was to pull hard on the strips while she wrapped.

"Ow!" Cal said. "That's too tight."

"Hush," Lillie said. "Don't be a baby." She continued winding, though a bit more loosely. Then she picked up another ribbon and did the same, then another and another until the ankle and foot were wrapped as snug and tight as if Cal were wearing a boot.

"Where's the shoe for this foot?" Lillie asked.

"Over there," Cal said, pointing to the hearth. "But it ain't gonna fit over all that."

"It will if you don't lace it up," Lillie answered.

She fetched the shoe, slipped it over the bandage and ordered Cal to stand up. He did so and took some careful steps forward, then smiled.

"It don't hurt as much," he said. "It really don't."

"Lillie," George said, "if that foot gets hurt worse, the overseer is gonna want to know why."

"It ain't gonna get hurt," Nelly said, with an approving glance at Lillie. "And the girl's right. We been treatin' him like a baby calf, and it's time we stopped. You done with your breakfast, boy?" she asked Cal. He nodded, used his fingers to scoop up the last bit of spoon bread from his bowl and gobbled it down.

"Then go play," Nelly said, shooing them out. "The both of you."

Lillie tugged Cal toward the door before Nelly could change her mind. They stepped outside, and when they were several yards away from the cabin, Cal asked, "Where do you reckon you want to play?"

"Nowhere," Lillie answered, her expression serious. "We ain't playin'. We're goin' to see Bett."

Cal looked at her quizzically, but she merely took him by the wrist and began walking as fast as the still-hobbling boy could go. She chose the shortest route possible—straight through the tobacco field, seeming not to notice the way the rain had turned the crop soil muddy—and slowed only once, when Cal needed a moment to rest his lame foot. When they arrived at Bett's cabin, Lillie wordlessly climbed the two little steps to the door and knocked. Bett opened it up and took in the sight of them.

"I got to go see my papa," Lillie said. "I got to do it now."

Bett nodded, opened the door and stood aside for them to enter.

"I know, girl," she answered. "I reckoned you'd be comin' today."

Chapter Twenty-five

LILLIE HAD WAITED a long time to speak the words she'd just spoken. She'd cried them out over and over again in the days after she first learned that her papa had died, but while those words had been full of terrible, grieving feeling, they were also empty of meaning. When Lillie spoke the same words today, she spoke them the other way 'round entirely. These words were empty of the sorrow and grief she'd felt before and filled instead with a cool and deliberate purpose.

"There ain't no more time to wait for a letter 'fore they come to take away Plato," she said flatly.

"I know," Bett answered. "But you got to come in 'fore you say anything more. It don't do to be talkin' 'bout such things out on the step." She opened the door wider and beckoned Cal and Lillie in.

Lillie entered, still holding on to Cal's wrist and pulling him with her. Cal looked wary but went where he was tugged. Bett closed the door behind them and regarded them sternly.

"This is serious business you come here on," she said.

"I know," Lillie answered.

"Dangerous business."

"I know. Still, I got to go see my papa."

"What are you sayin', Lillie?" Cal asked. "What do you mean, seein' your papa?"

"You puzzled it out, didn't you?" Bett said to Lillie, ignoring Cal.

"I did," Lillie answered.

"You puzzled it out last night, so that's why you come today."

Lillie nodded. "Backwards!" she said. "Them stones can send things backwards! You slow down enough, you come to a stop; you slow down more, you start things movin' the other way."

Bett nodded. "You is a smart child."

Lillie waved that off. "That means I can go see Papa today. I can catch him 'fore he went to war and tell him why he can't go. Then everything'll be like it was."

"Lillie!" Cal exclaimed. "I asked you what you're sayin'—what you're both sayin'! Her papa's dead, Miss Bett. Dead since spring. She don't even know where his bones is buried."

Bett smiled at Cal. "I know he's dead, boy," she answered

gently. "And dead is dead. But now and then, it ain't. This here could be one o' them times." Lillie nodded in agreement.

Cal spread his hands in confusion. "I don't understand," he said.

"Sit, children," Bett answered, pointing both of them toward her eating table, with its two simple chairs pushed up to it. "Sit."

Cal stepped toward the table, but Lillie stayed where she was and glanced about. The cabin was in its customary order, but Bett's work area was not. Bowls and spoons were set out on her counter, bags of flour and other supplies were open, and a small fire was beginning to grow in the oven. She looked at Bett expectantly.

"Are you fixin' to bake?" she asked.

"I told you to sit," Bett repeated. She looked troubled. Lillie had not seen this expression on her face before, and the sight of it quieted her. This time she did as she was told, and Bett stood before them.

"You done right to come here," she said, "and you done right to do it today. The men is comin' for your brother quick. I don't know if it's tomorrow or the next day, but I seen this kind o' thing before—over and over again. By the time the work horn sounds three mornings from now, he'll be gone."

Lillie looked startled and started to jump up, and Bett

gestured for her to stay where she was. "You got to listen to me, girl!" she snapped. She turned to Cal. "And you too, boy!" Lillie settled back into her chair, and Bett went on.

"It'll go hard on your mama when your brother's gone, harder than she knows. Mr. Willis ain't foolin' about the wolf's eye he's got for her, and without the boy to take her attentions, he plans to pay her some o' his own. An overseer botherin' a slave mama don't like no one in the way—and you, child, won't be nothin' but a nuisance to him. Come the spring, the Master will surely need to raise more money, and he'll surely need to sell off more slaves, and this time, you'll be among 'em. That letter o' yours was all you had, but after the business with your brother yesterday, time's even shorter than it was."

"Miss Bett," Cal said, "if what you say is so, there ain't nothin' to fix it, 'cept escapin'. I don't got no fight with that, but all this other talk 'bout seein' Lillie's papa, that just ain't talkin' sense."

"You're right, boy," she said. "But you're wrong too." She regarded him closely. "You as smart as I think you is?" she asked.

"I am," Cal answered, raising his chin a little.

"Smart enough to know things and not talk of 'em?"

"Yes."

Bett nodded. "You ain't got no cause at all to believe what I'm about to tell you, 'cept that it's the truth."

Then, in a slow and patient way, Bett told Cal the story of her oven—of the stones that came from Africa, of the charm they worked in that well-loved land and still worked in this enslaved one. She told him of the baking she'd done to save him from the slave driver's whip when the appraiser came to call. She told him of the baking that had quickened Lillie's feet and sped her to Orchard Hill and slowed the dogs and horses so that Benjy and Cupit could escape. She also told him that Lillie was right, that if you baked long enough and hot enough, you could slow things so much they'd run in reverse—far enough back to let a child go see a papa who was dead in this world but had been alive in an earlier one.

Cal said nothing, simply taking in all that Bett had said. Lillie was right that he was a smart boy, but smart boys could also be practical boys, not given to fanciful thoughts. Cal, however, had a feel for things that were so and things that weren't so—which was one of the other things Lillie liked about him. She watched his eyes as Bett spoke and could see by looking at them that he knew what he was hearing now had the feel of truth.

"That's why you got that fire goin'?" he asked quietly. "To send Lillie back today?"

"Yes," Bett answered. "I expected she'd figure it out, but what she ain't tellin' you is that I said it's dangerous. I reckon that's why she brought you—busted foot and all. Reckon she thought I wouldn't let her go 'less someone went with her."

Lillie nodded, and Bett looked hard at both of them.

"Lillie, girl," she said, "I'll send you back if you want, but you was right—only if this here boy goes with you. And only if you both know why I said it's a dangerous thing to do." She drew a breath. "The truth is, for a long time, I didn't even know it was possible to go backwards. I discovered it by accident one day when I fell asleep while a cake was in and didn't wake up till it was baked black. When I looked outside, there was slaves comin' to work in the fields what had already come there before I put the cake in. The overseer blew the startin' horn like the day was just beginnin' but he'd already blown it once before. It was only when I put out the fire in the oven that things caught up to where they was supposed to be."

"Then it worked," Lillie said.

Bett shook her head. "But you was right that before things can go backwards they have to come to a stop, and things that stop can get stuck." She looked for a moment as if she didn't want to say what she was about to say. "There was a barn cat what used to come 'round my cabin to catch mice for me—a good animal with a fine nature, and I liked him dear. I came outside after puttin' out the oven that day and he was just standin' there, froze solid as marble. The magic took hold o' him and never let go."

"He was . . . dead?"

"Not straight away, but he got there. It took that poor animal two days to cool down from cat temperature—and two days more for its cold eyes to stop shinin'. I expect that meant it was alive that whole time, knowin' it was trapped inside that stone and just waitin' to die. It ain't nothin' but luck that no people got caught the same way."

With that, Bett turned and stepped toward the small wooden trunk she kept at the foot of her little bed. She knelt down in front of it, opened it up, and pulled out something about the size of a large loaf of bread, wrapped in a soft cloth. Then she returned to the table and set it down. She carefully opened up the cloth to reveal the awful thing inside.

Staring lifelessly at Lillie, Cal and Bett was a cat—a stone cat. It was the size of a proper cat and the colors of a proper cat, and it looked as if it would feel soft and warm and living like a proper cat. But neither Lillie nor Cal dared reach out to touch it. Even from where they sat, the thing gave off a cold, dead chill, one that actually made them shudder, as if the very air of the cabin had gone wintry. Worse than that was the terrible look in the cat's lifeless eyes—a look of fear and misery and the need to cry out, if only the stone that imprisoned it would release its hold.

Lillie covered her eyes in horror. "Put it away, put it away!" she said. Even Cal could look at the thing for only so long before he felt sick and lowered his eyes too.

"This kind o' magic is like a log fire," Bett said softly. "If you're careful, you can keep it in place, but a spark can still pop free. Could be a cat what gets burnt this time, could be you, could be me. That's what you got to know—and that's why I showed you this poor thing." Bett then swaddled the cat in the cloth, carried it back to its place in the trunk and returned.

"One more thing, children," she said, and this time she looked at Cal. "If you go, you ain't just stayin' on this plantation and goin' back to before Lillie's papa went to war. What's done is done, and what's dead is dead. If it was his lot to be took by a bullet on a battlefield, he can't ever come here again—even with the stones helpin' him. It's you two what's goin' to the battlefield instead. You find him there, you talk to him and ask him what you got to ask him, and you get back here 'fore he dies—'less you want to be around to see such a thing."

Lillie nodded and both she and Bett faced Cal. He said nothing, considering all that Bett had said. Then, he looked toward Lillie. "I reckon I ain't no barn cat," he said with a smile. "And I reckon I wouldn't mind seein' what a little magic feels like. If Lillie's gonna go, Miss Bett, you'd best send me along with her."

Lillie burst into a grin. Without thinking, she grabbed Cal in a hug around his neck and kissed him hard on the cheek. Cal squirmed away and wiped off his face as if he'd been bit by something nasty—but he looked at Lillie in a way that said something else entirely.

"All right, children," Bett said with her own small grin. "You both go."

Wordlessly, Bett now stepped to her work counter and beckoned them to follow. With the practiced eye gained from a lifetime at the oven, she measured out the ingredients she'd need for a large and heavy dough, then pushed them to Cal and Lillie to prepare. She stood back while Lillie mixed and stirred, watching to make sure the girl remembered what she'd taught her, and clucking if she missed a step or got careless with one. When the dough was mixed, Cal and Lillie took turns kneading it. Sometimes Lillie's hands were in the bowl, sometimes Cal's, sometimes they both reached in at once. Their doughy fingers would collide and tangle, and Lillie would feel a small tingle go through her each time. Finally, the work was done and Bett turned to Lillie.

"Spit," she instructed, and Lillie spat in the dough. "Spit," she repeated to Cal, and he did the same. She gave the dough a last knead and slid the baking tray into the oven. Then she waved Lillie and Cal back to the table to sit.

"What comes next," she said, "is what's gonna be hardest for you children because what you got to do is nothing at all, 'cept close your eyes, stay quiet and think hard 'bout where you want to go and what you got to do." Lillie began to ask a question but Bett silenced her with a look. "Just do what I say, and the bakin' will carry you."

Cal and Lillie closed their eyes and at first noticed nothing at all. Lillie was able to steady her body, but her mind was racing, alive with the thoughts of what was to come. She shifted once, then again, the chair giving off a loud creak each time.

"Be still, girl," Bett said to her quietly. "Be still. Let it come get you."

Slowly, Lillie was able to let her body go slack, finding it all at once easier than she thought it would be and pleasanter too. Then, just as Bett promised, the baking seemed to be trying to gather her up. She could feel the warmth of the cook fire filling the cabin and swirling around her. She could hear the pop of a log and the crackle of the flame and they filled her head as if they were the only sounds there were to be heard. The smell of the baking soon followed, and it seemed a richer, sweeter smell than any Lillie had known before. The fragrance and the warmth and the sounds of the logs now thickened and grew, swirling together and crowding the cabin and pushing out anything else. Lillie felt her head grow light and her body grow buoyant, and she felt as if she were beginning to come unmoored and float straight up, even though she could still feel the hard wood of the chair beneath her. Her thoughts themselves soon began to melt away. The only things she knew for certain were that Cal was beside her, that he was surely feeling the same things she was feeling and that somewhere far away—but less far every second—her papa was waiting for them.

She was aware then of just one more thing: the touch of Bett's hand atop her own, patting it gently. "Travel safe, little Ibo," the old woman said. "And come home free."

A moment later, Bett stood in her cabin, alone.

Chapter Twenty-six

THE FIRST THING Lillie noticed before the darkness began to part was the smell of gunpowder. She still couldn't see anything, and she still couldn't hear anything, but the smoky, stony scent of the powder seemed to be everywhere. Gunpowder was always a smell Lillie reckoned ought to be unpleasant, given the nasty work it was usually put to, but it was one she liked all the same. Right now, there was plenty of it in the air for her to enjoy.

Then slowly, beneath the heavy air of powder, Lillie began to notice other things too. There was a damp smell; a warm, moldy smell; and there was the sharp, acrid tang of men who hadn't bathed in a long, long time. The men smelled of more than old sweat, though; they also smelled of fresh fear. It was a scent Lillie had learned to recognize long ago. It had come off her the night she had run to Orchard Hill. It had come off every slave at Greenfog ever threatened with the whip. Now it seemed to be rising up from everywhere.

Finally, Lillie noticed one other smell that closed her in and choked her throat and swept the air clean of all the other smells as if they hadn't been there at all. It was the terrible smell of flesh—horse flesh and human flesh. And it was flesh that was burning.

With that, Lillie became filled with fear, and suddenly her trip through the darkness was not the gentle, dreamy spin it had been. Now it was more like a plunge. She flailed her arms and kicked her legs and desperately grabbed about in the blackness for anything solid to clutch and hold. But there was nothing solid—just more darkness and more fear and the growing roasting animal smell. Then, fleetingly, her fingers brushed something. It was soft and it was warm and it felt familiar. She reached for it again and felt it again and grabbed on to it tight and immediately realized that she was holding fast not to something but to someone. That someone was surely Cal and when she realized that, she held tighter still, as if just by doing so she could stop her plunge. But holding Cal didn't help at all. The harder she held him, the faster she fell, and then she felt him holding her back—with the same urgency, the same fear. And still they fell. Now Lillie was sure they were both going to die— something that was probably all right since the poisonous air and the dizzying plunge were becoming too terrible, and if she and Cal did strike the ground and their short lives did end, at least those other things would end too.

And then, all at once, Lillie was standing. The fall had stopped, the spinning had stopped, and though the fearful smells were still everywhere, her own fear had mostly stopped too. She slowly opened her eyes and blinked around, squinting against a sudden flood of sun. The first thing she could make out clearly—the only thing she could make out clearly—was Cal's face, pressed close to hers. She pulled back from their tangled embrace and looked at him full. His eyes were still shut tight and while he was well and truly there in front of her, he seemed to be somewhere else too. For him, the fall through the darkness had not yet ended.

"Cal!" she said sharply. "Cal! Open your eyes!"

Cal seemed to hear her and tried to say something, but all that came out was the kind of jumble of words people mumble in deep sleep—the kind that make no sense at all.

"Cal!" Lillie said louder. "Cal, you got to wake up!"

Cal now jumped as if he'd been struck and his eyes flew open. He drew in a few startled breaths and Lillie gripped him tighter to prevent him from swinging his arms about if he still couldn't see her. Then he, like Lillie, began gazing blindly around himself—and he too seemed only to focus when his gaze came to rest on the face in front of his.

"Lillie," he said hoarsely, "Lillie, we ain't dead."

"No," Lillie said. "No, we ain't."

"I thought we was gonna be for sure. I thought we already was."

"So did I," she said. "I don't reckon we are, though—leastways not yet."

Lillie and Cal slowly loosed the hold they had on one another, stood back and only then began to look fully around. When they did, Lillie covered her mouth in both fear and wonder.

The children were standing in the middle of a vast, muddy, flaming battlefield. Everywhere they looked there was violence being done. Everywhere they looked, trees were burning and men were dying and great sprays of explosive fire were tearing up the earth. And yet all of it was completely silent and completely still. A terrible fight was unfolding before them, but it was a fight held fast in a frozen moment—as real as Bett's poor barn cat had once been, and yet as dead and stony-looking as that cat was now.

"We're in the war," Cal whispered in wonder. "The magic worked and we're in the war."

Lillie nodded mutely. Surely Cal was right; surely this was the war. But all the same, this couldn't be the war. War was supposed to be whooping men and charging horses. It was supposed to be fought on green fields under clear skies with flags and drums and bugles everywhere. The soldiers of the North were supposed to be wearing uniforms of midnight blue with gold buttons and bright swords. The soldiers of the South were supposed to be dressed in the cool gray of clean iron, with squared-off caps perched on their heads and shiny black boots on their feet.

But here the sky was a sodden gray and the ground was a sea of mud. There were soldiers everywhere, but most were capless, some were bootless, all were filthy and many were dead. Their uniforms might once have been blue or gray, but there was no telling them apart now, since they were all the same grimy shade of mud and earth. The landscape was an endless spread of blood and death and smoke and stink—a scene more of plague than of war.

"What is this place?" Lillie said in horror. She took a wary step forward and her foot sank almost to her ankle in mud. She pulled it out with a loud, wet noise, nearly losing her shoe to the ooze as she did. She took another few steps and Cal followed her, treading carefully with his bandaged foot. Both of them stared around in silence as they walked.

Off to their right, a huge fountain of mud and flame was roaring up from the ground, caught in mid-climb just instants after being hit from an exploding shell like the ones the Yankees were firing at Charleston. Soldiers on all sides of the blast were being knocked back or blown into the air— themselves stopped cold between the living world they all inhabited and the dead one some of them were surely about to join. Barely ten yards away, a fat oak tree, struck by another shell, had been snapped in two like a chicken bone. It was pitching forward and plunging to the ground, poised over a cluster of muddy soldiers who had taken shelter under it and would now be pinned beneath it. Elsewhere, fire raged from the remains of a supply wagon, which had been blown onto its side and lay in blazing ruins, its bags of provisions and other equipment spilled in the mud. The horse that had pulled it had also toppled over and was itself being consumed by the flames. The closer Lillie and Cal drew to it, the more sharply they could smell the animal's sizzling bulk. Cal stepped ahead of Lillie and held out his hand to the frozen fire.

"No, Cal!" Lillie cried out, but she cried it too late. Cal thrust his hand into the flame.

"It don't feel like nothin'," he said. "Like it ain't there at all."

Huddling closer together, the children walked deeper and deeper into the battlefield as the wreckage and death they'd already passed closed behind them and more of the same kept opening up. Lillie looked overhead and saw another shell—shaped like a bullet but big around as a tree stump—trapped in flight, heading for unlucky soldiers in an unlucky spot an untold distance away. Clouds of bullets as thick as gnat swarms hung in the air too, and judging by their pointed ends, they were headed in every direction at once. All over the field, men were being claimed by the gunfire—some freshly shot, clutching their wounds and falling to earth with their faces twisted in terrible agony, others still untouched but about to be shot, standing square in the path of a bullet that had not yet found its mark. Those same bullets, however, could do the children no harm. When Lillie approached a swarm of them that was too big to sidestep, she simply brushed them aside as easily as she'd brush a cobweb, and the bullets dropped to the ground and stuck in the mud with a wet plop.

"Like the slowbees," she said to Cal. "Just like the slowbees."

"This can't be where we're s'posed to be," Cal said. "There must be somethin' went wrong with the charm. We stay here, we gonna die with the rest."

"We ain't gonna die," Lillie answered. "We ain't supposed to die. The charm don't make that kind o' mistake."

Lillie could not know if what she was saying was true, but neither she nor Cal could know it wasn't. The only thing she knew for sure was what she felt in her belly—and what she felt in her belly was that this was exactly the place she was meant to be.

"C'mon," she said and pulled on Cal's sleeve, "or I'll leave you where you stand."

Lillie trudged on a few steps more, Cal limping behind her without protest, until suddenly, she stopped where she was—as still as one of the soldiers. Her eyes opened wide, her body tensed, and a single word came exploding out of her.

"Papa!" she cried, from every part of herself all at once. "Papa! Papa! Papa! Papa!"

And her papa, indeed, was there.

In a deep shell hole not far from where they were, the man who'd died early last spring stood. It was her papa's face; it was her papa's shape. He was splattered everywhere with blood, but judging by the way he held himself and the fierce look in his eyes, he was not injured. What he seemed to be covered with was other men's blood—and that made sense. Papa had joined the army as a battlefield nurse.

Lillie's heart boomed in her chest so hard and so fast she felt set to swoon. "Papa, Papa, Papa!" she cried again.

"It is!" Cal said. "It's your papa! It is!"

Lillie began racing through the mud now with Cal limping after her, both of them lurching and stumbling as fast as they could and gasping with the effort of it. At last, they reached the lip of the shell hole and tumbled into it and Lillie spun and fell and came to rest near her papa's feet. She looked up into Papa's face and drank in the sight of him. He had a stubbly beard he hadn't had before and his forehead bore deep, new lines. There were dustings of gray throughout his hair that Lillie had also never seen. But it was her papa all the same, as sure as if he'd never left.

And then, Lillie saw one more thing. It was a bullet, another bullet caught in mid-flight, this one heading straight toward her papa, frozen in place just inches from his chest. Cal, who had tumbled in the mud beside Lillie, saw it too, and he hobbled upright and helped her to her feet. Lillie's knees trembled badly as she rose and she feared they wouldn't bear her weight. Her hands shook too and she feared she couldn't use them. But she held her body steady and reached slowly out toward the bullet. Then, with thumb and forefinger, she plucked it from the air and dropped it in her dress pocket.

Instantly, the world exploded around them all in a storm of shell blasts, gunshots, snapping trees and the anguished cries of ten thousand men. Papa looked her square in the face with bright, living eyes.

"Quashee!" he said.

Then he grabbed Lillie and Cal, pulled them to the ground and threw his body on top of theirs.

Chapter Twenty-seven

THE SOUND OF the battle was a terrible thing—far worse than the sight and smell of it, if only because Lillie could at least close her eyes or pinch her nose and shut those things out. But there was no shutting out the furious roar of the shells and guns. It was a sound that wasn't just heard but felt—shaking the bones inside her and the ground below her and even the air above her, which seemed to hammer down with the force of a solid thing every time a cannon boomed or a shell burst.

Yet while Lillie felt the noise, she felt no fear. What she felt instead was safe—safer here on a battlefield where men were losing their lives than she had felt in even the deepest part of the quietest night in all the months since Papa had been dead. Because Papa was dead no more. Bett was wrong! It was possible to spare his life, and Lillie had done so! Even now, she could feel the bullet that had been meant for her papa harmlessly pressing against her hip as she lay flattened on the ground. It was a bother, perhaps, like a

pebble in her shoe, but no more than that. Far more powerful than the bullet were the arms of her papa, holding her
and Cal tight and shielding them from the explosions rain-
ing down everywhere. Lillie lay half buried in a smolder-
ing shell hole, and yet all she felt flowing through her was a
sense of protection and peace.

Finally—perhaps minutes later, perhaps hours—the explosions began to slow. There were longer and longer gaps
between shellings, gaps that were filled with the ongoing
rattle of gunfire. Then the guns stopped too and all there
was to hear was the screaming of the wounded men. That,
Lillie suspected, was a battlefield sound that never stopped.
Slowly, Papa's weight began to lift, and he sat up and looked
in wonder at the two children pressed into the muck beneath
him. He recognized Cal's face well, since he had known the
boy since he was very small, but for a moment he ignored
him. Instead, he looked only at Lillie, reaching down with
one arm and scooping her up as easily as he had when she
was a baby. He grabbed her in a fierce embrace.

"Quashee," he said. "Quashee, Quashee, Quashee."

"Papa," she said through her sobs.

"Quashee, I don't understand. It can't be you. It can't be
either of you."

"It is, Papa. It's us. We're here."

"It ain't possible."

"It is possible, Papa."

"But how? How did you get here? Why did you come here?"

"Papa . . . ," Lillie said, pulling back and looking him in the face.

Before she could say more, there was a sound of sloshing footsteps at the lip of the mud hole and the voice of an angry man barking down at them. "What's all this?" the voice demanded. "Who is this girl? Who are these children? Soldier, explain this!"

Papa, Lillie and Cal turned toward the sound. Standing above them was a broad, beefy white man, not quite as tall as Lillie's papa but more muscled. He had a thick mustache and long, muddy hair. Even through the filth that covered his uniform, Lillie could see three stripes on his sleeve.

"Sergeant," Papa stammered, "Sergeant, it's . . . they're . . ." He began to stand, helping Lillie up as he did; both of them found only poor purchase on the slick soil.

Beside them, Cal struggled upright and faced the sergeant square. "Drummer boy, sir," he said. "I'm a slave from near Charleston what got sent down here to help."

"There ain't no slave drummer boys!" the sergeant said.

"There is from Charleston, sir," Cal said. "Not enough white folks sent their boys; someone had to do the job."

"Who's the girl?"

"Runaway, sir," Cal said. Papa snapped his head toward Lillie, who looked down at the ground. "I got orders to carry her back to where she escaped from and collect the reward."

"What company are you with, boy? Who's your commander?" the sergeant asked with narrowing eyes.

Lillie froze, Papa stared—and Cal, for a moment, said nothing. Then he shrugged. "Don't rightly know, sir," he said. "Been with all of 'em, it seems. I just go where they sends me."

The sergeant nodded in disdain. "Well, if you're a drummer boy, you ain't a very smart one. Got no wits at all windin' up here, 'specially with that foot o' yours. Now, get off my battlefield and take that runaway with you."

"Yes, sir," Cal said.

"And you," the sergeant said, wheeling to Papa, "quit tendin' to children when you got wounded men to look after!"

"Yes, sir," Papa said.

The sergeant turned and plodded off, and Papa looked back to Lillie and Cal. "What's he sayin'?" he asked Lillie. "You can't be no runaway. He can't be no slave chaser."

"No, sir," Cal said, "I ain't."

"No, Papa," Lillie said. "We come to see you. We come to save Plato."

"Plato? What are you talkin' about?" Papa demanded.

"What happened to Plato? What happened to your mama?"

"They's all right," Lillie said. "They's all right now. But they won't be soon. The Master's gonna sell off Plato. Then he's gonna sell me off. They won't let us go free 'cause they say you're a thief. You was dead, so you couldn't tell 'em otherwise, but now you can!"

"Quashee, you ain't makin' sense," Papa said. "Look at me—I ain't dead."

"But you was!"

"And I ain't no thief."

"But they say you is!"

"Boy," Papa said, turning to Cal, "what kind o' story is this child tellin'?"

"It ain't no story," Cal said. "She's talkin' truth."

"It's Bett, Papa," Lillie said. "Bett sent us here to help."

Lillie then told Papa everything there was to tell—all the things she and Bett had just explained to Cal, and all the other things Papa could not know about: the slave appraiser and the shelling of Charleston and the hard times at Greenfog. She told of her trip to Bluffton and her visit to the one-legged Henry and her charmed run through the darkness to see his family at Orchard Hill. Finally, she told Papa of his own death, of the terrible sorrow it had caused and of how she had now prevented it. She pulled the bullet from her pocket and offered it to him, but he did not want to touch it, and Lillie tucked it back away. Papa said nothing at all as she told her story. He had no cause to believe such nonsense. But he was Ibo and Bett was Ibo and he'd always believed she had powerful ways. And the fact was, the children were here, and there was no other way that could be so. Finally he spoke, and to Lillie's surprise, he sounded cross.

"That old woman don't have no business workin' charms on a child," he said.

"But I asked her to," Lillie protested. "And now you're alive! You can come home."

Papa waved that off. "If I'm s'posed to get took by a bullet, I'll get took by a bullet," he said. "If I ain't, I ain't."

Lillie nodded mutely at the words. They were exactly like the ones Bett had spoken. She wanted to argue with him just as she'd wanted to argue with her, but she saw the same look of certainty on Papa's face that she'd seen on Bett's.

"What about Plato?" she asked instead. "What's s'posed to happen to him?"

"He's alive, child," Papa said. "Sometimes there ain't nothin' more'n that."

"What if he gets sold away from Mama and me?"

"And what if you and Cal get yourselves killed comin' here to try to fix things? What would your mama do then?"

"She's gonna lose us both to the slave trader anyway."

"Least you'll be alive."

"But Plato could be free!" Lillie protested. "Mama could be free! We could all be free! Don't that matter?"

Papa looked at Lillie, and now the certainty in his eyes wavered. The child had done a foolish thing playing with charms and stepping into a war. But that didn't mean she was a foolish girl. She knew her papa, and she knew his wishes, and she knew he wouldn't have gone to war himself if freedom for his family hadn't mattered more to him than anything else. Lillie knew the weight the very word carried with him—and the effect that simply saying it would have on him. Like any clever daughter, she knew the mind of her father.

"Little Ibo," Papa said with a look that was part love and part surrender, "you are a stubborn child. Tell me what you're plannin' to do."

Chapter Twenty-eight

PAPA HELPED LILLIE and Cal out of the shell hole and led them deeper into the battlefield to a patch of clear ground protected by a stand of thick trees. Many of the Confederate soldiers who had survived the battle were drifting in the same direction. As Lillie approached the spot, she could see a large tent with smoke and steam rising up around it.

"Cook tent," Papa said. "You children should have somethin' in your bellies."

Lillie followed, not interested in food after all she had seen this morning and not understanding how the soldiers themselves could have any appetite either. Yet the soldiers seemed to be hungry indeed and came streaming across the battlefield so fast that a few of them almost knocked her down. Suddenly, Lillie stopped in her tracks. Approaching the tent from barely twenty yards away was Henry—but this Henry had both his legs. He had yet to be wounded, yet to be sent home, yet to learn anything of the lonely life he'd be living in the furniture barn in Bluffton.

"What is it, Quashee?" Papa asked.

"It's Henry!" she said, pointing.

Papa looked in the direction she indicated. "Leave him be," he said. "If what you say is true, he don't need to know it yet."

Lillie nodded and simply watched in wonder as Henry trotted past and melted into the crowd.

"Now, don't stand about," Papa ordered. "Quiet times like this don't last no longer than it takes the Yankees to rest up and reload."

As Lillie and Cal waited, Papa gathered three tin plates with a strip of salt pork and a torn piece of bread on each. He unclipped a tin cup from his belt, dipped it into a barrel of water and filled it. The water looked brown and grimy in the barrel, but less so in the cup, and Lillie took it from Papa gratefully and drank it down. He refilled it and passed it to Cal, who did the same. A few soldiers looked at them curiously and Papa mumbled some words about a drummer boy and a runaway and that seemed to appease them. He then led the children to a spot next to a toppled wagon where they'd have a little privacy, and they sat.

"So they're sayin' I'm a thief," Papa said, not seeming troubled by the slander. "What do they say I took?"

"Coins," Lillie said, chewing on a small bit of the hard

bread, which felt grittier than the water did. "A whole bag of 'em. Yankee gold." She tossed off the last two words with a small laugh, as if the idea were too foolish to say out loud.

"Like these?" Papa asked, reaching into his coat pocket. He withdrew a drawstring bag, opened it up and spilled a shiny pile of golden money into his hand. Both children's eyes widened. Here in the past, where Papa was alive, the money was still in his possession. Back in the present—where Lillie and Cal lived and where Bett waited in her cabin for their return—Papa was already dead and the Master had the coins. The thought made Lillie dizzy. But she was dizzier still at the idea that what she'd been told about Papa and the gold seemed to be true.

"Papa!" Lillie said.

"Then they wasn't lyin'!" Cal whispered.

"Not about the fact that I got these coins, no," Papa said. "Five hundred dollars, the way I count it up—and I've counted it up a lot."

"Five hundred dollars," Lillie repeated in a wondering whisper. "Papa, where'd you get it?"

Lillie asked her question before she gave it much thought, and as soon as she did, she regretted it. It wasn't so much what she said as the way she said it. Her voice carried a whisper of doubt—a doubt that said she might actually think her papa could have stolen the money. She was ashamed of that tone and turned away.

"It's all right, Quashee," he said. "If my papa had turned up with five hundred dollars in gold, I'd have wondered if he stole it too. But I didn't steal it."

"How'd you get it, then?" she asked.

"I can't tell."

"Who did it belong to?"

"I can't tell that, either."

"Was it a man named Appleton?"

Papa looked at her in surprise and tried to hide it, but Lillie saw through him—and Papa saw that she had. "Where did you hear that name?" he asked.

"Henry," she answered. "He said the soldiers go to the Appleton land for supplies all the time. Said you went there to fetch water one day and come back with a bag full o' gold."

Papa thought that over. "I don't know nothin' 'bout what Henry thinks."

"Papa!" Lillie cried, so loudly that a soldier nearby turned. "Papa!" she repeated, lowering her voice to a fierce whisper. "I got to know! It's what I come here for! It's the only way to save Plato!"

Papa fell silent now and looked down. He seemed deep in thought and far away. When he looked up again, Lillie could see that his eyes were red.

"You know, your mama couldn't get by without you children," he said softly.

"I know," Lillie answered.

"And Plato can't get by without you and Mama. You reckon they really plan to sell him off?"

"Bett says it'll happen today or tomorrow."

"You reckon she's right that they'll sell you too?"

"She ain't been wrong yet," Lillie answered.

"And she reckons she was right sendin' you here where men is dyin' instead o' keepin' you home where you oughta be?"

"I know it don't seem safe," Lillie said, "but we ain't s'posed to get killed—on account of the charm."

"What kind o' charm can promise you that?" Papa demanded.

"The same kind what got us here."

Papa fell silent once more, then nodded to himself as if he had just made a decision. "All right, then," he said. "You both need to listen to me hard. I can't leave this battlefield. Times between shootin' like this is when deserters usually run, and the Army's got riflemen posted to see that they don't. A man lights out—'specially a slave man—he gets shot just like a Yankee. But you two can go—in fact you got to go. The fightin' what's comin' is worse'n what's happened already. You'll be killed sure if you stay here, and the Appleton farm is as safe a place as any. You go there, you talk to that farmer, and you see if he can't tell you what you need to know."

"But why can't you tell us?" Lillie pleaded.

"Because I gave my promise I wouldn't," Papa said. "Besides, who's gonna believe a slave child carryin' a tale that her papa did no wrong? You gonna have to have a white man's word on the matter, or it won't amount to nothin'."

Lillie nodded. She hadn't thought of that, but of course it was true.

"Boy," Papa said, turning to Cal, "can you move on that bad foot?"

"I'll keep up," Cal said.

"You good at navigatin' the woods?"

"Yes."

"What about you?" Papa asked Lillie. She knew nothing about navigating but lied and nodded. Papa saw the fib and turned back to Cal.

"You gonna have to get yourself and my girl where you're goin'," he said. "And you gonna have to be ready to use some o' that storytellin' I saw you workin' on the sergeant. You don't think you can do all that, you best say so now."

"I can do it."

Papa nodded, then reached down and ran his hand over the ground, smoothing out a patch of mud. With a shard of wood pulled from the toppled wagon, he drew a map from the battlefield to the Appleton farm. Cal and Lillie studied it carefully and listened closely while Papa told them about the landmarks they'd see along the way and the wrong turns they needed to avoid. The children traced the map with their fingers while Papa looked around to make sure no one was watching.

"You got it in your heads?" he asked at last. The children nodded, and with a sweep of his hand, he wiped the map clean.

Papa then walked Cal and Lillie as far as he could before he came in range of the riflemen hunting for deserters. Then he stopped and took Lillie by the shoulders.

"Tell your mama and Plato I love them," he said.

"They know that," Lillie answered, choking back tears.

"And I miss them."

"They miss you too."

"They got me, child. They got me in you. Your mama's a beautiful woman, and I know you was always disappointed that you favor me, not her. But you're a beautiful girl—the most beautiful one I ever seen. And you're the piece o' me what's gonna live no matter what."

"You ain't gonna die again, Papa!" Lillie said. "You gonna come home!"

"If I'm s'posed to, I'm s'posed to," Papa repeated.

Lillie threw herself against him and held him tight. He gathered her up in one more long embrace.

"Go now, girl," he whispered. "You gonna get through."

Chapter Twenty-nine

LILLIE AND CAL hurried through the battle-field as best they could, both of them struggling against the pull of the mud and Cal struggling with his wounded foot. They kept their eyes to the ground most of the time, figuring that the less they looked around themselves, the less they'd see of the waste and death everywhere. What's more, any soldiers inclined to stop them and question them might decide not to bother if they knew they'd have to call out to them and give chase first. It took more than an hour and a half of such hobbling running before the children began to reach the end of the muddy plain that was the field of war and encounter untrampled grass, unbroken trees and a sky free of smoke. They stopped to catch their breath, their hands on their knees and their heads hanging down.

"I didn't know . . . it'd be . . . so far," Cal panted.

"We got a while . . . still to go," Lillie answered.

They collected themselves, stood back up and then

hurried on, the directions Papa had given them for the rest of the journey running through their heads. Right turn, dry goods store, plank bridge, forked road, Lillie repeated over and over to herself—the words falling into the rhythm of her feet.

Right turn, dry goods store, plank bridge, forked road, Cal recited silently too.

At last they reached the bridge and raced across it—their footfalls making a terrible clatter in the otherwise quiet afternoon. "Over there!" Cal said, pointing ahead.

Lillie looked and saw that the forked road that was the last landmark was just where Papa had said it would be. One hundred paces down the left-hand side of it should be the Appleton farm. Lillie and Cal trotted and hobbled down the road and, as Papa had also promised, came upon a small sign bearing the single name APPLETON in red paint. Beyond it was a dirt drive and a large farmhouse.

"What do we do now?" Lillie asked.

That was a question neither one of them had considered. The farm looked tidy and quiet, with the shutters on the top floor closed and only a few on the ground floor open. There was a carriage house next to the main house and its door was partway open, but no one appeared to be inside. In the distance, Lillie could see the fields—far smaller than those at Greenfog—with just a few slaves at work. It was a quiet and peaceful scene—until it was suddenly broken by an angry voice.

"What do you want?" a man snapped.

Cal and Lillie jumped and turned to the sound, which seemed to be coming from off to their right. They could not see the person who was speaking.

"What do you want?" the voice repeated, more angrily this time.

"We don't mean no trouble," Lillie called back, her own voice quavering.

"I didn't ask what you mean! I asked you what you want!" came the answer, and now the man who owned the voice appeared. He had been inside the carriage house, hiding behind the partly closed door, and he emerged now with a shotgun at his shoulder, pointed directly at Cal and Lillie. The children took hold of one another and backed up a few steps. The man slowly approached, walking with a terrible limp, but holding the gun steady. He wore an old work shirt, a dirty pair of pants and a battered jacket. From where Lillie and Cal stood, the jacket looked midnight blue. With a start, Lillie realized it was the tunic of a Union soldier.

"What are you starin' at?" the man now barked. "Eyes on the ground and get off this land!"

"Yes, sir," Cal stammered.

He grabbed Lillie's arm and began pulling her backward. At first Lillie stood her ground, but the man waved the gun barrel at her and she too began to retreat. Then there was another voice.

"Lucas!" the voice cried. "Put that gun down!"

A man came bounding from the house, leapt down the porch steps and raced across the grass. "Lucas!" he said again. "Do what I say."

Lillie and Cal stood absolutely still as the gunman slowly lowered his weapon and pointed it toward the ground. The other man reached him, grabbed the barrel and wrested the gun away from him. "These're children! Do you know who they are? Did you even ask who they are?"

The man named Lucas shook his head. "I don't care who they are. What I care about is them askin' who I am."

"Well, so far they ain't asked. Now go inside the house," he ordered. Lucas stood his ground. "Go inside the house, I say, before I'm the one who turns you in!"

Lucas grumbled but did as he was told, stomping up the porch steps on his one good leg and one lame one, and going into the house. He slammed the door behind him. The other man unloaded the gun, put the shells in his pocket and then turned to Lillie and Cal.

"Now, what is it you want?" he asked.

Lillie cleared her throat. "We're lookin' for a man named Appleton."

"I'm Appleton," the man answered. "He's Appleton too," he added, jerking a thumb in the direction of the house.

"The Appleton what owns this farm?"

"That's me."

"I want to talk to you 'bout my papa," Lillie said.

Appleton cocked his head at her and studied her face. "I don't think I know your papa," he said. "I've got mostly women slaves working here, and the two men I do have are too old."

"He doesn't work for you," Lillie said. "He works for the Army."

"A slave man soldier?"

"Yes, sir."

"A nurse soldier?"

"That's him! Yes, sir, that's him!"

"Come over here, girl," the man instructed. He said it with a tone Lillie couldn't quite read. She took a wary step forward, and Cal held her arm and stopped her. The man smiled. He opened the shotgun once again and showed the empty barrels, then tucked it backward under his arm. "I ain't gonna hurt her, son," he said to Cal, "nor you."

He waved them over again, and Lillie and Cal approached. When Lillie was standing in front of the man, he studied her face once again. Then he smiled.

"This way," he said.

Without another word, he led them across the grass and up onto the porch and then, remarkably, opened the door of his house to them. Lillie and Cal had never been allowed to walk through the front door of a white man's house before. They stopped, having no idea how to proceed, then looked down at their shoes, which were covered with battlefield mud.

"Don't worry 'bout that," Appleton said. "There's nothing but rain and mud around here this time of year." He nudged them inside.

The children entered the parlor and looked around at the sheer loveliness of the place. Beneath their feet was a plank floor that was polished and smooth and covered with colorful rugs. The furniture was polished too, and softened with cushions that were woven with colorful patterns. There were bits of lace on the arms of the chairs and a footrest in front of one of them. A pair of oil lamps with tinkly crystals hung on the walls, and the cut glass caught the light streaming through the lace-curtained windows. Appleton pointed them to the dining parlor, where there was a long table with six chairs around it. There were more crystal lamps on the walls and a cabinet full of delicate-looking china. He pulled out the chair at the head of the table and motioned the children to the ones on either side of him.

"Sit," he instructed, and Lillie and Cal did as they were told. Then he called out over his shoulder. "Sissy," he said, "bring some water."

A slave girl appeared, gaped at Lillie and Cal, then hurried away and returned with a pitcher and three glasses on a tray. She set the glasses on the table and filled each one. Lillie and Cal looked down at their hands and squirmed in their chairs. A slave was serving slaves, and they could not meet the girl's eyes. Lillie murmured, "Thank you," when the glasses were full, and the girl vanished. Appleton now turned to Lillie.

"I expect you been told that you look like your father," he said.

"Yes, sir," Lillie answered.

He next turned to Cal. "This can't be your brother—the boy with the funny name."

"No, sir," Lillie said. "That's Plato."

"Plato, yes," the man said as if remembering.

"This here's Cal," Lillie said. "A slave boy."

"Happy to meet you, Cal," Appleton said.

"Thank you, sir," Cal said hoarsely.

"And I'm Lillie," Lillie said.

"I know," Appleton said. "I been told. You live in South Carolina, don't you?"

"Yes, sir."

"That's a long way. You runaways?"

Lillie and Cal looked at him and said nothing. The truth—that they'd come here by charm—would be taken as a lie. A lie—that they were runaways as he thought—would land them in worse trouble. They stayed silent until Appleton spoke, and what he said surprised them more than all the other surprising things that had happened today.

"It doesn't matter. More and more runaways now. And

there'll be more still as the war grows worse. You musta come down here to find your papa."

"Yes, sir," Lillie said. "To prove he ain't no thief."

"Who said he's a thief?"

"Everyone," Lillie answered. "They say he stole money from you. Yankee gold—five hundred dollars of it!"

Appleton nodded. "Your father does have my gold. And five hundred dollars is the right amount." He paused and Lillie held her breath, waiting for the man's next words like she'd never waited for anything in her life. "But he didn't steal a penny of it," Appleton said at last.

A burst of joy and relief exploded inside Lillie, and tears flooded her eyes. She wiped them with her sleeve, not daring to soil the lace napkin in front of her. But Appleton picked it up and handed it to her.

"Dry," he said, and Lillie dried her eyes. "Blow," he said, and she blew her nose.

"I have family too," Mr. Appleton now said, "but only a little bit. One of my sons died when he was a baby. My wife died of typhus in the first year of the war. My other son died at Antietam in the second year. All I got left is my brother, Lucas—and you met Lucas."

He inclined his head to the stairway that led to the second floor, indicating that Lucas was safely tucked away. "Lucas and me grew up here, but he was working in the North when the war broke out, and he enlisted in the Union Army.

He wasn't much cut out for fighting. The shelling drove him near mad, but he fought all the same. Coupla months ago he was sent down here for the fight at Vicksburg. . . ." Appleton now trailed off, as if he didn't want to admit what he had to admit. Lillie spoke for him.

"And he run away," she said.

Appleton nodded. "Deserted. Fighting so close to home was too much for him. He nearly got away clean, but when he wasn't but half a mile from here, he got caught by a shell. You seen his limp."

Lillie nodded.

"Same day he got here, your papa came to fetch water. He saw Lucas bleeding, close to death. He surely woulda died, but your papa had his nurse's kit with him and stayed to fix him up."

"Papa fixed a Yankee?"

"He did," Appleton said simply. "The Army of the North woulda shot Lucas if they'd caught him deserting. Army of the South woulda shot your papa if they'd caught him helping the North. But your papa stayed all the same, knowin' they might come lookin' for him." He patted Lillie's hand. "Lucas earned a lot of money—Yankee gold— workin' in New York. Don't you think your papa deserved five hundred dollars of it?"

Lillie beamed and nodded.

"So did I," Appleton said. "So did Lucas. So I don't

reckon it really matters if people think he stole it, long as you know he come by it the right way."

"But it does matter!" Lillie said. "The Army made the Master promise that my family could go free if Papa went to war, but now he says the money should be his and we got to stay slaves."

Appleton's voice went cold. "Your Master said that?"

"Yes, sir," Lillie answered.

"How'd he find out about the money at all?"

Lillie stopped. She suddenly realized she had no answer for that. She didn't want to lie to Appleton, but she couldn't tell about the charm that had brought them straight to the battlefield today. She couldn't tell him that Papa was already dead, but that here in the past he wasn't dead, or that the bag of coins was in the possession of the Master of Greenfog, but that here in the past it was in the possession of her papa.

"A white soldier saw the money and wrote a letter home sayin' her papa was a thief and word got sent to our plantation," Cal jumped in. "I reckon the letter got there before the mail roads got cut."

Lillie glanced at Cal, but Cal didn't look back. All at once Appleton rose and pushed back his chair. His face looked angry and the chair gave out a loud scrape against the smooth floor. Lillie was terribly afraid that he'd spotted Cal's lie and that now they were both in worse danger than ever. Appleton turned and strode into another room. He came back carrying a piece of paper, an inkwell and a pen. He sat back down in his chair.

"I'm writin' a letter to anyone who needs to see it saying it was me who got hurt. I fell off the roof and woulda died of my injury, but your papa stayed to mend me," he said sternly. "Any person takin' his money is takin' my money—and I'll pull the law in if I have to."

Appleton scribbled out the letter quickly, and Lillie marveled at the speed of his hand and the way the curly script fell from his pen. He read it through, nodded in satisfaction at what he'd written, and folded the paper up. He slid it inside a creamy white envelope.

"Now, you can't take this to your plantation yourself," Appleton said. "You both're runaways and it'll go hard on you if you show your face there again." He held the letter just out of reach. Lillie ached to snatch it from him and tell him that they weren't runaways at all, but again, she dared not. And again, Cal jumped in.

"No, sir, we can't never go back there," he said. "But if you was to give us a stamp for that letter, we could go somewhere near home to where the roads is still open and try to find a place to mail it. Then the rest of the family could get freed and meet us somewheres."

Appleton smiled. "You're a bright boy," he said. He walked back to the other room again and the children could hear a drawer opening and closing. Then he returned holding a stamp and stuck it to the envelope. He asked Lillie for the Master's full name and the plantation's proper name and wrote them out on the envelope as well.

Then he handed Lillie the letter. She smiled broadly and nodded in thanks she couldn't even express, but Appleton's expression remained serious. "You think you can carry that letter without losin' it?" he asked her.

"Yes, sir."

"Can you make sure she keeps track of it?" he asked Cal.

"Yes, sir."

Lillie slid the letter into her dress pocket. Appleton then rose, and Lillie and Cal did the same.

"Now, go," he said. "Get away from this terrible place and go back where there ain't no shootin'."

Mr. Appleton walked them to the front door and, while they were standing there, did something no other white person had ever done before: He reached out his hand to shake Lillie's. Lillie paused, then held out her hand and let it be swallowed up by the man's big, callused grip. He turned to Cal and did the same. At that instant there was a great double-clap of shellfire, and Lillie and Cal both jumped.

"It's thunder, children," Appleton said. "Just thunder. You'd best move on before the rain starts."

The rain never did start during the long slog Lillie and Cal made back to the battlefield. The clouds gathered as if they were set to burst, and the wind whistled as if it were set to blow. But the clouds, for the moment, held back their rain—something Lillie counted as lucky lest the letter in her pocket get ruined before anyone could read it.

Lillie and Cal said little to one another as they struggled back along the country roads, retracing their steps— forked road, plank bridge, dry goods store, left turn—and eventually plunging back into the smoke storm of the battlefield. They fought through long stretches of ooze where the mud was nearly knee-deep, found a patch of purchase here and there, and then waded back into the mire.

Finally, they saw the cook tent where Papa had fed them and, further on, the shell hole where they'd found him. Lillie picked up her speed, and Cal struggled to keep pace with her.

"Papa, Papa!" she cried, not seeing him but reckoning he must be somewhere nearby. "Papa!"

She strained to hear him calling back to her but got no reply, and she guessed that was not a worry since there was no telling exactly where he would be by now. It was only when she and Cal came within steps of the shell hole that they had a clear line of sight inside it. And it was only then that she saw two other slave nurses struggling up the slick, muddy sides of the pit, dragging a lifeless soldier between them. The man had a long, lean build and a bristle of beard and dustings of gray in his hair.

"Papa!" Lillie wailed, releasing a ragged cry from the very bottom of herself. "Papa!" she shouted again. She ran flat-out and leapt into the hole and fell atop the form of her papa. She grabbed him tight and screamed at the men.

"Leave him be, leave him be!" she cried.

"He's dead, child," one of the nurses said.

"Leave him be!" Lillie repeated.

"He's dead," the nurse said again. "Bullet got him two hours ago—long after the fightin' stopped. Musta' been one o' those guns what got dropped near a fire and just went off. No matter what, he's dead."

Lillie, holding her papa and sobbing against his muddy, bloody shirt, heard none of what the man was saying. She did not notice the rain at last beginning to fall, nor Cal trying to pull her free; nor did she notice that the bullet she'd carried all day in her pocket was no longer there. An instant later, she and Cal spun back into the void.

Chapter Thirty

L ILLIE AND CAL reappeared in Bett's cabin just the way they'd been in their last moments on the battlefield—with Lillie lying down as if she were clutching her papa and Cal holding tight to her. Papa himself was still in Mississippi.

"Papa, Papa," Lillie was saying between her sobs.

"Lillie, Lillie, let go," Cal was saying to her.

Both of them then felt Bett's warm, strong arms around them, and heard her murmuring to them.

"Hush, children, hush," she was saying.

They opened their eyes, blinking in the daylight of the warm, dry cabin at Greenfog.

"Hush, children," Bett repeated. "You ain't where you was. You're home now."

Bett helped Cal and Lillie up, seated them in the hard, wooden chairs at her eating table, and listened as Lillie tried to tell her story. Again and again, her sobs interrupted her tale, and again and again Bett would try to quiet her. The old woman seemed to know what the young girl was going to tell her and didn't want her upsetting herself with the effort. Cal stayed mostly quiet and stared ahead.

Bett helped Lillie and Cal clean themselves off and when they seemed more composed, she fed them warm bread, fresh milk and cold, just-picked apples. The children, to their own surprise, wolfed them down. They'd eaten nothing in the time they'd been away but the bit of salt pork and hard bread Papa had fed them, and now that they were out of danger, they were hungrier than they knew.

Even as Lillie ate, she found that Papa was the only thing on her mind, and when his face floated before her, her tears would flow again. In all the months he had been dead, she had often wished she could see him just one more time, talk to him just one more time.

But now that she'd gotten that chance, she wished she hadn't. She felt as if she were learning all over again that Papa was gone—and understanding all over again that he would never be back, even though she'd begun to make her peace with that months ago. She resolved at that moment that while she would tell Mama everything that had happened today—and carry Papa's message that he loved her and missed her—she would say nothing to Plato until he was older. The boy did not need the sorrow Lillie was feeling.

The letter from the farmer was still in her pocket and had escaped the rain that had begun falling in Mississippi.

Lillie took it out carefully and pulled the precious paper from its neat little envelope. The man's flowery script was hard to read, but Lillie was able to make out most of it. He wrote about the care Papa had provided him—leaving out any mention of Lucas, as he'd said he would. He told of the money he'd given Papa, and he went on to address the Master in a manner Lillie had never heard any other person use with him.

"You will take heed that the five hundred dollars in Union gold in your slave man's possession is my property, which I gave freely to him," he wrote. "Upon his discharge from the Army, that sum belongs to him. Upon his death, that sum belongs to his family, who shall be freed according to the terms of Army conscription. You will take further heed that I will view any interference with those terms as a theft of private wealth, and I will proceed accordingly." The letter was signed "William T. Appleton." Lillie reflected that until this moment, she did not know the man's full name, and now that she knew it, she liked it fine. It was strong and simple and it suited him well.

Lillie was thrilled by the words. The Master was now required to return the money to Mama and the family and set them free, but first he had to see the letter, and that would not be easy. Lillie could not simply hand it to the Master, who would not believe it was real and would surely have her flogged both for fibbing and for knowing how to read at all.

Bett, however, had an answer. She took the letter from Lillie and, later that day, gave it to a kitchen maid, who gave it to a parlor maid, who waited until the Master was away from his library and placed it atop the stack of plantation correspondence he read and answered each afternoon.

"What is the meaning of this?" the Master boomed as soon as he returned to his desk and read the letter. The Missus ran in to see what the disturbance was, and the two of them stayed behind closed doors for the better part of the hour—the Master pacing and shouting, and the Missus offering soothing words. He called the parlor maid in and questioned her closely about how the letter got there, and she coolly revealed nothing.

"I cleans around the letters, sir," she said. "I never touch them. Besides, I couldn't read them to tell one from the other nohow."

The maid quickly reported back to Bett that the Master had seen the letter, and Bett reported that back to Lillie.

"Then we's free!" Lillie exclaimed.

"You ain't nothin' of the kind," Bett said. "Remember what your papa told you 'bout the weasel. It don't let go o' the chicken till it has to, and the same is true of a master and a slave."

Bett was right, of course. The Master of Greenfog would not consider releasing three of his slaves and handing them five hundred dollars on the say-so of a letter he didn't trust in the first place. But the farmer's phrasing had been so firm he dared not ignore it, either. Instead, he stalked to his stable, mounted his horse and galloped to Bluffton, where he visited the telegraph office and sent a message all the way from Charleston County in South Carolina to Warren County in Mississippi, addressed to the man named Appleton. The telegraph cables, so far at least, had not been cut by the war.

"Letter received," the Master instructed the telegraph man to tap out in code. "Authenticity in doubt. Please confirm."

He rode back to Greenfog, and two days later a boy from the telegraph office arrived with a response from Mississippi.

"Letter authentic. Gold was mine. Proceed as instructed or I shall proceed as promised."

Lillie and Mama and Plato knew nothing of the exchange of telegrams during those two days, and they had no choice but to go about their business and wait for some kind of word. Throughout that time, Lillie found that her thoughts and her dreams were filled with feverish images of the war and the battlefield and her muddy, dying papa. One night she awoke, screaming and sobbing, and Mama was suddenly beside her—holding her head and stroking her hair as she did when Lillie was a child smaller than Plato.

"Your papa ain't here," Mama whispered. "But your mama is."

Finally, on the third day after Lillie's return, the Master told the housekeeper to tell a kitchen maid to fetch Lillie and Mama and Plato up to the Big House. When they arrived, he was waiting for them on his porch—having no intention of receiving slaves in his library or even in his foyer. He stared at them coldy, with nothing but a nod for a hello. Then he read the letter from Mr. Appleton aloud. Lillie smiled to herself when she noticed that he left out the parts in which Appleton gave him instructions and threatened him with what he would do if he didn't obey. A Master who had spent his life giving orders to others seemed not to want his own slaves to hear him taking them.

Mama gasped. "What does this mean, Master?" she asked when he was done.

"It means you're free, Franny," the Master said sourly. "You and them as well." He gestured absently at Lillie and Plato.

He reached into his coat pocket and reluctantly handed Mama the gold coins. Lillie's eyes welled when she saw the drawstring bag that held them. It was the same bag Papa had shown her just days before—still bearing traces of battle-field mud. The Master looked much sorrier at the prospect of losing his gold than at the prospect of losing his slaves, and Lillie took heart at that. Even before he had summoned them, she and Mama had discussed an idea.

"Sir," Mama said now, "if you want some o' this gold

back, we'll give it to you—'cept we want to trade it for two other slaves." The Master didn't have to ask if those two slaves were Bett and Cal, but he asked anyway.

"Yes, sir," Mama answered. "Them's the ones."

Bett, they all knew, was almost worthless to the Master, but he demanded fifty dollars for her, which was far more than she would ever fetch at auction. Cal had a lot of years of labor ahead and the Master demanded two hundred dollars for him. Even that was less than he could have gotten if he sold the boy when he was fully grown, but the Master was in need of cash now and settled for the lower price. Mama returned the payment for both of them before the coins had even grown warm in her hands. Then the Master ordered them to wait where they were, while he retreated to his library to write out the manumission papers for the five of them. He handed them to Mama and assured her they were in order. Later, in their cabin, Lillie and Mama read them through carefully. The papers were properly drawn and signed and named the entire family, plus Bett and Cal, as the slaves to be freed.

All five were instructed to be off the Master's land by the very next morning. Lillie and the others used the one night they had left to pack their possessions and say their good-byes. Lillie ran to see Minervy, hugged the girl tight and told her to look after the babies and try to be brave. Minervy cried and promised she would. Lillie never set eyes on Sarabeth again, and that was fine with her. Sarabeth had been a better daughter to her father than she had been a friend to Lillie, and while that might be as it should be, she had done Lillie a terrible wrong all the same. The good and bad in all of that was more than Lillie wanted to sort out when she was feeling such joy.

Cal spent a final night in Nelly and George's cabin and realized only when he was leaving the next day that they must have become true parents to him—otherwise he'd not be feeling the sadness he was. He cried as he said good-bye to them, but took care to finish up before he saw Lillie.

By the time the work horn blew the next day, Samuel's wagon was hitched and waiting and the five of them were piling their bags aboard. As they were doing that, they heard footsteps crunching through the soil and turned to see Mr. Willis approaching. They froze at the sight of him—his whip coiled in his right hand, his expression a mixture of amusement and contempt.

"I reckon this is good-bye to the lot o' you," he said as he drew near. He stopped and spat in the dirt at his feet.

"Yes, sir," Mama said.

"Can't say I'm sorry to see any o' you go," Willis went on with a small laugh, and then gestured to Plato. "Though this one woulda fetched a nice price."

Plato pressed himself against Mama, who held him tight. Willis then looked at Mama squarely. "Course I do reckon I'll miss seein' your face, Franny," he said. He took a few steps toward her, reached out and took hold of her chin. Mama shuddered, but Willis didn't notice and turned her head first one way, then the other. "You was a pretty one," he said.

Before she could think, Lillie stepped forward. "Mr. Willis," she said in a clear voice. "That's a freedwoman you're touchin'. She's my mama, and her name ain't Franny—it's Phibbi." Then she glanced toward the Big House, where the Master would just be getting up and would expect a quiet day, with no sign of the five freed slaves when he emerged for his morning walk. He would not care for Mr. Willis causing any unpleasantness and disturbing those plans. Willis followed her eyes—and her thinking—and looked back at Lillie with an icy expression. Then he released Mama's chin with a snap, spat in the soil again and strode off.

Without another word, Lillie and the others climbed into the wagon. Two hours later, they were in Bluffton. While they were there, they stopped at the furniture store where Henry lived and gave him one hundred of the remaining two hundred and fifty gold dollars. That would not be enough for him to buy his wife and child back, but it would get him much closer—and allow the family to reunite much sooner. Shortly before nightfall, they all said their good-byes to Samuel, who turned his wagon around and headed back to Greenfog. Mama hired another wagon heading North—uncertain for the moment where they would all finally stop, but reckoning that Pennsylvania sounded like a fine and friendly place to live.

It would be only one more year before the war would be over and all the slaves on all the plantations would be free. In that time, however, the Greenfog slaves would still need their Friday bread, and the Master did allow the oldest of his kitchen maids to move into Bett's cabin and take over the work. Bett had schooled the woman well in the ways of baking over the years, and the two of them had hugged good-bye on the morning Bett left. With all the farewells, no one had paid any mind to the heavy-looking, loaf-sized bundle Bett was carrying among her few belongings. But the first time the new baker woman tried to use the oven, she did notice that a single brick was missing from inside it.

Author's Note

S LAVERY WILL ALWAYS count as America's greatest crime. It was a period defined by greed and cruelty and inhumanity. But for the slaves themselves and the people who tried to help them, it was also a time of courage and sacrifice and sometimes even joy. *Freedom Stone* is a work of imagination, but it's also one in which I have tried to include both of those sides of the Civil War South.

To the extent that I have succeeded in doing that, I owe thanks to what I learned from some fine historical works. Among them are: *The Slave Community: Plantation Life in the Antebellum South*, by John W. Blassingame; *Roll, Jordan, Roll: The World the Slaves Made*, by Eugene D. Genovese; and, most remarkably, *The Interesting Narrative of the Life of Olaudah Equiano*, the 1789 autobiography of a slave who won his freedom and then told his tale. It is a moving and extraordinary book.

As always, I also owe thanks to my friend, confidante and agent, Joy Harris, of the Joy Harris Literary Agency.

There is none wiser or better, and I am lucky to know her. Thanks too to Michael Green of Philomel Books, for giving *Freedom Stone* the thumbs-up, and to Jill Santopolo whose suggestions and recommended edits were always smart, insightful and precise. It is a far better book for having spent time in her care. For reading the manuscript and offering advice, appreciation goes to Steve Kluger and Garry Kluger, as well as to Kevin McAuliffe, the kind of grade-school teacher every child deserves but only the luckiest ones get.

Finally, my deep love to Alejandra, whose strength and love of family brought life to the character of Mama; and to Elisa and Paloma, who enchant and amaze me daily.